Taking Liberties

By the same author:

Forbidden Fruit
A Sporting Chance

Taking Liberties
Susie Raymond

BL

First Published by Black Lace 1999

2 4 6 8 10 9 7 5 3 1

This edition first published in Great Britain in 2009 by
Black Lace
Virgin Books
Random House, 20 Vauxhall Bridge Road,
London SW1V 2SA

www.blacklace.co.uk
www.virginbooks.com
www.rbooks.co.uk

Addresses for companies within The Random House Group Limited can be found
at: www.randomhouse.co.uk/offices.htm

The Random House Group Limited Reg. No. 954009

A CIP catalogue record for this book is available from the British Library

ISBN 9780352345301

The Random House Group Limited supports The Forest Stewardship Council [FSC],
the leading international forest certification organisation. All our titles that are
printed on Greenpeace-approved FSC-certified paper carry the FSC logo.
Our paper procurement policy can be found at www.rbooks.co.uk/environment

Printed and bound in Great Britain by CPI Bookmarque Ltd, Croydon CR0 4TD

Chapter One

*B*eth stood up and glided across the office, her movements slow and deliberate. Behind her, through the
open doorway into her boss's office, she could sense
Simon watching her again. He had done a lot of that
lately. In fact, it was a wonder that he ever got anything
done at all; his mind clearly wasn't on his work when
she was around. She grinned slyly to herself.

As she stooped over the drawer of her filing cabinet,
Beth could feel his eyes burning into the back of her
thighs. She straightened slowly and began to amble back
to her desk. Out the corner of her eye, she surreptitiously
examined him in return, admiring his well-proportioned
physique and dark good looks.

Being brunette herself, Beth was usually more attracted
to fair-haired men, but there was something about brown
eyes that always drew her like a magnet. Simon had the
deepest, darkest coffee-brown eyes she had ever seen.
When he watched her, as he was doing now, it was
almost as if she were being sucked helplessly into them,
powerless to resist. Soon, she promised herself. Very
soon now.

Once she was back out of sight behind her desk she
allowed herself another quick grin and reached for the

next document in her in-tray. As she resumed working her way steadily through the mound of accounts awaiting her attention, she hummed contentedly to herself. She had always been good at maths and she took quiet satisfaction at the way the neat columns of figures flowed from her pen and bowed to her will. It was all so easy, so logical. She had been away from the financial world for far too long and it was good to be back.

Taking a short break, Beth sipped her already cold coffee and glanced happily round her domain. It was a pleasant room, if a bit on the small side. The dark wooden desk and leather chair pleased her, even though they weren't anywhere near as plush or expensive as those in Simon's office. It was a warm day and she wriggled slightly in her seat, enjoying the feel of the cold leather on the bare skin of her thighs.

She slipped her feet out of her shoes and smiled as she rubbed her toes gently along the carpet, luxuriating in its velvety softness. If she did that in Simon's office, her toes would disappear in the thick pile. She had trouble simply walking on it in her high heels. Of course, nothing was too good or too expensive for Simon Henderson. Even the visitor's couch would put most luxury beds to shame. She smiled again, then put her empty mug back down and returned to her work. Images of Simon's liquorice eyes and wide, sensuous lips danced tantalisingly in her mind, full of promise.

Five minutes later Beth finished bringing the Simpson account up to date. She leant back and glanced thoughtfully out of the window. Being Saturday, the high street was busier than usual and from five stories up she had a good view. As she watched the weekend shoppers scurrying frantically to and fro like ants with their whinging children in tow, she sighed softly. Despite the apparent bustle, you couldn't help noticing how run down and neglected the area had become in recent years. Small towns like this, with their tiny family businesses, were part of a dying era. They just couldn't compete with the huge, modern shopping malls springing up everywhere. No wonder Simon was planning to move to a brand-new business park further out from the London area. There was nothing to keep businesses here any more.

Thoughts of Simon reminded her that it was time to provide him with a little further distraction. As she reached out to gather up the stack of financial projections and investment options she had just been working on, her mind filled with the pleasures soon to come and her skin began to tingle.

'Since you are going to be away all next week, we really need to get the Simpson account put to bed before you go.' His words from the previous day ran through her mind. His choice of expression had not gone unnoticed. Nor had his hands, which had wandered on to her thigh before she had twisted out of his reach.

'I know it's a bit much to ask,' he had added, 'but perhaps you wouldn't mind if we both came in tomorrow morning, just to finish up?'

He must have known how flimsy the excuse had sounded. The money in the Simpson account was already securely invested and would be perfectly all right for the week she was due to be away on her training course. Besides, if it had really been all that important, he could quite easily have returned to the office the previous afternoon after his lunchtime appointment with a client.

Of course, he must also have known that there would be hardly anyone else in the building on a Saturday and no clients would be knocking on their door. Whatever Simon wanted her in the office for this morning, Beth was certain that it had little to do with customer care. It would seem that her teasing over the past weeks was finally about to bear fruit. This was the moment she had been waiting for.

Beth slipped her feet back into her high heels and stood up. She smoothed down her short skirt and carefully checked her appearance. Satisfied, she walked leisurely into his office, her hips swinging from side to side.

As soon as he spotted her, Simon reached for a client file. He opened it quickly and pretended to be concentrating avidly on its contents. His face looked slightly flushed and Beth hid her smile at the thought of what he may have been up to with his hands under the desk. Her eyes twinkled mischievously.

'Here's the Simpson account. I've completed the financial projection up to the end of the month. I think you'll find everything in order.'

As she spoke, Beth examined his hard, athletic body and perfectly proportioned features, trying to assess his thoughts. His dark hair, normally so immaculate, looked slightly tousled, as if he had been running his fingers through it. Her own fingers itched to smooth it back in place.

'Thank you, Beth.' His slight smile was full of hidden possibilities and his liquorice eyes glittered in a way that made her whole body tingle with longing.

He watched her closely as she reached across the desk to place the documents on the far side in the only available space. It would have been much easier to reach from the other side, but less easy for him to reach her. As she leant over, she kept her legs straight so that her skirt lifted slightly to reveal a brief glimpse of lacy stocking top.

She took her time, pretending to tidy up a few pens and pencils and put them back into his pen holder. Finally, she stood upright again and ran her hands down her sides so that her blouse pulled tight over her nipples. Simon's eyes narrowed and his whole body seemed to tense as he stared at her breasts. She heard him sigh gently as she turned to walk back to her own office. There was a soft rustle of clothing as he stood up.

'What's your hurry?' he questioned. 'We haven't finished yet.'

Even though she was expecting it, Beth pretended to jump in mock surprise as Simon made a sudden grab for her from behind. She allowed him to put his hands round

4

her waist and run them up towards her breasts until the tips of his fingers were just touching the outer curves. Although his hands were large and firm, his fingers were surprisingly long and slim, lightly tanned and silky smooth. She twisted away and turned back to face him.

'Don't do that.' She forced anger into her voice. 'What would anyone think if they walked in?' As she turned away again, Beth reached out and brushed a pile of papers with her hand. With a soft thud, the whole heap landed on the floor.

'Damn,' she cursed under her breath. Bending deliberately from the waist, she started to gather them up. She took her time, certain that he would be enjoying the view. Suddenly, she heard the sharp click of the office door locking. How in the world had he got over there so quickly and quietly? Although surprised, she pretended not to notice and continued to gather the scattered documents.

Finished, Beth stood up slowly and put the papers back on his desk. As she smoothed her skirt down over her hips again, she could sense Simon hovering just behind her. Without warning, he put his hands around her so that her arms were effectively pinned to her sides as he began to caress the swell of her breasts. Beth could feel the outline of his erection thrusting urgently into her buttocks. She resisted the urge to push herself hard against it and began to struggle feebly in an effort to escape his grasp.

'Simon! Stop it. What if somebody comes in?' It was just possible, albeit unlikely, that a cleaner or someone from one of the other companies with whom Henderson Finance shared the six-storey office block might come by.

'They can't. I've locked the door.' His voice was thick with desire. His hands began to move inwards towards her already hardening nipples.

'Oh!' Beth gasped. She prayed that he would think her cry was caused by her shock and not because of the exquisite tingling sensation that was running down her spine at the feel of his fingers on her nipples. She increased her half-hearted efforts to escape.

Clearly excited by her struggles, Simon grabbed a handful of her blouse. Beth gripped his hand in hers, as if trying to pry his fingers loose, and pulled hard. The buttons immediately began to pop out of the carefully enlarged buttonholes. Beth squealed and twisted away so that the pressure on the buttons increased. The cotton snapped on the final button and the garment gaped open.

Beth faked another squeal and placed her hands across her chest as if trying to protect her tiny white bra. Simon made another grab for her and Beth automatically put her arms out in front of her to push him away. His fingers hooked over the front catch of her bra.

'Stop it.' Beth twirled and tried to duck under his arm. The bra lifted up and one of her breasts popped out. 'Oh!'

Simon's eyes widened at the sight of her naked breast. He tugged harder and the carefully doctored stitching on the catch gave way. The bra snapped open and her other breast bounced into view.

Beth quickly covered her breasts with both hands. In the struggle, her skirt had ridden up over her stocking tops and she suspected that he might even be able to see the bottom of her silk thong. She had chosen it carefully; the elastic wasn't very strong and she was sure that he wouldn't have any trouble pulling it off.

Keeping her arms up in front of her, Beth took a small step backwards. Simon grabbed for her again. As she pulled away, she gave her shoulders a quick shrug so that her blouse slipped off into his fingers and her bra straps began to slide down her arms. Pretending to lose her balance, Beth stumbled back over the cushioned settee.

Her skirt rode up even more. Beth pushed herself along the cushion until her hem was up around her buttocks and the soft elephant cord was gently caressing the tops of her thighs. She pretended not to notice her skirt and concentrated on her naked breasts, fondling her swollen nipples as she tried to cover them with her hands.

Simon's eyes were fixed on the small triangle of white silk covering her mound. She could feel her breasts heaving with excitement as she stood back up, exposing even more thigh. Casually, she shook the bra off her arms. It fell to the floor beside her feet.

Simon seemed to be staring at her as if in shock. Her tattered blouse was still clutched between his shaking fingers and his face was deathly pale. For one awful moment, Beth was afraid he was about to lose his nerve and start apologising. She gazed down ruefully at herself and made a feeble attempt to straighten her skirt. Her breasts danced and bobbed tantalisingly in front of her.

She pouted seductively. 'Now look what you've done. That really was very naughty of you.' Her voice automatically adopted the tone one might use when scolding a naughty child. She noticed with satisfaction that his eyes were moving restlessly back and forth between her breasts and crotch. She leant down casually and picked up her bra.

'You've broken the catch. I won't be able to wear this again.' She dropped it in the waste-paper bin and then quickly covered her breasts with her hands again, as though she had suddenly remembered her exposure.

'You are going to give me my blouse back, aren't you?' she queried, as she held out one arm towards him and tried, in vain, to conceal her breasts with her other hand.

Simon stared blankly at the blouse still clutched between his fingers, then raised his arm as if he were about to give it back to her. Obviously, he needed another little prod in the right direction.

'Or are you going to make me work topless?' she continued. She lifted her hands and glanced down at her puckered nipples. 'It would be a bit hard to concentrate while I'm trying to cover these up,' she added.

It worked. Simon immediately pulled his hand back.

Beth gazed up into his eyes. His face was flushed and his breath was coming in short little pants.

'Not for what I've got in mind,' he whispered hungrily.

Beth could hear the longing in his voice. She didn't have to glance down to know how his penis was straining against his flies. She was convinced that all he needed was one more little push and he would lose his final inhibitions. She shivered with a combination of fear and excitement. She had been anticipating this moment for weeks.

Beth reached out for her blouse. She hesitated in apparent confusion, then quickly tried to cover herself again. As she stood shivering in front of Simon, she did her best to look nervous and indecisive. Almost absent-mindedly, her fingers began to tease her nipples again.

Simon glanced down at her skirt and Beth followed his gaze. The top button had popped undone during their brief struggle so that he could see a glimpse of her panties. Beth noticed his whole body was quivering. Another surge of desire threatened to engulf her when she saw the almost desperate expression on his face.

'You don't need that, either.' He dropped her blouse to the floor and reached out to grasp the corner of her skirt. He pulled hard and the skirt opened. He let it fall to the ground beside her blouse, leaving Beth standing in just her panties and stockings. She stepped back.

Immediately, Simon made another lunge for her. Beth dodged, squealing indignantly. As she bent forward, she placed one hand across her breasts and turned her head away to hide the look of satisfaction on her face. Her other hand slipped down between her thighs and, in her excitement, her fingers began to squeeze her mound as if to try to stem her own growing passion. If anything, it made things worse.

Simon pushed his fingers under the elastic of her thong and began to peel it down over her buttocks.

'Or these,' he added softly.

'No. Stop it,' she protested weakly as she twisted away

from him again. With both her hands crossed over her breasts, Beth began to dance nimbly around the chairs and desk. Simon lumbered after her, his hands everywhere.

As soon as she reached the visitor's couch again Beth deliberately lost her footing and fell forward. Simon pounced. As he pushed his finger under the elastic of her panties, Beth wriggled back, so that they began to slip down towards her knees. Simon immediately let go of her and stood up. Without taking his eyes off her exposed mound, he raised his hand and started to undo his belt.

Beth stared up at him, mesmerised, her eyes unblinking. Yes, she thought excitedly. That's it. Tie me up with your belt. Strap my hands behind me so that I can't defend myself and run your fingers all over me until I beg for mercy. She felt another surge of longing race through her.

Simon released the catch on his trousers and slowly undid his zip. She noticed the shiny wrapper of a condom in the palm of his hand and almost sighed with relief at his forethought. She watched silently as Simon slid his pants down over his erection and his stiff cock sprang free. She wasn't disappointed.

When he saw the direction of her gaze, he smiled and ripped the condom wrapper open with his teeth. Wordlessly, he smoothed the sheath down his rigid penis. Beth shivered again as he grasped himself in his hand and moved his fingers slowly down himself, checking the fit. She had always known that it would be fun, pushing him like this. She hadn't anticipated the powerful extent of her own arousal.

As Simon grabbed her panties to finish tugging them off, Beth squirmed back away from him, still feigning resistance. She rolled off the settee and landed on her stomach on the floor. Simon bent over her and continued to pull at her underwear. Beth squeezed her legs together to try to stop him. She didn't want him to think it was

9

too easy. Her own excitement was building urgently. Her thighs were already damp and her nipples were aching to be sucked.

Simon gave another sharp tug on her undies and suddenly they were down at her ankles. Changing tactics, Beth opened her legs as wide as she could to make it difficult for him to get them over her feet. In doing so, she totally exposed her sex lips to his burning gaze. She heard him groan and felt a rush of moisture flowing from her.

As Simon grabbed one of her legs and tugged her underwear off, Beth whimpered in mock fear and tried to wriggle across the floor. He was too quick for her. As he grabbed both her legs to pull her back, he crossed her ankles and forced her to turn over. She gazed up at him, doing her best to look helpless.

'Please don't,' she whispered.

Simon ran his eyes hungrily down her naked body while his hand continued to fondle his erection.

'You don't mean that.' Slowly, he leant back over her and began to tug at her stockings. As soon as he had pulled one off, he tied it to the arm of the settee and looped the other end round her right wrist. Beth immediately tried to free herself, but Simon grabbed her again and whipped the other stocking off. He knelt over her chest so that his erection was only inches away from her mouth.

She twisted and bucked under him until she felt his crotch resting on her breasts. She continued to squirm, kicking with her feet and trying to wriggle out from under him. Swiftly, he tied the other stocking to her left wrist and attached it to the desk leg. His cock was so close to her face that it was all she could do to resist sucking him into her mouth.

'That should keep you where I want you,' he whispered.

Trapped, Beth began to wriggle her bottom up and down in an attempt to escape. Please don't let him see how much I want this, she breathed silently as he moved back so that he could examine her whole body.

As she continued to roll her hips from side to side, Beth made a futile effort to cross her legs to protect her mound from his burning gaze. Another whimper of desire burst from her lips and she could only hope that he would think it was one of fear. She rolled on to her side away from him, and started to tug against the restraints holding her wrists.

'Behave yourself.' Simon raised his hand and smacked her buttocks. Beth jumped at the force of the blow and her eyes began to water at the unexpected sting.

'Ow!' she cried. She gritted her teeth as he smacked her again. 'Stop it. Let me go.'

Simon ignored her. He ran his fingers slowly up the back of her legs and rested them on her buttocks. Beth squirmed and rolled on to her back again to try to trap his hand underneath her.

Simon grinned and grabbed her right breast. Beth gasped and tried to free her arms from their restraints to protect herself. She lifted her leg as high as she could to push him away. She could hear his breathing growing heavier and more laboured as she continued her half-hearted struggle. Clearly, he was enjoying it as much as she was.

'Stop it. Untie me,' she demanded in the sternest voice she could manage. 'Look. I'll pretend nothing has happened if you just untie me now.'

'Nothing has happened, yet.' Simon moved closer and pushed his fingers between her legs. 'But we'll soon change that.'

Beth clamped her thighs together as tightly as she could. 'Let me go,' she repeated in a deadly whisper. She did her best to ignore the tingling sensation his touch was causing.

Simon gave her a small smile and moved down towards her feet. She noticed that one of his hands was busy fondling his cock again and the sight of his bursting erection throbbing between his fingers caused her to gasp aloud. He pulled her ankles apart roughly and knelt between her feet. Slowly, he began to work his way back up her legs, forcing them wider and wider apart. She felt the fingertips of his free hand caressing her thighs softly.

Beth shuddered from tip to toe. He was so big and so hard. She lifted her head up off the floor as far as possible so that she could watch his prick throbbing and twitching in his hand. She couldn't remember ever being this excited before. Not even with Jonathan and his two friends. Her breath was coming in short little pants and she had to bite her tongue to stop herself moaning with anticipation. She waited impatiently while he ripped open his shirt and pulled it over his head without bothering to undo all the buttons.

'Don't you dare,' Beth hissed as he took his cock back in his hand and guided it towards his target. She made another supreme effort to wiggle free, but he pushed her down easily and squeezed her right breast painfully.

'Lie still.'

Beth fixed him with a cold stare, as if daring him to go the whole way. As she felt the tip of his manhood begin to penetrate her, her whole body trembled with another spasm of excitement.

'No!' She uttered what she hoped would sound like a cry of total despair.

Simon ignored her pleas and squeezed her breast even harder. 'Keep still,' he commanded hoarsely.

Keep still! Jesus. She knew she mustn't let him realise how much she was enjoying it, but how could she keep still when his cock was teasing her like that? She tried, without success, to suppress another shiver of longing.

Slowly, ever so slowly, Simon pushed himself into her. Beth wanted to shout aloud for the sheer pleasure and success of it. She gritted her teeth so that all that came out was a subdued moan.

Simon reached under her and grabbed her buttock with his free hand. As he leant forward over her and began to kiss her, he squeezed her bum with his fingers and forced his full weight down on to her. Beth gasped as he began to pump slowly in and out. His body pressed down on her and his mouth covered hers so that there was nothing she could do but let him have his way. Gradually, he began to thrust harder and faster.

'Oh, Christ,' he moaned. 'I've wanted you for so long.' She sensed him slowing and changing the rhythm as he tried to prolong his pleasure. Instinctively, she tightened her legs around him and thrust her pelvis up to meet his strokes, squeezing him with her muscles. He groaned again and a feeling of triumph shot through her as he stiffened and came.

Just the thought of his climax was enough to push Beth over the top to her own release. She was sobbing helplessly. He must have known that she had enjoyed it as much as he had. Just so long as he didn't realise that she had deliberately planned the whole thing.

Simon slid himself out and lifted his weight off her. Without saying a word he stood up, pulled his pants up and walked across the room towards the little kitchen area.

Beth closed her eyes and lay completely still, gloating over her success. She made no attempt to cover herself or to stifle her little sobs of pleasure as her mind savoured every moment of the experience. After a few minutes, she heard the sound of the kitchen bin closing and then his footsteps returning. She opened her eyes.

Simon had picked up his shirt and tie and was pulling them back on over his head.

Realising that he was just going to leave her there, Beth slipped her wrists from the ineffective restraints of her stockings and stood up slowly. She was surprised at how shaky her legs still were from the intensity of their lovemaking. She couldn't remember when it had last been quite that good, if ever.

Beth picked up her skirt and wrapped it round her. Only one button remained intact and her thigh was completely exposed. Her blouse wasn't in much better condition. The whole outfit was good for nothing but the rubbish bin. Perhaps she could claim for new clothes on company expenses!

Despite her earlier plans for him, Beth knew that she was too weary to even try to turn him on again. Without saying a word, she headed out into her own office. Through the open door, she could see that Simon had finished dressing and returned to his own desk. She wondered what was going through his mind.

What would he do now? Was he wondering what to say to her or what she might say to him? Would he try to pretend that he hadn't meant it to happen, that he had just lost control? Would he dare try it again? Could he do it again? Despite her weariness, her clit tingled.

It was just over a month now since the interview that had led to this job. The advert had sounded perfect. Just exactly the opportunity she was looking for. Her brief but intense fling with Alec had come to a natural end and Beth was ready for something new in her life.

Her job in the newsagents seemed completely dull once young Jonathan was no longer there and she had resigned within a couple of weeks of him moving away.

Beth couldn't believe how much she still missed Jonathan. They had had so much fun together – even if she had lived in constant fear of what would happen if anyone had ever discovered that she was having an affair with a sixteen-year-old schoolboy! Not that there had been anything dirty or sordid about it. At the time, she had been lonely and insecure after her marriage breakup and Jonathan had been, well, Jonathan had been sweet and young and very innocent, and totally consumed by his insatiable passion for her. While it lasted, what they had enjoyed together had been both very special and very beautiful. It was a memory that she would always treasure.

The real motivation for her change of career, though, was her ex-husband, Tony. Ever since he had discovered how much she had changed in recent months, he had been finding one feeble excuse after another to visit her. He had even gone so far as to let himself in with the spare key one day while she had been in the shower.

Just because he still paid her maintenance, it didn't mean he had any rights. She regretted the way she had led him on when she had first discovered how much he now wanted her. If she were ever to be free of him, she needed to find a way to make herself financially independent and there was little chance of that while she was working in a newsagent.

It had been her best friend Ann who had come up with the idea of her returning to the financial world.

'After all, you used to earn good money once,' Ann had reminded her. 'And you've never lost your interest in financial matters. If you hadn't married Tony, you might have really got on as a career woman.'

A quick refresher course in office skills had soon brought her CV up to scratch, and then it was just a matter of finding the right company. She had hardly been able to believe her luck when she had seen Simon's advert for a personal assistant in the local paper.

Although his name had sounded vaguely familiar, it had only been when she had attended the interview and come face to face with him that she had remembered Simon Henderson.

Beth had known straight away that he did not remember her. Why should he? They hadn't seen each other for years. Not since she had married Tony and left work to become a housewife. She had been a bit on the plump side in those days and not an obvious choice for someone like him.

Simon had been the office heartthrob and all the girls had yearned after him. For a while, before Tony, Beth had been hopelessly infatuated with him. Apart from taking advantage of her to run his errands and do all his dirty work, as he took advantage of everyone, Simon hadn't even known that she existed.

She wasn't really surprised to discover that he had done so well for himself. He had an unpleasant talent for sucking up to those in power and advancing his own career at everyone else's expense. She could still remember how he had once outmanoeuvred Tony for a promotion he most certainly didn't deserve. And now, here he was, the director of his own financial advisory company. How typical of the man.

Right from the start, her interview had gone well. It was obvious that Simon was interested in more than just her experience and qualifications. He had hardly been able to take his eyes off her breasts from the moment she had walked in the door, and his pointed comments about 'needing someone who would give everything to the job' had not escaped her notice. Well, as her friend Gerri always said: if you've got it, flaunt it. She had relished how avidly he had watched her body while they chatted.

Her initial reaction, once she had recognised him, had been to leave. He had always been an arrogant bastard; he certainly wasn't her ideal choice for a boss. It irritated her that he so obviously did not remember her at all. He must have noticed from her CV that they had once worked for the same company. Even though she had only been a junior member of the team, she would have thought that he might have shown some spark of recognition.

It was such a good job, though. Just what she was looking for. Jobs like this were few and far between. It was only after she had actually received his job offer that Beth began to realise just what an opportunity she had for a bit of extra fun. As she sealed the envelope with her acceptance letter inside, Beth made herself a promise. He might not remember her now but, by the time she had finished with him, Simon Henderson would certainly never forget her again.

Thirty minutes later, Beth had finished the last of the outstanding work in her tray. She gathered up everything that required Simon's immediate attention and headed back into his office. While she waited for instructions, she stood well within range of his hands and began to fiddle awkwardly with her gaping clothes, deliberately drawing attention to her semi-nakedness.

Simon pointed to one of the letters. She was pleased to see that his finger was shaking.

'What have you done about this?' he demanded, obviously doing his best to ignore the state of her clothing. His voice was shaking even more than his finger.

Beth leant over the desk and let her skirt open wide. Simon's eyes homed in on her thighs. She leant over further and her left breast partially flopped out of her blouse.

'I sent confirmation yesterday,' she replied, then jumped with surprise as his hand began to slide gently up her leg. She made no attempt to pull away.

Simon spun his swivel chair round to face her and put his knees either side of her legs. One hand started to caress her thighs while the other played with her pubes. Beth pursed her lips and struggled not to react. Although she could clearly feel the muscles of her bottom tightening and relaxing at his touch, she doubted that he would notice. She gasped with shock and pleasure as he pushed his finger on to the bud of her clit. She was afraid even to look at his groin in case her face gave her true thoughts away.

'It was entirely your own fault earlier,' he told her, as he continued to explore her.

Beth closed her eyes and prayed that he wouldn't stop. She said nothing.

'You've got such a fabulous body. I get a hard-on just thinking about you.' He lifted the hem of her skirt, pulled her down on to his lap and began to kiss her neck.

Beth could feel his erection rising up urgently underneath her. One of his hands was fondling her sex, the other her breast. The goosebumps were springing up all over her skin at the feel of his lips. It was almost

17

impossible not to show him how much she was enjoying herself. God, he had wonderful fingers.

'You didn't really mind, did you?' he whispered.

Beth found she was having trouble breathing again. She tried not to so much as move against his fingers, lest she involuntarily gave him the answer he wanted.

'I'm sorry, Beth.' He removed his fingers. Beth almost collapsed with a mixture of relief and frustration; she had been so close. She melted into his lap. Before she could say anything, he put his hand under her arms and lifted her up off him.

Beth tried to stand but Simon twisted her round and continued to push her forward so that she fell across the desk. Instinctively she stuck out her hands, pushing everything on to the floor. Passively, she allowed him to manoeuvre her into position.

'I have to have you again.' Simon pulled the hem of her skirt up and tucked it into her waistband, then put his hand under her crotch to lift her up. Beth lay across the desk with her buttocks twitching. He slid his hands down over her hips and pushed her legs apart.

Beth obediently opened them and stood on her toes to give him the best possible access. She knew she was already damp with desire. He must realise how ready and willing she was. Had he been apologising for what he had done, or for what he was about to do? Beth felt a tinge of apprehension mingling with her desire.

'Please, not again,' she whispered softly, determined to play her role to the end.

Simon stood back, staring at her apparent surrender. Beth stifled a small whimper as her climax began to build up inside her again. She was sure that, if he so much as touched her there, she would come. She wouldn't be able to help herself. She whimpered softly again, pleased that she seemed to have mastered the art of turning her groans of pleasure into sobs and whimpers of surrender.

'You do understand, don't you?' She heard his zip

18

open and his trousers fall to the ground. 'Tell me you don't mind.'

Her whole body was shaking with her desperate need. Just get on with it, she begged him silently. She could barely breathe. Every muscle was trembling and twitching. She couldn't hold off any longer.

He started to fondle her buttocks again and Beth felt the tears welling up in her eyes.

'You've got a gorgeous bum, Beth.' As Simon bent forward and ran his tongue over her buttock, she felt both his hands still stroking her. He kissed the other cheek, then bit it gently. It was the final straw. With a deep, low-throated moan, Beth climaxed. Exhausted, she collapsed down over the desk, her legs almost too weak to support her.

Seemingly oblivious to what he had done, Simon pushed her further on to the desk and guided his cock into her. Beth was so numb she hardly felt him penetrate her. She was so wet that there was no resistance as he slipped effortlessly in and out of her with his thighs slapping rhythmically against her.

He pushed her against the desk with his hands, groaning and pumping faster and faster. Startled, she found herself responding yet again.

'Please,' she sobbed. 'Oh God.' For the first time, a feeling of panic swept through her. Surely she couldn't survive another orgasm so soon? She was afraid that, if she came again, she might actually pass out from the pleasure. Tears were running down her cheeks as she tried to wriggle out of his embrace. There was no escape and that knowledge increased the intensity of the experience.

'Please!' she panted as another climax tore through her.

Simon continued to pump harder and harder, his breathing ragged. His fingers were everywhere, squeezing and pinching her exposed flesh. One hand fondled her bottom and breasts alternately; the other held her hip, pulling her hard on to him. His thighs slapped loudly against her buttocks and he grunted loudly at every stroke.

As his climax approached, he began to groan urgently in time with his thrusting, increasing the pace as he slammed in and out of her. Finally, he gasped and rammed himself into her as deep as he could. Another gasp and it was all over. He slumped over her, totally spent.

Beth wasn't sure how long it had lasted. It had seemed like hours. She was so weary that she didn't even notice him withdraw. She was still lying there with her skirt up over her bottom when she heard him say goodbye. She fell asleep over the desk.

A police siren woke her. It took a few seconds for her even to remember where she was, then a rush of elation swept through her at the extent of her success. She could hardly believe what had happened, or how much she had enjoyed what he had done to her.

She groaned as she stood up and tried to ease the aches from her cramped muscles. She was so stiff she could hardly walk. Gingerly, she made her way over to the kitchen area and gratefully gulped down a glass of cold water. She began trying to rearrange her tattered clothing. It was a futile effort.

Had he any idea how much she had enjoyed herself? She almost writhed in shame as she remembered the way she had responded to his caresses. That wasn't quite what she had planned.

It was bad enough knowing what a conceited, arrogant bastard he was. She might not have seen him for years, but she could still remember all the office gossip of his many conquests. Even in the few weeks since she had started working for him, she had already seen how he behaved with some of his female clients and how they fussed and preened themselves for his benefit. She certainly hadn't expected to discover that he had anything to be conceited or arrogant about!

20

As she finished dressing, Beth was already contemplating her revenge. She knew she was being somewhat unreasonable, since it had been she who had led him on, but, somehow, when she got back from her training course, she was going to find a way to teach Simon Henderson a lesson he would not soon forget.

Simon took his time driving home. His thoughts were in utter turmoil.

He had known from the first time he had seen Beth that he had to add her to his list of conquests. He had always had a bit of a thing for brunettes. Beth's long, dark hair was complemented perfectly by her golden-toned complexion and those deceptively innocent hazel eyes. It was strange that he didn't really remember her from when they had worked together before. Why hadn't he had her years ago?

God, she had a fabulous body. Tall, slim and firm in all the right places. If he hadn't known that she was 38, he would have guessed her to be in her late twenties, early thirties. Next to her, his fair-haired wife seemed dull and mousy.

He remembered the way she had whimpered and struggled helplessly against him, pretending that she didn't want him to, when all the time . . . The memory inflamed him. Beth had been every bit as good as he had anticipated, maybe even better. He had loved that innocent little-girl act she had put on for him; loved the feeling of power and control it had given him.

As he felt himself hardening, he wondered if he should go back and take her again. She had probably already left by now. His wife would have to do. Maybe he would rip Marie's clothes off and take her into the garden; she hated doing it outside. The very thought of it made his cock throb urgently.

21

Chapter Two

*F*ortunately, since she was due to be away from the office all the following week, there was no need for Beth to make any immediate decisions about Simon.

The course itself, in advanced financial-management software, was probably the most popular in their profession and held at one of the best training centres in the country. It was a brilliant opportunity to improve her CV and Beth knew how lucky she was to be given a place so quickly. Simon must have pulled a few strings to get her in. She felt no qualms about allowing him to pay for a course that would allow her to move on, as soon as possible, to better things. He had always been a master at using other people for his own ends. Now it was her turn.

The following Monday morning, as she packed her bag and prepared for the journey up to York, she couldn't help wondering how Simon would expect her to show her gratitude. Having had his way with her once he would, no doubt, believe he was entitled to enjoy her body as and when he pleased. It seemed ironical that such a bastard should also be such a fabulous lay. Her knees felt weak at the thought of what he had done to her.

* * *

Since she was unfamiliar with York, Beth took a taxi from the station. She was so preoccupied with her thoughts and plans that she scarcely noticed the admiring glances the taxi driver gave her in the mirror as he skilfully negotiated the rush-hour traffic. Her ex-husband had been pestering her again over the weekend and her determination to make herself financially independent of him was stronger than ever. She really needed to make the most of this course.

The training centre turned out to be quite near the heart of the city. It was a plain, modern brick building of indeterminate architecture and it stuck out like a sore thumb against some of York's more beautiful buildings. Beth noticed that the tiny car park at the back was already full and she was relieved that she had chosen to come by train. She had always hated driving in unfamiliar places.

As soon as she had checked in at the main desk and received her identity badge from a plain-faced, bespectacled woman who seemed to have forgotten how to smile, Beth nervously sought out her assigned classroom.

Several of the other trainees, all male, had already arrived and they stood around smiling sheepishly at each other and sipping foul-tasting coffee from flimsy polystyrene cups. Gradually, as ten o'clock approached, the classroom filled.

Beth chose a desk near the back of the room on the left so that she would be able to see out of the window. She settled herself as comfortably as she could on the hard, wooden chair and took out her notebook and pens. Giving up on the coffee, she allowed her eyes to roam around the room, eyeing up the men.

Most of them seemed slightly younger than her, but she noticed a few appreciative glances here and there and she gave an encouraging smile to those that looked the most interesting. She was not really surprised to discover that there was only one other woman. The financial world still tended to be somewhat male dominated.

23

One of the men who had been watching her ever since she had arrived walked over to her desk and bent forward to examine the name badge pinned over her left breast.

'Oh, Beth.'

Beth stood up politely and examined his badge in return.

'John, is it?' she responded with a friendly smile. 'Nice to meet you.' They shook hands as she appraised him openly.

At first glance, he was not really her type. Perhaps 30 to 35, he was tall and rather thickset with short, light-brown hair and hazel eyes similar in colour to her own. He had an attractive face with a square jawline and an enigmatic smile that hinted at a deep and thoughtful personality. She had the feeling that he was a man who knew just how to get what he wanted out of life. She also sensed that his interest in her was more than just casual politeness.

Another of the men spotted the opportunity to meet her and ambled over to join them.

'And who is this lovely creature, then?' Beth felt his hand brush her arm as she turned to face him.

Even taller than John, he was of much slimmer build with collar-length blond hair and pale blue eyes that were magnified by his tear-drop-shaped glasses. He was dressed casually in dark trousers and a soft leather jacket and his face had the tanned, weathered appearance of someone who spent a lot of time out of doors. Beth guessed him to be about the same age as John, maybe slightly younger. The man raised his hand to her name badge so that his little finger was resting lightly on her breast.

'Beth. That's a nice name.' A second finger made fleeting contact with her breast.

Beth smiled innocently and stepped back out of reach.

'Why, thank you –' she checked his badge '– Steve.'

Just then, the door opened and the instructor walked

in. To Beth's surprise and delight, she was female; a pretty blonde, probably in her mid-to-late twenties. She was very slim and had a rather boyish figure, emphasised by the mannish suit she was wearing. At least Beth would have more than one other ally against the men, although the other female trainee didn't look like she would create much of a diversion – but she wouldn't provide any real competition, either.

As they began to take their seats and settle down, Beth noticed that the men did not seem to be paying the instructor much attention. She wondered whether it was her masculine clothing that was putting them off, or if they just didn't like the idea of a female instructor.

'OK. Good morning, everybody. Welcome to Top Spot Training. My name is Lisa Williams and I will be taking most of the course this week.' She glanced round slowly, as if appraising the potential of the group.

'The primary aim of the course is to familiarise you with version 4.1 of Softtrend X. For anyone who doesn't already know, Softtrend X is fast becoming the *de facto* trends-analysis package in the financial sector. Since 4.1 has several major new features we've got rather a lot to get through so I will be moving at a fair old pace. Just call out if you don't follow anything. Also, there will be plenty of time to ask questions during the practical sessions. You'll notice that you've each been provided with a laptop for that.' She looked round again, her green eyes flashing. She seemed to have a slight trace of an accent that suggested she might be Swedish or Dutch.

'Now, before we get stuck in, I think it would help if you all quickly introduce yourselves. Maybe we can start here?' She pointed to the mousy woman who had seated herself in the front row.

As the introductions progressed, Beth began to doodle absent-mindedly in the margin of her notepad. Without realising what she was doing, she found herself scribbling down the names of those men who most interested her and including an odd and suggestive comment or two about them to help her remember who was who. She put a star beside Steve's name then, after a moment of hesitation, another star beside John. There was something about him that intrigued her. She had no intention of sitting alone in her hotel room every night.

When it was her own turn, she was pleased to notice that the room fell silent. She was fairly certain that more than one man was making a note of her own particulars, too. She kept her comments short and to the point and did her best to gloss over how short a time she had been back in the financial world.

As Beth sat back down, Lisa gave her a warm smile of thanks before she moved on to the next person. It was only after everyone had had their say that Beth realised she was the only one Lisa had smiled at. She noticed that one or two of the men were beginning to pay Lisa a bit more attention now that she had taken her jacket off and they could see her pert figure and the outline of her bra under her white blouse. Beth decided that it was likely to be an interesting week.

Lisa handed out a set of training notes and got stuck in to her first lecture. As she turned her back to write up a few pointers on the whiteboard, Beth let her eyes wander round the room again. She caught Steve staring at her and remembered the way he had allowed his finger to brush lightly over her breast while he had examined her badge. Cheeky sod. He reminded her of an older version of Jonathan with all that soft blond hair. Her pulse quickened.

She swivelled her head to look at John and caught him examining her again too. Did he and Steve already know each other? Even though John was a self-employed consultant while Steve worked for a large finance company, they hadn't acted as if they had only just met. Perhaps they had operated together before. Maybe they always worked as a team.

She noticed that Steve was talking quietly to another man and quickly consulted her notes. Brian. Well, Brian had been giving her more than the occasional appreciative glance. She rather liked the look of him. It was probably his gentle brown eyes and that friendly, carefree smile. He was dressed more formally than the other two, but he wore his dark business suit well. It was funny how some men looked good in a suit while others just looked like failed sales reps. She noticed a few silvery hairs at his temples and guessed him to be around her own age. She checked her notes again and saw that, like Steve, he worked for a big London finance house. Yes, she might enjoy whiling away a long evening with him.

Lisa finished writing up her notes and turned round to explain the first piece of practical work she wanted them to try. As she spoke, Beth glared apprehensively at the laptop on her desk, wishing that she could get over her instinctive dislike of computers and praying that she was not about to make a complete fool of herself.

To her great delight, however, she soon discovered that the work was easily within her capabilities. She had not realised how much she had already learnt from Simon. It was lucky that he was such a whiz with computers. As she typed away, she watched Lisa moving round the room, giving help here and there. Finally, she arrived at Beth's desk and crouched down to talk to her. She rested one hand on the back of Beth's chair and one on her desk, just inches from her knee.

'OK? Anything I can do to help?' She gave Beth another encouraging smile.

Beth could not resist. She had to find out, one way or the other. She turned to face Lisa and crossed her legs so that her knee was almost touching the instructor's leg.

'No. Nothing at the moment.' She leant forward so that she could whisper in her ear.

'Actually, I did quite a lot of studying before I came. It's very important for me to do well. The size of my pay rise depends on it.' Her nipple just brushed the back of Lisa's hand. She heard Lisa take a sharp breath and saw her give Beth's body a more than casual glance.

'Well, if there is anything I can do,' Lisa repeated, 'I'll be very happy to help. Anything at all.'

Beth smiled and Lisa patted her on the knee.

'I mean it. Any time, Beth.' Lisa gave her a conspiratorial look and her hand slipped a few inches up Beth's thigh.

Beth grinned. Despite her lack of familiarity with computers, she was fairly certain that she should be able to pass the course without any trouble and the pay rise was just a figment of her imagination. If she were being completely honest with herself, she could not resist the opportunity for teasing.

She had already learnt how much she enjoyed turning men on, but this was the first time she had ever tried to entice another woman. It thrilled her more than she could believe. Of course, a woman had to be harder for her to seduce than a man. Lisa's responses wouldn't be ruled by her prick, as a man's so often seemed to be. She smiled to herself.

At the morning break Lisa wheeled in a trolley of tea, coffee and biscuits from the corridor. Beth immediately found herself surrounded. She felt Steve brush his hip up against her and noticed that John's eyes were riveted on her cleavage. Brian wasn't exactly keeping his eyes to himself, either.

Although she was enjoying their attention, Beth couldn't help wondering whether she would be able to cope with all three men at lunchtime. Taking advantage of a brief lapse in their concentration, she excused herself politely and moved over to where Lisa was sipping her coffee – thankfully, this time, from a china cup. Out of the corner of her eye, Beth noticed looks of disappointment on the men's faces and she suppressed a grin.

After she and Lisa had chatted about the course work for a while, Beth asked where she could find a good place to eat for lunch.

'Oh, I usually go to a little place just around the

corner,' Lisa replied. She barely hesitated before adding, 'Why don't you join me?'

'Thank you. I'd love to.' Remembering the way Lisa had responded to her earlier, Beth felt a warm tingle of anticipation.

The rest of the morning seemed to drag, but finally one o'clock arrived and the class ended its morning session. As soon as they had left the building, Beth and Lisa headed up the main road towards the restaurant. Beth was still grinning at the look of disappointment on the men's faces when they realised that she would not be joining them. She liked the idea of them having to keep their hands to themselves over lunch. Or perhaps they would find another use for their roaming fingers. She started wondering who had got the most to offer and was soon fantasising about inspecting each of them in turn. In her mind's eye, she could see them wanking away for her while she made her selection.

'Is there something funny?' Lisa questioned, seeing her smile.

'No. Just a thought.' Beth quickly dismissed the image and forced her thoughts back to Lisa. Was she correct in her assumption that Lisa was interested in her? If so, how far was she prepared to let things go?

By the time they reached the restaurant, they were chatting away together as if they had known each other for years. Beth discovered that Lisa's mother was Dutch and that she had been brought up in Holland, which explained her slight accent.

Lisa confidently led her to a small booth in one corner. She stood aside to let Beth slide in first, then slipped herself in beside her. The waitress immediately came over with the menus. As Lisa leant over to point out the best items, she moved her hip right up next to Beth's. She was so close that Beth could feel the heat of her thigh and a small thrill of excitement ran through her.

Lisa half turned in her seat and pushed her leg up against Beth's. She patted her on the knee.

'Actually, I usually just have a cheese salad,' she said. 'They have a wonderful selection of cheeses here.' As she spoke, she moved her body again so that her hand was fully resting on Beth's thigh, just above her knee.

'Well, why don't you order for both of us?' Beth replied softly, doing her best to keep the tremor out of her voice at the unfamiliar touch of another woman.

Lisa gave her a beaming smile and turned to signal for the waitress. As she turned back, her hand slid, seemingly accidentally, halfway up Beth's thigh. As if suddenly realising what she was doing, she quickly apologised and slipped it back down before removing it.

Although she knew full well that it was no accident, Beth had decided to play along. Lisa had almost reached the top of Beth's stocking before she had stopped herself. Beth wasn't sure just how far she would have let her go. Her leg was still tingling and she was surprised to sense a slight dampness in her panties. She wasn't attracted to Lisa, exactly, but she was certainly excited by the forbidden aspect of it all. She realised that she really wanted to know what it would be like with another woman. She wanted to see if she could seduce Lisa or, better still given her own lack of experience, let Lisa seduce her.

She started to fantasise what it would be like. Would she dare? Could she do it? How would it make her feel? Excited, Beth placed her hand on her own leg and began to slide it gradually up towards her stocking top. Out the corner of her eye, she noticed that Lisa was watching her with a knowing smile. Another little tremor of desire rushed through her and her panties grew even damper.

The waitress returned with their order and Beth removed her hand to pick up her knife and fork.

'So, what are your plans for this evening?' Lisa asked her, as they began to tuck in. 'I'd be happy to show you around if you like. I've lived here quite a while so I know my way about.'

Beth thought quickly. She was more than tempted, but

decided that she needed time to think through the implications.

'Thanks for the offer,' she replied, 'but, to be honest, I'm completely shattered after the journey up here this morning. I think I'm just going to have a hot bath and get a good night's sleep.'

Lisa looked disappointed. 'Well, perhaps we could get together another evening?'

'Yes. Why not?' Beth was certainly not going to close the door on the possibility. 'I'd like that. When I am not feeling so drained.'

Lisa immediately appeared to cheer up and as they ate they chatted happily, their conversation ranging from topic to topic: music, food, holidays, everything except, surprisingly, men. Beth realised that it was the first time she had ever chatted for so long with another woman without the subject coming up.

As the meal progressed, Beth realised that she was taking quite a liking to her instructor. Lisa was very amusing outside the classroom. By the time they were on to the coffee, she had Beth in fits of laughter over some of the things various trainees had got up to in the past. Beth reached out and put her hand on Lisa's knee.

'I think I am really going to enjoy this week, Lisa. You are so much fun to be with.'

Lisa immediately covered Beth's hand with her own and pulled it up higher on her thigh. Beth's feelings of arousal increased and intensified. It was like when she was first touched by Jonathan: exciting and naughty.

'Well, I suppose I had better get back,' she joked breathlessly. 'The teacher is a bit strict. She might put me over her knee if I'm late.'

'Yes, she would enjoy that. She can be very demanding.' Lisa gave Beth's knee a final pat. 'I'll get the bill.'

'Oh no, really, I can't let you do that.' Beth reached for her shoulder bag.

'I insist.' Lisa snatched the bill and headed for the cash desk.

31

Beth watched her walk. She had a nice figure, she decided. Perhaps a bit boyish, but that was good. She wondered if Lisa always dressed in such a masculine manner. Would it be easier to make love to another woman if she dressed and acted more like a man, or would it be more fun to imagine herself in the masculine role, seducing the female? She imagined herself sliding her hand slowly up under Lisa's skirt the way Lisa had been doing to her earlier. She found the idea surprisingly stimulating.

On their way back to the training centre, Beth brought up the subject of women wearing trousersuits.

'I used to wear jeans all the time but now I find they make me feel a bit sexless,' she confessed, nonchalantly. 'I always wear skirts and stockings now because they make me feel so feminine.' Not wishing to sound too critical, she continued quickly, 'Mind you, if I had your job then I would probably wear trousers, too. With your figure, the men just wouldn't be able to concentrate otherwise.'

Beth hoped it was enough of a hint. She felt quite pleased with herself. It had been just the right thing to say about Lisa's figure. She could tell that Lisa was pleased with the compliment as well as a little thoughtful.

'I usually dress up in the evenings,' Lisa replied slowly. 'But not at work. To be honest, it's not really company policy.'

'I see.' Beth smiled. Contrary to what Lisa had just said, Beth had noticed several other female members of staff wearing dresses. She felt sure that Lisa had got her message.

They strolled the rest of the way back to the training school in silence, each seemingly lost in her own thoughts. By the time they reached the classroom, Beth had made her decision. She was going to go through with it.

'How about tomorrow night?' she suggested nervously. 'My treat.'

'Oh, I'm sorry. I can't. I have to see my mother.'

Beth looked disappointed.

'I can make Wednesday though,' Lisa added quickly.

Beth hesitated. She didn't like not being completely in control. Besides, now that she had made her decision she wanted to act on it. Perhaps she should have agreed to tonight? She really was exhausted.

'Wednesday is fine,' she said. 'Will you pick me up? I'm staying at the Hilton. I can let you have my room number tomorrow.'

'Yes, of course. Shall we say seven o'clock?' Lisa's face suddenly looked flushed and her green eyes were sparkling with excitement.

'Yes. That's great.' Beth wondered if it was really her mother Lisa was seeing. She was surprised at the twinge of jealousy.

Beth enjoyed the rest of the afternoon. Although it was far more comprehensive, the new software wasn't really all that different from the earlier version that Simon had on his office PC. Once she had got used to using the laptop, she had no trouble with the exercises Lisa set for them. To her, manipulating the stock market and predicting company trends had always seemed like some sort of a game. Although slightly sceptical of the real advantage of the some of the fancier software gimmicks, especially the AI relational database, she had no difficulty in creating fictitious companies and predicting the probable market trends.

During the tea break, she quickly found herself surrounded by John, Brian and Steve again. Although they kept the conversation strictly on financial matters, she was aware of the desire smouldering in their eyes as they cast appreciative glances over her body. The proximity of so much masculinity focused on her made her tingle all over.

To her surprise, Brian was the first to ask her out. For

some reason, she had expected Steve to be the first off the mark.

'Well, not tonight.' She turned him down gently. 'Perhaps tomorrow?'

Both Steve and John extended invitations of their own shortly afterwards.

'I know. Why don't we all go together?' Beth suggested brightly. She could tell that the men were not too happy with that idea. The possibilities from her point of view made Beth feel quite weak.

'It's either that or not at all,' she insisted. 'How can I possibly choose between you?'

Defeated, they laughed and agreed. Beth wondered what the evening would bring. She studied each groin again surreptitiously, trying to guess who had the most to offer. Unless he had any extra padding down there, she thought it was probably John.

Beth finished her work early and asked Lisa if she could go to her hotel. She was suddenly feeling extremely grubby and weary after the excitement of the day, and she couldn't wait to get into a hot tub. Lisa followed her out.

'Take the stairs, Beth, the lifts can be a bit slow.' She followed Beth into the stairwell. 'I'm really sorry I can't make tomorrow but I always see my mother on Tuesdays.'

Before Beth could reply, Lisa gave her a quick kiss on the lips. Although it took her by surprise, Beth didn't pull away. She smiled when she saw the flush on Lisa's face. She noticed that the other woman was panting slightly and studying Beth's reaction carefully. Beth did her best to keep her own face neutral. Her lips tingled as her leg had done earlier at the other woman's touch.

'I suppose I'd better get back to work.' Lisa's hand lingered momentarily on her arm.

Beth took a couple of steps towards the stairs and felt Lisa's hand slip reluctantly from her arm. She looked round over her shoulder. 'OK. I'll see you tomorrow then. Thanks again for lunch. Bye.'

The hotel was quite close to the training centre and it didn't take Beth long to find it. She checked in at reception and was given room 309 on the third floor.

'Turn left from the lift. It's the end, corner room,' the bored-looking receptionist told her. 'Do you want someone to carry your bag?'

'No. It's not heavy. Can I get a sandwich sent up?' Beth was suddenly too tired even to bother about dressing for dinner.

'Yes, madam. Here's the room service menu.' He handed her a small leather folder. 'Just ring down when you have decided.'

'Actually, I'd love a prawn sandwich,' Beth replied without looking at the menu. 'Brown bread, preferably.'

'Of course, madam. How many rounds?'

'Two, please. And some coffee.' She suppressed a grin when she saw his eyes linger over her breasts. He would be quite good-looking if he took that sour look off his face.

'I'll have it sent up in about ten minutes.' His eyes finished their journey down her body and she was gratified to notice that his expression was distinctly less bored than it had been a moment earlier. She could sense him still watching her as she walked over to the lift.

Beth made her way up to her room and looked around curiously. It had two wide beds, a television, a kettle and a few nicely decorated cupboards and drawers. There was a separate bathroom and the view out of the windows was terrific. She could practically see the whole of York spread out before her and, being on the corner, she could see in both directions. She pressed her nose to the glass and peered out.

To the east, she could see the castle wall and a glimpse of the river glistening in the late evening sunshine. She turned her head and gazed up the main street. It really was a beautiful town, full of character and with such diversity in the buildings. Beth had never seen such clean streets. They put London to shame. She was almost tempted to go out for a stroll, but couldn't quite summon up the energy after her long day. Besides, her food would be arriving shortly. Her tummy rumbled hungrily; she adored prawns. Especially when Simon was paying.

Beth bounced on both beds and chose the one nearest the window. She unpacked her bag quickly and put her blouses and skirts into the cupboard and her underwear in the drawers. By the time she was finished, there was a knock at the door and a young girl's voice called, 'Room service.'

Beth picked up her purse and opened the door. The girl brought the tray in and placed it on the table. Beth smiled gratefully and gave her a tip. The girl thanked her politely and left, closing the door quietly behind her.

Beth locked the door and then stripped off her top layer of clothes to avoid getting any prawn juice on them. She sat down on one of the beds. There was a full-length mirror on the far wall and, as she ate, Beth studied her figure.

Her breasts looked great in the crop top. It had been a good choice. A bra would have made Steve's attentions to her badge less interesting. The material of the crop top was so fine that she had been able to feel his touch as if she had not been wearing anything. Better, actually, because the silk was so smooth.

She had to admit that it had been a neat move of his with the ID badge, managing a surreptitious caress of her breasts. Of course, it was always awkward for women, not knowing where to pin a badge. Men just stuck it on the lapel of their jacket. Maybe there should be a new rule, making them wear it on their flies? Now, that would be more like it! She pictured herself bending down to inspect each name in turn while her fingertips lingered on each one, getting the measure of them ... She raised one hand and stroked her breasts lightly, enjoying the sight and feel of her nipples hardening as they moved under the soft silk. Her nipples were not as big as she would have liked, but big enough. Lisa had smaller breasts than her. What would it be like to touch another woman? She looked at her legs in their stockings and tried to imagine Lisa's hands caressing them. A small shiver ran down her spine.

Beth finished eating her sandwiches and then started to fondle her buttocks. She slid her finger inwards until she met the elastic at the top of her crease and wondered if all three men had been trying to figure out what she was wearing under her skirt.

The sudden thud of a door closing in the corridor outside broke her train of thought. Smiling at her outrageous fantasies, Beth finished her coffee and went into the bathroom to run the bath. She undressed deliberately, practising her striptease and imagining an audience of men watching her, their hands busy in their laps under the table.

God, she was feeling horny. She regretted not agreeing to go out with one of her invitations. Still, it had been a long journey that morning and, anyway, she liked to plan what she intended to happen before she went out.

Beth stepped into the bath and gradually submerged her whole body. She was glad she had thought to bring a sponge. She washed the dirt of the day off and soon felt clean and relaxed. Her thoughts drifted to her planned revenge on Simon Henderson. She was going to enjoy that. She started to go over the details in her mind then dismissed them, returning to the next day and her triple date. She began to plan what she intended to happen. Should she take the lead or let them think they were in control? What should she wear? She was fairly sure that she could expect a lot more flirting and accidental touching during the day. If she wore a tight skirt, it would have the advantage of showing the outline of her stockings and garters to encourage them.

Of course, whatever she wore, Lisa would see her, too. She had a date with Lisa on Wednesday. What did you wear to excite another woman? She had never really considered it before. Well, that was Wednesday's problem. She returned to the following day: tight silk skirt, stockings and garters – perhaps the lacy top and no bra. Then again, the lacy top only came down to her midriff. Remembering Steve's brief caress earlier, she began to fantasise about him accidentally catching his finger in the top and pulling it up until she was totally exposed to everyone. Hmm, perhaps not. Maybe she had better wear something else.

She settled on a low-cut satin blouse and lacy half bra. That should keep them interested, yet not give too much away. Of course, she could stick close to Lisa all day. That would frustrate the men. She wanted to be sure that she teased them sufficiently to get them really excited for their date. What would she wear for them, then? She reviewed her limited wardrobe again in her mind.

How about her short, loose skirt? A quick twirl and it would fan out around her, showing everything! She could wear it with the bare-midriff top, and just a thong and stockings underneath. It was a good thing that the weather was so mild. She would suggest that they take her to the restaurant Lisa had told her about, one where they also had dancing. There would be plenty of opportunity for wandering hands on the dance floor. Then, back to her room, not one of theirs.

Beth lay back in the hot bath and pictured each of the three men in her mind. They were all quite handsome, although she thought she probably liked Steve's rugged good looks and silky blond hair best. There was something about that smile of John's, though. Instinct told her that John would be a very interesting man to get to know better. She really would have to decide whether to take control or let them. She thought about Simon and how good it had felt letting him think he was in charge. Would she be able to keep all three under control? She would need to be very strict.

She pictured them lined up in a row, waiting for her

38

to make her selection. Perhaps she could have a contest to see who had the most to offer. She could sit on the bed, her skirt up round her thighs, with Steve and Brian on each side of her and John in front, looking up her skirt. She let her imagination have free rein.

'OK. One at a time, drop them. You first, Brian. I want to inspect your credentials.'

She could clearly picture the smile on John's face. They both already knew he had nothing to worry about. She couldn't wait to see for herself.

She imagined the other two protesting, trying to make excuses. Perhaps she would be forced to give them a little more encouragement?

Beth pushed her hand down under the water and put it between her legs. She imagined the look on their faces if she started to play with herself in front of all of them. She would get them all hot and panting for it, then insist they obey her or leave.

She began to caress her clit with one finger. She pretended it was Brian touching her, while John and Steve looked on enviously. She would let him fondle her, even allow him take her hand and place it on his cock. She would squeeze his hardness and feel him growing in her hand. Beth shuddered and pulled her fingers away.

She could see them lined up, red faced and desperate. She conjured up a picture in her mind of each of them in turn beginning to unzip himself. If she was not very much mistaken, John especially was destined to be quite a handful. She remembered the more than obvious outline at his groin and suddenly felt almost dizzy with longing. The fantasy was so real.

She pushed the tips of her fingers into her vagina and imagined that John was thrusting his huge prick deeper and deeper inside her. There was a loud crashing noise and Beth slipped under the water in shock. She came up spluttering and opened her eyes. Her fantasy men disappeared. What the hell was that?

'Room service. Have you finished with your tray, madam?' Someone was knocking on the door.

Damn. Now she would have to wait until tomorrow to see if she had got it anywhere near correct. Why on earth had she turned them all down tonight? Ignoring the door, Beth moved her hand back down under the water and lay back contentedly. As John's erection magically reappeared in her mind, Beth sighed with anticipation and resumed fondling her tingling clit.

John, Brian and Steve met up that evening in the bar of the hotel in which they were staying. Brian ordered a round of drinks and they sat at a corner table to unwind after the long day.

It was not the first time the three of them had been on a training course together and, for a while, they chatted about their work and caught up on each other's news. Soon, they moved on to the day's course work and began speculating about Lisa.

'She's quite a looker, in her way,' Brian commented. 'But she seems a bit hard. Somehow, I don't fancy my chances.'

John nodded thoughtfully. 'Actually, I suspect Beth is more likely to appeal to her than you are,' he suggested. Brian's eyes widened at the implication.

'She's quite something, isn't she? Beth, I mean. How old do you reckon she is?' continued John.

Brian blew the froth off his beer and took a long, satisfying gulp. 'That's great. Just what I needed.'

Steve shrugged. 'Early thirties, maybe? She certainly is gorgeous. I still can't believe she's agreed to go out with us all tomorrow.'

Brian licked the beer off his upper lip and frowned. 'I just wish she'd agreed to go out with me alone. No offence, but I did ask her first and having you guys along will just cramp my style.'

'Maybe she's got a thing about having more than one man at a time,' Steve suggested hopefully. He sighed heavily at this somewhat optimistic fantasy. 'She certainly is one classy lady. Not only beautiful but intelligent too, by the look of it. Did you notice how fast she finished the practical work this afternoon? I was still only halfway through when she left.'

John watched them both thoughtfully. He, too, would have preferred to take Beth out on his own. He had the feeling that Beth was a woman who enjoyed playing games and he had more than a few games of his own in mind.

'I think you'll find that there is a lot more to Beth than meets the eye,' he told his companions softly. 'And, I don't think she is anywhere near as sweet and innocent as she pretends, either.'

No one with a body like hers could be that innocent. Those eyes of hers were enough to drive a man insane. She had been playing with them all, even Lisa. He raised his beer glass in a toast.

'Cheers.' He took a small sip and examined the other men over the rim of the glass.

'Something tells me that tomorrow night is going to be very special,' he added softly. 'Very special and very memorable.'

41

Chapter Three

*L*isa kept them all hard at it the following morning, so that Beth found she had little time to dwell on her various dates to come. Determined to frustrate the advances of the men until later, she kept close to Lisa during the mid-morning break. Since it was such a lovely day, the two women took their coffee outside and sat on a low wall in front of the training centre. Beth took advantage of the opportunity to question Lisa more closely about the aims and goals of the rest of the course. If she could get any advantage out of her friendship, she was determined to make the most of it.

As if by mutual consent, neither of them mentioned their date for the following evening. Beth realised that she was growing increasingly nervous about the whole thing. Short of asking Lisa outright, she couldn't see any way of finding out just how experienced she already was with other women. Despite her erotic thoughts about fondling Lisa's legs, Beth could not really see herself in the dominant role. She wouldn't know where to begin.

No, for once, she was going to have to take the submissive role. She promised herself that she would do whatever Lisa did or told her to do. Possible scenarios immediately flooded her mind and Beth shuddered, partly in fear, partly in anticipation.

When they returned to the classroom, she found it difficult to concentrate on the lecture. Her thoughts kept returning to images of herself caressing Lisa's silky thighs. By lunchtime, she was so eager to get on with the experience that she was tempted to suggest to Lisa that they go to her hotel room right then. While Beth hovered indecisively, Lisa gathered her things together and hurried off without saying where she was going. Beth wondered if she had a date with someone else.

Resisting the temptation to follow her and see what she was up to, Beth sneaked away before any of the men could suggest lunch. After a quick sandwich, she whiled away the time window shopping in the nearby shopping mall. She went into several boutiques and was unable to resist trying on a gorgeous red silk blouse that would go perfectly with the skirt she intended wearing that evening. She examined the price label ruefully, knowing it was far too expensive for her budget. Then she shrugged. She would just have to find a way to lose it on her overall expenses. Simon owed her some new clothes, anyway.

That afternoon, the course continued to go well. To her delight, Beth was beginning to discover that she was well ahead of most of the group and was sure that she would not have any trouble gaining her certificate. Of course, her friendship with Lisa gave her a better insight into what was required. Still, it annoyed her that she wasn't really learning anything new, yet needed to complete the course just to get a piece of paper to say she had passed. It was all such a waste of time. However, the fact that it was also wasting Simon's money did much to pacify her. Besides, considering the other possibilities that were opening up to her, the compensations promised to more than make up for it.

She amused herself during the afternoon tea break teasing yet avoiding close contact with her three male admirers. It was time to forget Lisa for now and concentrate on the potential delights of the coming evening.

'So, which of you is going to pick me up tonight?' Beth questioned as they were packing up their belongings at the end of the day. She had decided to let them take control at first but she needed to retain the option to change her mind later. It would be easier if she could think of a way to get them back to her room, rather than going to one of their rooms at a different hotel. She could already feel herself growing excited wondering which of them would try to take her first. She wanted all three at the same time. Would they do that?

She thought about Simon again. She hadn't struggled that much with him. Tonight would be different. After they had got so far, then she would really put up a fight. Perhaps they would force her into submission or hold her down? Maybe two of them would hold her while the third took her? She tingled all over at the idea.

'We'll all meet up first, then come for you,' John told her.

Beth smiled to herself. Obviously, they didn't trust each other not to take advantage of being alone with her. She told them which room she was in so they could call up for her from reception. It was important that they knew her room number for later, too.

As soon as Lisa released them, Beth rushed back to the hotel to allow herself plenty of time to get ready. She had another long soak in the tub, improving further on her fantasies, then lingered over her dressing and make-up.

Everything went according to plan. A call came just before eight o'clock. By the time she had locked her door behind her, the three men were already on the landing waiting for her. Beth asked if one of them would hold her key, since she had nowhere to put it. This had the added advantage of drawing attention to her clothing. She saw them all scanning her, looking for pockets. As she had decided the day before, she was wearing a mid-length black button up skirt, long enough to cover her stocking tops unless she twirled. Her new blouse was cut low and a little too tight so that there were gaps between the buttons when she stretched. As she moved, the men could see quick flashes of her skimpy bra.

'I'll look after it.' Brian was not slow to take up the opportunity on offer.

Beth handed the key over and watched nervously as he dropped it into his top pocket. It was out of her control now.

Beth could smell the drink on their breath as they crowded in the lift. As he casually placed his arm round her waist, Brian tried to slip his fingers between the buttons of her blouse. She twisted out of reach and scolded him in a joking, friendly way.

Escaping Brian, however, meant that she had stumbled against John, who began to caress her thigh with his fingertips. By the time they had reached the ground floor, all three of them had taken the opportunity to fondle her. Laughing, she stepped out of the lift ahead of them.

'I can see that I have got my hands full tonight,' she complained cheerfully.

'Not yet,' Steve countered suggestively. Beth ignored him and tried not to look down at his crotch.

They were using Brian's car and John was quick to open the door for her. She rewarded him with a brief flash of stocking top as she climbed in. One should always encourage a gentleman.

Beth had already told them about the restaurant that Lisa had recommended to her. There had been no disagreements and she had had the feeling that it did not really matter to them where they went to eat. Perhaps their thoughts were already on the after-dinner entertainment? They were not alone in that. She was already tingling all over again.

Although there were lots of jokes and laughter in the car, the conversation was rather forced and unnatural. Beth found herself wondering if they had already made the decision that they were going to have her, no matter what. She thought they probably had.

She smiled to herself, slightly nervous of what was about to happen but also exhilarated. She remembered that Simon had taken her twice. Would they all want to have her more than once, too? Could she take it? She had felt so drained after Simon that she had just sprawled over the desk. Now, here she was, deliberately provoking three men. This was far more exciting and dangerous. If things got out of hand, she would stand no chance of stopping them

She thrilled at the idea. Although she hardly knew them, she instinctively felt sure that she could trust them not to harm her. She wanted all three at once. It made her feel weak just thinking about it. By the time they arrived at the restaurant, Beth had vividly imagined half a dozen ways they might take her and she was already damp with her arousal. She just hoped that they would not disappoint her.

As she was sitting in the front seat, there was not much opportunity for any of them to take advantage of her during the journey. Beth half-twisted round in her seat, so that she could talk to John and Steve in the back. Her skirt rode up a bit and she noticed Brian giving her little admiring glances from time to time.

She leant forward, allowing both the other men to get a good view down her top. She carefully avoided looking at their trousers. That would only show inexperience. Besides, it would also let them know that she was deliberately teasing and give the game away.

Steve dominated the conversation. He was really quite witty. Beth found that she enjoyed his dry sense of humour and laughed at his jokes. As she had guessed, he was a keen sportsman and sailor. He kept them all amused with his exaggerated tales of adventure on the high seas in his small yacht. She wondered what it might be like to spend a weekend sailing alone with him.

All the men kept eyeing her hungrily and she was

certain that they assumed she didn't realise how much she was revealing of herself. Considering the way their eyes were running all over her, she would have had to be totally stupid not to realise. It was always an advantage to be underestimated.

When they finally arrived at the restaurant car park, Steve leapt out of the back seat and held the door for her. She slid out of the seat, her skirt riding up so that he got more than a quick glimpse of panties as she stepped out.

Since he was holding her hands to help her out of the car, it was a few seconds before she could smooth her skirt down – long enough for the other two to hurry round to enjoy the spectacle. She couldn't have planned it better herself.

While Brian was locking the car, Steve and John quickly got either side of her. They took hold of her arms and pulled them round their waists.

'Your lucky day, with a man on each arm,' Brian joked when he saw what was going on. 'Not so lucky for the chauffeur,' he added ruefully, as they set off across the tarmac.

As they approached the door, Brian started talking with the *maître d'*. Beth was sure she saw some money exchanging hands. Certainly, the *maître d'* was all smiles as he asked them to follow him.

Even though the restaurant was relatively quiet, he led them to a secluded booth well away from the main dining area. Beth slid on to the bench seat with Brian and Steve on either side of her. John sat opposite and slightly on her left, presumably to make the most of her gaping blouse.

As the *maître d'* left, he signalled to the wine waiter.

'I don't really think I should drink anything,' Beth confessed quickly. 'I tend to get a bit silly after just one G and T.' She tried not to smile at the looks they were giving each other.

'Very silly after two and practically under the table at

three,' she added. 'Do you think I could just have an orange juice?' She knew that she was not meant to notice the little nod Brian gave John.

'I prefer to get them from the bar,' John announced as he stood up. 'That way I can see what they are doing.'

'I'm sorry?' Beth pretended to look confused.

'If you don't watch them, they pour you a short measure or give you one drink and charge you for another,' he explained. Steve and Brian nodded agreement.

'I see. Well, just an orange juice for me, then,' Beth smiled.

Brian and Steve both asked for lager and John went off to fetch the drinks, his face a picture of innocence. Beth could read his mind like a book. He had obviously done this before. He thought he could add alcohol to her drink without her realising. Was he in for a surprise! Not only could Beth actually drink with the best of them, but she had already had a milk shake and a quick sandwich to line her stomach before leaving the hotel. If they wanted to play games, let them. It would be even easier for her to take advantage of them if they thought she was drunk. Pretending to chat with the others, she watched John at the bar and saw the barman turn round to the bottles with a glass. So, she had guessed right.

John brought the drinks back, his face still expressionless.

'Everything OK?' Steve questioned.

'Yeah, no problem.' Beth pretended not to see the wink John gave the other two men.

'You mean they didn't try to fool you?' Beth queried innocently, knowing exactly what was meant. She did her best to look bemused when they all laughed at her comment.

She tasted the drink carefully and felt a slight warmth at the back of her throat. It was probably vodka.

'Thank you. That's very good.' She took another long gulp and put the glass down. 'I really needed that. I've been dry all day.' She quickly polished off the drink then pulled a face. 'It's a bit sharp.'

'Don't you like it?' Steve questioned anxiously.

'Oh yes. It's just a bit sharp, but very good. I wonder what brand it is? I'll have to remember to order it in future.'

All three men began laughing and Beth quickly joined in. 'Oh dear. I think I've got the giggles now,' she spluttered. 'It's not that funny.' This caused another paroxysm of mirth from the three men. Beth continued to look bemused.

Finally, they calmed down and settled down to order. Beth chose pâté with toast followed by a chicken salad. The others also ordered and sat back to enjoy their drinks. Music was playing softly in the background and one or two couples had gone out on to the dance floor.

'Would you like to dance, Beth?' Brian took her hand and pulled her from the booth before she had a chance to respond.

'As long as it's slow.' Beth accidentally missed her footing and made a grab for the side of the booth to steady herself, bending over to give them all a quick flash of stockings and panties. She had practised these sorts of manoeuvres at home for Simon's benefit and was certain she was so good that no one would ever guess she was doing it on purpose. Since they all thought she was a bit drunk, it gave her even more opportunity to be careless.

She half stumbled into Brian's arms. Instead of leading her to the dance floor, Brian started dancing with her in the small space behind the booth. He pulled her close and placed both hands on the small of her back.

Beth waited to feel his fingers over her buttocks and was surprised when instead he slid both hands down and pulled her even tighter against him. It was a neat move, effectively trapping her arms under his. She wriggled, trying to get free, but could not escape. Eventually, when she realised that her struggles were only adding to his enjoyment, she gave up and let him fondle her. As his fingers continued to caress her softly, he clasped her buttock tightly with one hand, pulling her close against his hardness and making it difficult for her to get away without making a scene. She allowed him his small victory. When he tried to slide a hand round on to her breast, however, it was Beth's turn to hold him tight so that he failed.

'Why don't we go on to a nightclub or something later, just the two of us,' Brian whispered. 'We don't need the others.' The feel of his breath in her ear made Beth shiver.

'It's hardly fair,' she replied. 'After all, I did agree to go out with all of you. Maybe another night,' she added.

The music ended and Brian held on to her, reluctant to release her. Beth was just about to slip out of his grasp when Steve appeared, cutting in. The music started again and, like Brian's, his hands were soon all over her. He started to lift her skirt and Beth was forced to twirl out of his grip, slapping the material back down and pretending not to notice that this had only caused the other side of the hem to lift.

'You mustn't do that, you naughty man,' she reprimanded him girlishly. 'Someone might see.'

Just then, the food arrived so they left their impromptu dance floor and went back to eat. As soon as Beth sat down, Steve and Brian moved close, thigh to thigh. She pretended to ignore them and concentrated on her pâté, which was delicious. She had been really enjoying the dancing and was sorry that it had had to end. Hugged up so close to them it had been impossible not to notice the obvious physical effect she was having on them. She was certainly getting them going, that was for sure.

She had noticed the little beads of perspiration on their faces, the intense expressions and the triumphant glitter in their eyes as she surrendered to them. She was also intensely aware of the animal scent of them; a scent not masked by their aftershaves. It was far more intoxicating than the doctored orange juice.

Apart from the insistent pressure of their thighs, the first course passed without any further incidents. Feeling cramped, she tried to move her legs, but it just seemed to encourage Steve to push even harder.

Beth had almost finished her second orange juice when John asked her to dance while they waited for the main course. As she stood up she used both hands on the table to push herself upright, giving him a great view down her blouse at the same time.

'Just so long as you promise to behave yourself.' She deliberately slurred her words slightly.

John grinned. 'It's a promise.'

She had to slip past Steve to get out. He wasted no time in taking the opportunity to push his hand up under her skirt to give her buttocks a quick pat. Beth squealed indignantly.

John pulled her tight against him as he steered her around the floor. She was intensely aware of his excitement pushed hard against her as his hands began to squeeze her nipples.

'John. Don't. Somebody might see.'

'Not unless you make a fuss,' he responded, giving her left nipple another tweak.

'Ow. I mean it. Stop it,' she repeated in a more demanding voice.

John reluctantly removed his hand. He pulled her even closer so that his lips were against her ear.

'Your little-girl act might be fooling the other two, but it isn't fooling me,' he whispered softly. 'You are no more drunk than I am and you know exactly what you're doing.'

Beth stiffened. 'I don't know what you mean,' she protested weakly.

'There you go again,' he responded as he continued to fondle her breast. 'Not that I mind,' he added, as his lips gently caressed her neck. 'Your little games are very endearing. I promise I won't let on.'

Beth didn't reply. She made no further attempt to thwart him. Her pulse was racing as the implication of his words sunk in. She pushed herself hard against his hand as though to try and block anyone else from seeing what he was doing and pretended not to notice that he had undone her top button.

'That's it, Beth. Surrender to the inevitable.' She was infuriated by that smile of his.

When Beth and John finally joined the others, Brian quickly slipped his hand under her as she sat down, so that she found herself perched on his over-inquisitive fingers. She leapt to her feet again.

'Brian, stop it!' She took his hand and placed it firmly on the table. Brian and Steve roared with laughter. Beth continued to hold his hand while she sat down again.

'Now, stop it. It's not fair.'

By the time her bottom made contact with the seat again, Steve's hand was there. She grabbed it quickly, so that she was now holding both their hands. Of course, this meant that she could not smooth her skirt down. The plastic cushion of the seat was cold and hard against her bare thighs. She shivered with excitement.

Steve and Brian now had a great view of her legs and stocking tops.

'You're spoiling the evening,' Beth muttered petulantly. 'I don't mind a little fun, but you are going too far,' she scolded them all unconvincingly.

Despite what John had said, Beth was pleased with her performance. She could tell that Steve and Brian, at least, didn't know quite how to take her comments and behaviour, the drunken giggling and the girlish modesty. Her voice was saying one thing, her body language quite another. She was driving them both to distraction and loving every minute of it. How far did she dare push it?

The main course arrived and the men returned to

casual chatting and joking, their comments very much on the suggestive side.

'Would you like another drink?' John asked her as she emptied her glass.

'It's my round.' She was determined not to let John get the better of her. As she stood up to go and fetch the drinks, Steve grabbed her skirt, pulling it up. Beth instinctively sat down again. She discovered that there was no skirt under her at all. The hem was practically around her waist and she could feel a cold draught on her exposed buttocks.

'Be careful,' she protested. 'You almost ripped my skirt off.'

Brian winked at her. 'That was the general idea,' he admitted. 'John will get the drinks.'

Just then, the *maître d'* headed towards their table. Beth quickly rebuttoned the top of her blouse and attempted to straighten her skirt.

'Is everything all right?' the *maître d'* enquired.

Beth was tempted to tell him that things were coming along nicely but, instead, she smiled innocently and replied, 'Oh yes, delicious.'

'Do you want anything off the sweet trolley,' he questioned, 'or would you prefer just coffee?'

'We'll have three coffees,' Steve replied. 'The lady is just going to have another orange juice.'

Brian sniggered and Beth smiled, marvelling at how stupid they must think she was as they winked and nodded to each other over her supposed drunkenness.

She tried to pull her skirt down under her, but Brian stopped her. She sighed and reached for the drink John had now placed in front of her. John leant over the table and pretended to study her bracelet. He took both her hands in his.

'You've got lovely hands, Beth,' he told her.

She was just about to thank him when Brian and Steve put their hands on to her legs under the table. Beth tried to pull away but found that John was gripping her wrists tightly.

The two men slid their hands slowly up her legs and on to what were, by now, the wettest pair of panties she had ever had.

'Stop it,' she whispered urgently as realisation dawned.

'Stop what, Beth?' Brian questioned in mock innocence as he tried to force his hand between her clenched thighs.

Beth immediately crossed her legs but this only gave Steve a better attack. She felt his fingers trying to find their way underneath her panties and she immediately squeezed her legs tighter. All that did was to make her own arousal even more urgent. She shifted her buttocks from side to side and bit her bottom lip.

Steve had almost got his fingers on to her clit now. She crossed her legs in the other direction and felt Brian's fingers start to explore her again.

'Stop it. John, let go.' Her voice was not loud enough for anybody to hear except for the three men at the table.

'I like holding your hands, Beth,' John told her. 'In fact, I can't see ever letting you go.'

Beth shifted her buttocks again, wiggling all over the seat, her excitement tinged with fear at how far they might be willing to go. John was so strong that she could not move her hands at all. She knew she could still put an end to it if she really wanted to, however – but she didn't want to. The fear was real enough, though.

Brian had managed to get his fingers right down inside her panties. She tried to cross her legs again, but Steve was waiting for this. As she uncrossed them, he placed his left leg over her right leg. Brian had both hands under the table and was pulling her left leg wide apart. He put his own leg over it so that she found herself both trapped and totally exposed. She could feel their fingers caressing her flesh but could do nothing but squirm. She hoped that they would think she was trying to escape. In fact, she was just wriggling with pleasure. She glanced

54

round nervously to make sure no one was paying any attention to them. It seemed incredible that she was practically being finger-fucked in the middle of a restaurant and no one seemed to be aware of what was happening. She felt Brian trying to pull her panties down.

Beth knew she needed to put a stop to that. She didn't want to be stripped in public, too! She slumped down in her seat as far as John would let her so that, although they had got her underwear half off, they couldn't get any further. She tugged her arms again.

'John, please let go. You don't realise what they are doing.'

'I've got a pretty good idea, Beth.'

Beth felt her heart starting to thud. She stared at him in shock.

'Pull her up, John, so that we can get her knickers off,' Steve whispered.

John began to pull on her arms and Beth felt her buttocks lifting off the seat. She tried to resist but there was little she could do. She clenched her buttocks as hard as she could but could not stop the waist elastic from slipping down around her thighs. She sank back down on to the seat, her legs like jelly. At least they couldn't get the knickers any further.

'I'll get the bill then we'll take her out to the car,' Brian muttered thickly. Beth recognised the look of lust blazing in his eyes. His words sent a cold shiver up her spine. She felt weak with excitement and fear at what they might be planning to do to her.

Had she gone too far? Maybe she could still get away. As Brian moved away, John slipped in and pushed her back on to the bench. Beth froze as he lifted her skirt. He ran his fingers over her newly shaved mound, then smiled wolfishly.

'Nice. I like a woman who remembers to shave.' He pushed his finger up inside her waiting dampness and Beth felt herself melting at his touch.

Steve stood up and, with a lingering glance at her breasts, headed off towards the loo, leaving the two of them alone. John smiled coldly and nodded his head towards the exit that led out to the car park.

'Once we go through that door, Beth, then you become our plaything for the night.'

Beth stared at him, without speaking.

'We are going to take you back to your hotel room and use you for our own gratification,' he added softly. His finger caressed the outline of her swollen nipple.

Beth swallowed. She realised that he was giving her a final chance to back out. She could call the waiter over and then just walk away. She wasn't even sure that she could walk, unaided.

'But then, you already know that, don't you? It's what you intended all along,' John continued as Beth digested his remarks. She felt his other hand slide on to her thighs. Before she realised what he was doing, he had pulled her panties down to her ankles. She gasped and locked her ankles together.

'Step out of them.'

Beth was horrified. 'No!' She exclaimed.

'You can't walk with them around your ankles,' he told her. He reached down and lifted one leg to get her started.

Without taking her eyes off him, Beth did as she was told. She bent down to pick them up, but John pushed her firmly against the seat.

'Leave them.' As he took her arm to guide her out from behind the table, Beth gulped.

'I can't just leave them.' She imagined the waiter or even the next customer finding her damp underwear in a heap on the floor. God. She could never come here again. Everyone would know what they had been doing to her.

John half-supported, half-carried her towards the exit. She was midway across the room before she remembered her skirt. John's hip was pressed against her and she sensed that most of her left buttock was exposed. Frantically she tugged the material back down.

Oh God, her knickers! She had not intended to let them do that to her. She had decided that they could take control, though, hadn't she? She swayed against him, feeling dizzy and light-headed. She needed some fresh air; she couldn't think straight. She should have put a stop to this before it was too late. She knew she couldn't back out now; she wanted it as much as they did. John continued to guide her confidently towards the exit. As they reached it, she felt Steve return and take hold of her other arm. The door closed behind them and Beth swallowed hard. She was totally committed now.

Chapter Four

Outside in the car park, John and Steve continued to steer her towards Brian's car. She hadn't noticed when they arrived that Brian had parked in such a secluded slot. The car park was empty except for a few cars in the far corner belonging to the other diners.

It had turned chilly. The wind had picked up and she could feel it tugging at her clothes. Cold air crept up under her skirt and caressed her naked flesh. Considering how small her thong had been, it was incredible that the lack of it should make such a difference. She knew she was being over-sensitive. She also knew she was with three men who were all well aware that she was no longer wearing any panties.

After a few paces, John stopped and pushed her up against the side wall of the restaurant. Brian, who had the car keys, was still paying the bill. When Beth saw the predatory look on John's face, she barely stopped herself from crying out. Jesus. Surely they weren't intending to take her here in the car park? Not that she would stop them – nor that she could stop them. Still, it hadn't been part of her plan. She started to panic. What if they were seen? She began to imagine everybody in the restaurant coming outside to watch. She pictured the men calling out encouragement while the women looked on with feigned disdain and barely suppressed envy.

'Take your bra off,' John commanded.

'I'm sorry?' His words confirmed her predicament.

'Take your bra off, now,' he repeated loudly.

Beth shook her head. 'You must be joking,' she whispered as she glanced round again just in case anyone was already watching. Steve and John were now either side of her, making it difficult for her to escape.

John reached for her blouse and wiggled his fingers through the gaps between the buttons so that his fingertips were just touching her breasts. Beth took a deep breath.

The look of shock on her face was quite real. It was no longer necessary for her to play-act. He had already given her a chance to back out. By saying nothing, she had as good as told him that it was OK for them to have her. Now, it seemed they were going to make her strip right here.

'No.' She grabbed his hand with hers. All she succeeded in doing was to push his fingers harder on to her breasts. She gasped. She was having trouble with her breathing again. She could hear each breath rasping in and out noisily; she was practically panting for it. She let go of him and John released her blouse. She looked round at Steve. His glasses had misted up in the cold air. As he removed them to wipe them dry, she stared into his eyes and shivered at his hungry, expectant look. She turned back towards John and saw the same expression echoed in his face.

Seeing her watching him, a slightly sardonic grin broke out across John's lips. He parted them, exposing his tongue. Slowly, he ran it over his dry lips. The gesture was deliberately crude, provocative. She heard Steve swallow noisily as she started to move her hands up towards her breasts.

Trying to stop her fingers shaking, Beth slipped them inside her blouse and opened the catch of her bra. The click as it came undone seemed almost deafening. She flinched as a cat jumped up on to a nearby wall and began to wail. She could almost sympathise with the desperation in its call. She couldn't believe how excited she was becoming.

Beth closed her eyes. The cat fell silent. She could hear Steve shuffling his feet impatiently beside her. In fact, the air was now so quiet that she could hear the sound of his fingers moving against the material of his trousers. She realised that he had put his hand down inside his flies to adjust himself. She could imagine his erection straining uncomfortably against his pants and almost feel his excitement as he touched himself with his fingers. She felt a ripple of longing between her thighs.

Beth undid the buttons on her sleeves. She heard a sharp intake of breath.

'She's going to do it.' Steve's words were so soft she could barely make them out. John didn't respond, but she heard his breathing quicken. She pushed her hand up inside a sleeve and grabbed the shoulder strap to her bra.

A car pulled up on the other side of the car park and Beth jumped as the doors opened, then slammed. She could hear voices talking and joking as a couple headed towards the restaurant. John moved in closer, until she could feel his warm breath on the side of her neck. She reached up her other sleeve for the second strap.

With a sharp tug, Beth whipped the bra down her left arm and out of the cuff of her sleeve, like a magician pulling a rabbit from a top hat. She kept her elbow into her side as she held the bra out for them without showing anything. John took it from her without a word and let it drop to the ground. At the rate they were going, she would be leaving a trail of discarded clothing all the way back to the hotel – a bit like an X-rated paper-chase.

Beth realised that her breathing had returned to normal. She was feeling much calmer and more in control again now. She had evaded their intentions so easily. She almost grinned as she heard John's disappointed snarl.

'Oh, very clever, Beth,' John congratulated her. 'But, I think we'll just undo these top buttons anyway, don't you?' As he spoke, he reached for the top button of her blouse.

'Will you do it, or shall I?' he asked her. 'I don't mind either way, but if I do it, I might just get carried away and undo all of them.'

She might have won the first round but, obviously, John was not going to let her enjoy her small victory for long. Beth moved her fingers slowly up over her stomach and under her breasts until she reached the top button. She took her time, knowing that, for the moment, she still held the power.

She heard Steve smacking his lips as the first button popped undone. As she moved her hands down, she could feel her breasts. Any second now, she would be exposed. She slipped the button open and hunched over, trying to keep the material together across her chest. The blouse was so small and tight that it wouldn't take much now for her breasts to slip right out.

'Make her undo the next one,' Steve whispered hoarsely to John. It confirmed her suspicions about who was in control: John.

The restaurant door crashed open, making them all jump. Beth only just managed to stop her left breast falling out. She clutched desperately at her blouse.

'There you are,' Brian called as he began walking towards them. 'I hope I haven't missed anything.'

Nobody said a word. John took Beth's hand away from her clutched blouse and opened it slowly. Beth found herself beginning to tremble as his fingers moved closer to her breasts. She shuddered at the first touch, suddenly desperate for him to fondle her.

John grinned and stepped away so that they could all admire his handiwork. Brian's low-pitched whistle immediately reminded Beth of why women think of men as wolves. Brian's whistle sounded like the call to feed.

'Beth decided that she didn't need her bra anymore,' John finally responded to Brian's question.

'So I see.' Brian said. 'This lady has a bit of a habit of dropping her clothes about the place, doesn't she? The poor waiter almost had a nasty accident just now when he tripped over her knickers. You should have seen his face when he picked them up and realised what they were.'

Beth opened her eyes and stared at Brian in horror as his words sank in. She could sense that they were all waiting for her reaction.

'Yeah, I can imagine,' said Steve, his excitement palpable. 'What did he do with them?'

'You mean after he had sniffed them and licked his lips?'

Beth could sense her cheeks burning. She knew Brian was being deliberately coarse just to upset her. It was working. She tried to turn her face away. Even though it was getting quite dark, there were several lights on outside the building and John had managed to place her right under one of them. She could not escape their knowing grins.

She glanced down at herself and was thankful to see that she was still more covered than revealed. Without the bra, though, her nipples were quite obvious, as was the gleam of perspiration in her cleavage. Damn John!

'He was in seventh heaven,' Brian continued. 'He rubbed them all over his face. He even started licking them. I hope you don't want them back, Beth. You would break his heart.'

She knew they were still watching for her reaction. She couldn't stop the horror showing on her face. Supposing the waiter came out before they left?

'Excuse me, madam. You seem to have dropped your knickers. Shall I help you put them back on?' She shuddered with embarrassment, both at her thoughts and at the smirk on John's face – on all their faces. She could sense that they were waiting for her to say something. Her lips were very dry and there was a lump in her throat that she couldn't seem to swallow.

She knew that she was twitching all over but could do nothing to control it. She felt like a fish caught on a hook. They were reeling her in, inch by inch, and she could do nothing but struggle helplessly on the end of their line. She had never been so aroused.

The three men were still chuckling, revelling in her discomfort.

'What did he do then?' Steve demanded.

'Well, for a second, I thought he was going to start jerking off there and then,' Brian continued crudely.

Despite herself, Beth felt her curiosity aroused. What would the waiter want with her damp underwear?

'He pushed them down the front of his trousers,' Brian continued. 'I expect he's going to keep them for later.'

Steve leant against the wall and stared at her. 'What do you think he's going to do with them later, Beth?' His words were very slow and deliberate. He reached out and ran one finger down her throat, across the front of her blouse and on to her right breast. 'Do you think he wrapped them round his dick?'

Steve pushed her blouse out of the way so that she was fully exposed. Slowly and deliberately, he began to rub the knuckle of his finger over her nipple. As he started to peel back the other side of her blouse, he repeated his question.

Beth found she couldn't speak. Her whole body was trembling. All she could think about was her panties nestled up against the waiter's cock. She didn't know whether to believe it or not. She tried to mouth a few words but only succeeded in spluttering.

'You know what I think?' John suggested. 'I think that, at the first opportunity he gets, he'll nip to the loo, pull his pants down and wank himself with your knickers.'

Beth jumped at his words and twisted her head round to face him, her eyes wide with disbelief.

'You'd like that, wouldn't you, Beth? Like to watch him wanking all over your undies?'

Beth stared at each of the men in turn, not knowing what to do or say. Should she admit to enjoying the idea? She knew that was what they wanted her to do.

She had a quick vision of the waiter slipping her panties on and pulling them up over his tight little bum. There wouldn't be enough material to cover him. That thought excited her, too.

Finally, she found her voice. 'Please can we go now?' She was suddenly desperate to get back to the safety of the hotel room. She wanted them to throw her on the bed and take her, one after another.

'Please. Before the waiter comes out. Take me to my hotel.' Before I lose all self-control and start ripping your clothes off, she added silently.

'Hmm. Not quite yet, Beth.' John was taking charge again. She knew he was toying with her. Knew he knew what she wanted. Was he trying to make her beg? She would, too. She knew she would. Right now, all she could think about was getting one of them to take her. Even here in the car park.

'I think we should have a little contest first,' he announced.

'Contest?' Beth questioned incredulously.

'Yeah. Let's see if you can guess who's got the biggest one and whose is the thickest.'

'Biggest? Thickest?' Her voice rose an octave on each word. 'What do you mean?'

'I think you know what I mean. Come on. Don't try to tell me you haven't been wondering who's got the most to offer?'

'No, I haven't,' Beth denied the accusation. Her face started to change colour again.

John raised his eyebrows. 'I don't believe you,' he told her. He moved closer and stood right in front of her.

'Nice nipples,' he commented.

Beth opened her mouth, then covered it with her fist. 'Oh.' She had completely forgotten how totally exposed she was. Her face flamed.

John placed his hands on her hips then slid them down her thighs. Crouching slightly, he reached the hem of her skirt and started to move inwards towards the buttons on the front. Beth instinctively drew her legs tighter together.

To her surprise he didn't try to put his hand up her skirt, just opened the bottom button. His fingers moved up to the next one.

'Admit it, Beth.' She felt another button slip undone. Still she said nothing. His hands began to move up again.

'Yes,' she spluttered.

'Yes, what?' He opened the third button. Then, no longer needing to crouch, he stood up and stared into her eyes.

Beth still hesitated. 'Yes. I have been wondering who has got the biggest one,' she whispered finally.

Her words were not fast enough to save another button from opening. John stepped back. The next one was just inches away from her mound. Her stocking tops would be clearly visible when she moved and, if her skirt rose even a fraction when she walked, nothing would be safe from their eyes.

'Well, now's your chance to find out. I want you to give each of us a good grope and tell us who wins.'

'No.' Beth feigned shock, praying he wouldn't open the next button.

John ignored her. 'If you're wrong, we will just have to spank you when we get back to the hotel,' he continued.

'I won't do it,' Beth insisted boldly, already shaking with excitement and anticipation. She stared defiantly at him.

'Yes, you will,' John insisted confidently. 'Because, if you don't, Steve and Brian are going to take an arm each and spread you across the bonnet of the car.' He paused to let that sink in.

Beth could see that Brian and Steve were delighted with the idea and were already moving forward to grab her.

'Then, I'm going to lift your skirt up and spank you until you do obey me.'

As he finished his threat, Steve and Brian grasped her arms. Beth struggled frantically, digging her heels in and pulling and pushing against them. It was hopeless. Within seconds, they had dragged her across the tarmac and spread her, face first, over the front of the car.

Her breasts had completely popped out of her blouse at the first tug and the metal of the car wing was cold and hard against her skin. The breeze rushed up between her parted legs, teasing her trembling flesh. She lashed out with her feet, but the two men easily sidestepped her. Using the same trick that they had pulled in the restaurant, Brian and Steve hooked a leg around each of hers, pinning her in place.

'I'm going to enjoy this,' John smirked. Beth heard him spit on his hand and rub his palms together.

She whimpered softly as he lifted her skirt very slowly, inching his way over her thighs and buttocks until the material was up round the small of her back. He patted her gently.

'Yes. I'm really going to enjoy this,' he repeated.

Beth surrendered. 'OK. I'll do it, if it means that much to you.' She tensed her buttocks, waiting for the sting of his hand. The anticipation was worse than the action. The wind continued to ripple over her buttocks and caress the soft flesh between her thighs with its invisible fingers. The dampness between her legs was cold as ice.

John patted her softly again. 'Well, never mind. I expect I shall get another chance later. You're not the most obedient woman I've ever met.'

Steve and Brian let go of her arms and released her legs. They watched her closely as she straightened up, tucked her breasts in to her blouse and smoothed her skirt down. She looked around uncertainly, not sure where to start. Steve was closest. She was determined to make John wait until last.

Beth moved forward and bent down to unzip him. She felt John's hand on her bum. She straightened up and twisted away.

'I won't do it if you keep molesting me,' she protested.

John smirked and stared meaningfully at the car. 'Yes, you will,' he contradicted her. 'You will do whatever we say or . . .' He flexed his fingers. 'Anyway, that's not why I stopped you. You have to do it by touch alone. No peeking.'

Beth gulped. That wasn't the way it had happened in her fantasy. She wasn't sure she had intended to let them be quite this much in control. The quiver of her bottom lip revealed her indecision. She drew a deep breath and almost lost her breasts out of her gaping blouse again.

'All right.' She moved over to Steve and gripped his waistband with her left hand. Gingerly, she plunged her fingers down inside the top of his trousers.

'Remember, Beth. If you get it wrong . . .' John left the threat dangling in mid-air.

She wondered if they had already compared themselves. Was this some sort of man-thing? The biggest gets to go first? She fumbled around in Steve's pants until she touched his naked cock. She jumped and pulled her hand away in shock. God knows why. What else had she expected to find down his trousers? Warily, she pushed her fingers back and ran them down to the base, trying to make some mental measurements as she squeezed and stroked his unseen penis. His hard flesh twitched and jerked between her fingers and she could hear his laboured breathing. She couldn't believe how exciting it was.

Reluctantly, she withdrew her hand and walked over to Brian. Her fingers moved more confidently this time, quickly gripping his hardness. She was fairly sure that his was thicker, but could not decide whose was longer.

She certainly couldn't tell which of them was throbbing the most. She made a mental effort not to allow herself to squeeze her own thighs together. She knew John was watching her. She noticed that the look on their faces had changed from hunger to dumb pleasure at her touch and she experienced a surge of elation at the effect she was having on them.

'This is impossible,' she exclaimed as her fingers began their journey down John's front. As she had expected, it wasn't difficult to guess who was the largest; she had always known it would be John. She wasn't going to admit it to him, though, just yet. Without removing her hand, Beth reached out with her other arm and grabbed Steve. Pushing her fingers back down his pants, she made a great show of comparing the men. It wasn't really fair, because they had both grown even stiffer in the last few minutes. Reluctantly, she released John and tested Brian again, just for fun. She was thoroughly enjoying herself again now, revelling in the looks on their faces. As she fondled him, John had that expression of intense concentration she so loved. When she released him, she heard the long sigh that told her he had been holding his breath. She could see the sweat breaking out on Brian and Steve's brows. She wondered if she could make any of them completely lose control. It was tempting, but her own need was also becoming more urgent. She had a better use for their passion.

'John is the biggest and Brian the thickest,' she declared. 'Steve is the hardest,' she added quickly. She didn't want him getting a complex. It might adversely affect his performance. She looked around, loving the lust blazing in their eyes, the heavy sighs, the foot shuffling. That had certainly got them all on the boil!

'Well, am I right?'

John shrugged. 'How would I know? We'll find out later, won't we?' He frowned. 'I hope you're wrong. I've still got a strong urge to smack that very sexy bum of yours.' He patted her again.

Beth made another futile effort to contain her breasts.

'Let's just get back to the hotel,' Steve rasped urgently. Beth noticed that he had pushed his hand into his trouser pocket and was fondling himself. She shivered with excitement at his desperation for her.

Brian took the keys out of his pocket and unlocked the car. John moved closer. 'Steve, you get in the other side. Beth can go in the middle.' He opened the back door for her as Steve and Brian walked round to climb in the other side.

As Beth moved to get in, John flicked her skirt up. Holding it, he slid in beside her. She jumped as her cheeks made contact with the cold leather and quickly put her hands in her lap, trying to pull as much of her skirt over her as she could. Her breasts flopped free again.

As Steve slipped in beside her, she found herself wondering what was in store for her during the journey. She knew that it would not take much to push her to orgasm and she didn't think they were much better off. She tried to keep her face as expressionless as possible. Looking neither right nor left, she stared regally out at the front windscreen and let her mind run free.

I bet it will be John first, she told herself. He was obviously the leader. Brian next, perhaps? Brian started the engine and pulled off.

Her desire was building back up swiftly. She had never been at this level of sexual tension for so long without climaxing. She gripped her skirt tightly over her mound and began squeezing her legs together in her enthusiasm. The tensing of her body alerted John. He pulled her hands from her lap and placed them on her knees.

'Not yet, Beth. Later, for all of us.'

Beth flushed, not only for the implied threat of what she was clearly expected to do for them, but also because he had noticed her loss of self-control.

'What was she doing, John? Trying to inspect your dick again?' Brian laughed excitedly.

'No. Something else.'

'I didn't see anything. What was she doing?' Steve demanded. His eyes looked huge behind his spectacles.

Beth began to shake. Please don't tell them, she begged John silently with her eyes.

'Tell them, Beth.'

She shook her head.

'Tell them.'

Beth dropped her head on to her chest. She was so humiliated that she could feel tears burning behind her eyes.

'Find a quiet spot and pull over,' John ordered. 'Beth needs a little persuading. That bus stop will do.'

Beth's head jerked up. There were plenty of other cars about and the street lighting was good. If they were to put her across the bonnet now, people would see. Jesus. It might even get into the newspaper. Public exposure was all right in a fantasy . . . She stared desperately into John's eyes.

'Tell them what you were doing or everybody is going to get an eyeful.'

Beth was horror struck. 'I wanted to go to the loo. I was squeezing my legs to hold it.' The excuse sounded lame even to her.

'Pull over,' John commanded.

Brian obeyed. As soon as the car had stopped, he turned round expectantly. All three men stared at her.

'Last chance, Beth.' John obviously had no intention of letting her off the hook. Beth gave in.

'I, I was masturbating,' she whispered miserably.

'I'm sorry? What was that? We didn't quite hear you.'

'I was masturbating.'

'Better. But, I still didn't catch the last word. Why don't you run it by us again.' John was clearly enjoying himself.

Beth gritted her teeth. The tears were running down

70

her cheeks. 'I was masturbating,' she repeated loudly. She buried her head in her hands.

'There, there, Beth,' John reassured her. 'That wasn't so bad, was it? You must admit these little urges of yours. Like wanting to take your clothes off or wondering who has got the biggest cock and how much you want us all.' He grinned.

'You've been wondering who is going first, too, haven't you?'

'Yes,' she admitted quickly, still terrified at the idea of being publicly spanked.

'You see? Confession is good for the soul,' John told her, his hazel eyes sparkling with mischief. 'Now, show Brian and Steve what you were doing.'

Beth had managed to stop sniffling. All she wanted to do was to get back to the hotel as soon as possible. She replaced both hands in her lap and squeezed herself a couple of times. For a moment, she thought John was going to make her move the covering hand, so they could see exactly what she was doing. John, however, just smirked.

'Here. Dry your eyes and blow your nose.' He handed her a hankie and Beth dutifully dabbed her eyes and cheeks and wiped her nose.

She felt the car pull off. She cursed her stupidity. John was doing it on purpose. He was deliberately looking for any excuse to delay them and she had played right into his hands. He wanted her to beg for it. No way. She wouldn't beg and she wouldn't give him any more excuses to delay them. She would let them do whatever they wanted with her, once they got back to the hotel room.

To her surprise, they didn't touch her again, although she was acutely aware of their eyes devouring her, of their knowing grins and of the longing smouldering in their eyes. The silence was even worse than their comments.

'Whoops, I almost forgot.' John's voice made her jump

71

again. 'Brian, perhaps you could pull over again. Beth needs a pee.'

'No,' she exclaimed quickly. 'I'm fine. I'll go when we get to the hotel.'

Brian had already started to slow down.

'Oh, all right then. If you're sure? Carry on, James. Drive slowly. We wouldn't want to shake Beth up too much, would we?' John glanced at her again. 'Now, you are quite sure? It's no trouble.'

If she hadn't wanted him so much, Beth would have cheerfully strangled John.

'No. Damn it! No! I'm fine. Just get me back to my room.' She leant forward. 'Put your bloody foot down, can't you? This is a BMW, not a sodding hearse.' Beth rarely swore. Only when she was really provoked or under severe stress. It had never seemed more appropriate. If they didn't get there soon, she really would have to go for a pee.

She felt the car pick up speed. She squeezed her thighs tightly together again. The movement caused John to give her a sideways glance. She sat perfectly still, legs clenched, not daring to relax them in case he decided to stop again.

'You know, I've never actually seen a woman masturbating.' Steve started the conversation again.

'I have. Well, on films, anyway,' Brian replied.

'Not the same.' John patted her knee.

'No, they are not really doing it there,' Steve commented.

'Yes, they are,' Brian argued. 'You can tell a fake.'

'You reckon?'

Their deliberately crude conversation about female masturbation continued the rest of the way to the hotel. Beth did her best to ignore it but could feel herself getting wet with anticipation.

'We'll soon see.' Brian pulled the car into an empty slot. 'Beth is going to give us a little show now, aren't you, Beth?'

Beth did not respond. The talk had given her time to settle. She was feeling much more in control of herself now; calmer than at any time since they had first pulled her panties down. Holding her head high, she put a martyred expression on her face and clenched her teeth together. She promised herself that, no matter what, she would not beg again.

Steve climbed out the car. Beth began to slide across to follow him.

'This side, Beth.' John held her arm. 'You wouldn't want to get out in front of the main door like that, would you?'

She hadn't noticed where Brian had parked. She glanced down at herself in dismay then looked up at his face. Again, she experienced the urge to throttle him. She was sure that he knew just how close she was to total surrender. She would not let him win.

As she started to follow him out, he blocked the door, delaying her again. 'Wait until Brian is round here, too.'

Beth fixed him with an icy stare. She had no intention of giving them another public peep show. Let them wait.

'Right, now come out backwards and don't touch your clothing at all.'

Beth hesitated, then, remembering her promise to herself not to cause further delay, she did as she was told, ignoring the ribald comments and lecherous grins.

John was still laughing as he slammed the car door and took her arm. He led her towards the main entrance. 'You two had better walk in front or our Beth will create a bit of a sensation. We don't want her arrested for flashing, do we? I've got an urge that needs satisfying first.'

Steve and Brian laughed coarsely as they took up position in front. They moved quickly. Beth could feel her breasts bouncing up and down and she put her arm across her chest to try to stop them. She knew she must be flashing everything as she scurried to keep up with them.

73

Once inside the hotel, they made straight for the lift. Beth closed up as much as possible to the men in front. She didn't dare look round to see if anyone was behind them. She knew that this was her last chance to change her mind. It wouldn't be all that difficult to break out of John's grip. Her nails were long and sharp and it was only a few paces to the women's toilets. But no; there was no backing out now.

The lift door opened and an elderly couple stepped out. Beth turned her head so she would not have to look at them. They crowded inside.

It's not far, Beth kept telling herself over and over again. Steve moved up beside them and took her other arm. As he pulled it down to her side, she felt her nipples slip into view again. Only a few more paces to go. The lift stopped and John and Steve guided her firmly along the corridor.

She was so keyed up, she could barely think straight as Brian rummaged in his pocket and produced her key. Finally he opened the door and they led her inside and placed her face down on the nearest bed.

Beth lay motionless. This was it. Who would be first? She waited to hear the tell-tale sound of a zip opening. She wanted to be held down by two of them while the third took her from behind. She was growing more excited by the second. What were they waiting for? She could hear nothing but their breathing.

'Well, who's first then? How about me? After all, I did pay the bill and do all the driving.'

'Yeah, and?'

'Take it easy.' It was John's voice, naturally, taking control. 'There's plenty of time. Beth will take care of all of us at least twice, won't you, Beth? Wiggle your bottom if you agree.'

Beth didn't move. She sensed the smack coming and tightened her buttocks. After the third stinging blow, she wiggled her hips feebly.

'Good girl. Right. Before we do anything else, Beth

74

needs to know if she guessed right about us. Strip off, gentlemen.'

She wasn't surprised that Steve and Brian did not seem too keen on that idea. She was more surprised that they had continued to let John take charge of everything for so long. She hoped that they weren't about to start fighting over her.

'You two have got no finesse, that's your trouble. Beth wants to know who's got the most to offer her.' Beth heard John drop his coat over the chair. A deep surge of longing rushed through her. Who cared which one had the most to offer? She just wanted someone to get on with it.

John carried on undressing. Finally, she sensed the other two giving in. She resisted the urge to turn over and watch them. She heard a click and then music started playing.

'Come and see if you were right, Beth.'

Beth slid off the bed. Another of her skirt buttons had come undone and her crotch was clearly visible. She had already surreptitiously opened the rest of her blouse buttons. If John was determined to make her tease them, so be it. She was good at that. Besides, she was sure that Steve and Brian were not going to play John's games for much longer.

When she saw John's body, she had to bite her tongue to stop herself gasping. She had thought he was a bit on the tubby side, but now she could see that he was all muscle. He looked as if he could break the other two men in half if he wanted. No wonder they were letting him take the lead. God, his chest was bigger than hers! She gulped, hardly daring to look any lower.

'Well, did you get it right?' John questioned.

Beth dropped her eyes and made a pretence of scanning all three men, before returning her gaze to John. She almost licked her lips in anticipation. She nodded silently.

'Good. Now let's get on with it,' Steve demanded

impatiently. 'You can go first. Then Brian, then me.' Beth noticed the sweat glistening on his naked skin.

'I'm not sure that's entirely fair, is it? I mean, just because I've been blessed with more muscle than most, why should I automatically go first?' John replied. He smiled at Beth, clearly aware of her discomfort and enjoying it to the full.

'I think we should play cards for her.'

'Cards?' Steve and Brian spoke together.

'Yes. The first one to win five hands gets her.'

Beth whimpered under her breath. Where did this man get his self-control from? He wasn't even fully aroused yet, as the other two were. Perhaps he was all mouth and muscle? She felt a small rush of disappointment.

'OK. Let's get on with it,' Brian reluctantly agreed.

'As we are playing for the pleasures of your body, Beth, it seems only fair you should show us the prize. Strip, woman, strip.'

Beth didn't even hesitate. Before John had said 'strip' the second time, she had ripped her blouse off and begun to drop her skirt. As she started to peel her stockings down, she remembered that, in her fantasy, she had done this slowly and reluctantly. She was far too desperate for that.

'Not very ladylike, Beth. Anybody would think you were in a hurry,' said John. Beth did her best to ignore his sarcasm. She just wanted them to get on with the card game before she lost control completely.

'Now then, Beth. Why don't you make yourself comfortable on the bed? Kneel here with your thighs apart and your ankles together.' He patted the duvet encouragingly. 'That's it. Now, bend over and touch the bed with your nipples.'

Beth turned her head and pushed her breasts down on to the duvet cover.

John smiled appreciatively. 'Well, lads. That's what we are playing for.' He slipped his hand underneath her and ran his finger gently over her clit. Beth shuddered and fought the climax that was threatening to engulf her.

'Yes. I think she is just about ready for the winner.'

Beth kept perfectly still as they dragged a table and some chairs over. She heard the noise of cards being shuffled and dealt, and then Steve's voice asking for more cards. She didn't dare look up at them.

Brian won the first hand. Then there was a delay because no one had any paper or pen to keep the score. While John was searching around, the other two inspected the prize, touching and tormenting Beth until she began whimpering again, writhing around the bed as she fought her approaching orgasm.

'Right. Brian, Steve, John.' John called their names out as he wrote them down. The game continued.

After the second hand, Steve had the bright idea that Beth should entertain them while they played.

John pursed his lips thoughtfully. 'No. She's already boiling now. Let her start and she won't need us, eh, Beth? That's right, isn't it?' Beth chose not to reply.

He was right, of course. All she needed was a few seconds. Steve's suggestion would have been a lifeline. Once she had taken care of herself, she would be able to take control of the situation again. Damn John! She had more than met her match this time. She bit her lip, then flushed when she saw he was still watching her. Her eyes dropped hungrily to his crotch.

'Tell you what, though,' John added. 'Beth, why don't you kneel in front of us?'

Beth pushed herself up into a kneeling position.

'No, facing us, Beth,' he told her in a slow, patient voice.

Beth turned around and put one arm across her front. Quickly, she placed her other hand over her mound. John smiled. Wordlessly, he leant across and parted her legs, then moved her hands on to her hips.

The game continued with the occasional break so that they could rearrange her body into other poses; each man clearly trying to outdo his companions with the imaginative positions they placed her into. Beth said nothing, not daring to refuse, no matter how humiliating their demands became. When Brian finally won, she almost shouted aloud with relief.

'Have you got protection?' John asked.

'Yeah. I've got plenty.' As he spoke, Brian threw an open pack of condoms on the bed. They spilled out beside the box Steve had also produced. Beth realised that there must be nearly twenty condoms on the bed.

Suddenly, Brian grabbed her, pulled her up and penetrated her from behind. The shock of it caused her vaginal muscles to contract, gripping him like a vice. She felt him pushing deeper and deeper into her and she clamped her lips tightly together to stop herself from crying out with sheer pleasure and relief.

She could sense the other two men watching and imagine their own excitement building. Part of her wanted to prolong the show as long as possible, torturing them with anticipation; part of her was so desperate for her own release that she knew she couldn't hold out. She gritted her teeth and closed her eyes, willing herself to resist.

Brian groaned urgently and increased his stroke. His hands reached round and caressed her swollen nipples and a small whimper fell from her lips. It was no good. She couldn't help herself. With a loud moan, her powerful orgasm rippled through her shuddering body.

Her obvious pleasure was too much for Brian. His cock jerked and she heard his urgent sigh of release. Beth pushed her head down into the duvet to smother her gasps.

'There. I told you she was ready.' John patted her arm. 'Your turn, Steve. Just a quick one first. We can take our time later.'

Beth just lay there, passively, revealing in her enjoyment. To her surprise, Steve entered her gently, almost reverently. From some of his comments earlier, she had half expected him to be the least considerate. Almost immediately, she sensed that he was not going to be able to last long. His whole body was rigid with his urgent need for release. Memories of Jonathan rushed into her mind. She had never been able to get enough of his desperate lust for her.

Steve built up speed quickly, pumping in and out of her with an urgency that enflamed her. 'Oh Christ,' he whispered. 'You drive me crazy.' His fingers caressed her breasts and his teeth nibbled her neck, sending little shivers down her back.

When he came, his climax was so violent and his moans of delight so intense, she was afraid that they must have woken everyone in the hotel.

Then, it was John's turn. She wasn't surprised when he rolled her over on to her back. She knew he wanted to watch her reaction. As soon as he penetrated her, she felt her muscles contracting again with the shock of his size. John wasn't having any of that. He pushed harder, forcing himself deeper and deeper. Beth put her fist in her mouth and bit her knuckles to stop herself crying out with sheer delight.

He increased his thrusting, pushing harder and harder until they were both gasping for breath and their sweat was mingling on their hot, straining flesh. Considering how long he had waited for this, Beth was impressed by John's restraint. She fought to match him, tensing her muscles and writhing from side to side as the pressure built and built. Then, with one final thrust that seemed to fill her whole being, they both climaxed together.

As he withdrew, Beth fell back exhausted with her eyes closed.

Before she had had time to recover, Steve and Brian lifted her up and carried her into the bathroom. She noticed that Steve's erection was already beginning to swell again and a wave of panic swept through her at the idea of them all taking her again so soon.

Brian lifted her into the shower and pushed her down

on her knees. All three men squeezed in beside her and began to soap her all over, while Brian took charge of the shower attachment to spray her body down, aiming the jets teasingly between her thighs and over her swollen breasts. Beth sighed with pleasure as the hot water caressed her aching limbs and revived her body.

Brian picked up the bar of soap and handed it to her.

'Why don't you make yourself useful,' he demanded. Hesitantly, she began to wash his legs and genitals, while Steve soaped her breasts and John took advantage of her buttocks with his fingers.

As her energy and enthusiasm gradually returned, Beth began to take a more active role, running soapy fingers over any penis that came within reach. Before long all three were fully erect once more and thrusting urgently against her slippery skin.

John rinsed her down then lifted her up and wrapped her in a soft bath towel.

'There, doesn't that feel better?' He dried her gently from top to toe and Beth was amazed at how excited she was becoming by his tender caresses. He was such an enigma, this man. So masterful, yet so gentle. She could see his own excitement rebuilding as he worked over her and, again, she marvelled at how big and hard he was.

The three men dried themselves off quickly and led her back into the bedroom. John pushed her on to the bed. He picked up a pillow and threw it to Steve.

'Push that under her.' He reached down and grabbed her hand. Beth gasped as he placed it on to his penis. 'Don't let go.'

As John knelt down beside, her, Brian did the same the other side. She felt her other hand being lifted and placed round his erection. She automatically closed her fist and squeezed gently, her eyes still fixed on John's cock. She slid her fingers slowly up his rigid shaft, shivering as she felt him twitching at her touch.

Steve pulled Beth's legs apart and she felt his hand opening her outer lips. His full weight came down on her body as he penetrated her. She pushed up to meet him and he began moving slowly in and out.

Beth whimpered softly and squeezed the other men even harder, tightening and loosening her grip in time with Steve's thrusting. He increased his stroke and she whimpered again, louder this time. This was so much better than she had ever imagined; her fantasies had not even come close.

She had no idea how long Steve lasted. She barely noticed when Brian released her hand from his cock and took his place at the bottom of the bed. She heard Steve move across the room to the loo and she instinctively tightened her grip on John's cock as Brian pushed himself slowly into her. She closed her eyes and let herself go.

'The best last, eh, Beth?'

Hearing his words, Beth realised that Brian had gone and John was about to penetrate her again. She sighed with anticipation and reached out behind her to grab the headboard. John slid in, deeper and deeper, further than she would ever have thought possible. She pushed herself up to meet him, hanging on to the bed as if she were tied up. She bit her lips to stifle her moans. John began thrusting confidently.

Some time later, through the haze of her own pleasure, she felt John climax and withdraw. She didn't move, just lay there, sated and motionless, with her hands still gripping the headboard.

She could hear the men moving around and talking in low voices. With supreme effort, she turned her head and looked at her travel clock. They had only been back in the hotel for a little over an hour. It seemed more like a week.

Beth felt her head being lifted up and a cup was pressed to her lips. Coffee! Some sweet angel had made her a mug of coffee. Beth let go of the headboard, pushed herself up and gratefully grabbed the mug from John's outstretched hand.

81

'Thank you.' She took half the scalding liquid in one gulp. John watched silently. She stared openly at his penis curled up against his body. Even like that, it was still huge.

'Drink it all up, Beth. You need your strength.'

Beth looked up at him, her eyes huge. 'No more,' she begged.

John smiled. 'Sorry. We've got a little bet on to see who can take you the most and no one wants to lose.' He licked his lips. 'Besides, don't forget you promised to entertain us, too.'

Beth looked puzzled.

'What you were doing in the car, remember?'

Beth reddened and shook her head in disbelief. Not now. Not after all they had already done to her.

John looked round thoughtfully. 'The second bed will make a good place for us to watch from. When you're ready.'

The strength flowed back into her limbs as the coffee revived her. She finished the mug and placed it on the bedside table. She was sharply aware of the three men lined up in a row on the second bed with their eyes devouring her. Despite her fatigue, she experienced a small tremor of lust at the way they were watching her. Time to get a little of her own back.

Taking a deep breath, Beth lowered her hand and placed it between her legs, using her thumb to stroke her clit.

'Don't forget, we'll be able to tell if you fake it.'

Beth jumped at John's words and stopped.

'Don't stop.' Steve was sitting on the edge of the bed, leaning forward eagerly. His cock was thrust up in front of him like an additional spectator.

Beth turned to face them and then lay back, sprawled across the bed. She drew her legs up, revealing herself totally. OK. I'll give you a good show, if that's what you want, she promised them silently. I'll give you such a good show that you will all be wanking helplessly before I'm done with you.

She started slowly, building up. Soon she was totally immersed in her own gratification. She could hear their laboured breathing, the occasional exhalation. She raised her knee and started to slide her finger over her clit. She could imagine them fondling themselves as they watched her and the images it conjured up sent waves of desire rushing through her. She increased the pressure, using her other hand to play with her nipples. She heard a loud gasp from one of the men.

She removed her hand from her sex lips, put it to her mouth and sucked her fingers. She heard another gasp. She put her hand back between her legs and pushed the tip of her damp finger inside her vagina, arching her back and thrusting against her hand as if fucking an invisible lover. Her senses were so keyed up that she thought she could hear the sounds of the men's fingers moving up and down their stiff cocks.

She removed her finger and pushed herself upright until she was kneeling in front of them with her legs together as she rubbed her mound. She had not been wrong. All three of them were moving their hands rapidly up and down their throbbing erections. Their faces were dark with lust, their breathing fast and shallow.

She felt rather than heard the tiny mewing noises she was making in her own enthusiasm. Watching them watching her, seeing what they were doing because of her, was almost more than she could bear. She was already burning with the need for release again. Beth parted her legs and pushed her fingers up urgently inside her moist sex.

All three men gasped and increased their own move-ments. Her own mewing sounds changed to a cross between a purr and a whimper. Falling back on her ankles, Beth cried out softly as she climaxed.

'Yeah. Oh yeah,' Brian sighed urgently.

What happened next became a jumble in her mind. Afterwards, all she could remember was a medley of hands and pricks; of being pushed and pulled this way and that as the three men used every part of her pliant body for their own enjoyment and release.

Long before they had finished with her, Beth had drifted away on a cloud of sated exhaustion.

She never even heard them leave.

Chapter Five

*B*eth had trouble waking up the next morning. The insistent jangling of her travelling alarm clock seemed to take forever to penetrate her consciousness. As she sat up and gazed groggily round the hotel room, confused memories of the previous evening flooded into her mind.

Beth groaned as she slipped her feet out from under the duvet and padded slowly into the bathroom to shower. She felt as if she had just taken part in a world cup final, playing the part of the ball.

After three cups of strong, black coffee and a pile of thickly buttered toast, she was feeling much more human again. Thank heavens for room service. What a night! Not even her wildest fantasies had come close to the reality of it. She polished off the last of the coffee and glanced at her watch. She would have to get a move on if she didn't want to be late.

She pictured the knowing grins on the men's faces if she failed to appear on time. They would be convinced that they had been too much for her to handle. No way was she going to give them that satisfaction. John had already humiliated her quite enough.

She had got her own back though, she reminded

herself smugly as she wiggled into a soft jersey dress and pulled up her stockings. The look on their faces when she had masturbated for them! Talk about desperate. Had any of them actually lost control, watching her? She couldn't remember. She couldn't remember anything much of what had happened after that.

By supreme effort, Beth managed to arrive at the training centre before any of them. It was a small victory, but it pleased her enormously. She was even more delighted when she saw the condition they were in. All three of them looked half-asleep. Steve and Brian looked as if they were suffering hangovers. Funny; she didn't remember any of them drinking all that much. They had been far too busy trying to get her drunk.

She forced herself to smile at each of them in a friendly, detached sort of way. Steve and Brian managed a feeble nod in return. John, of course, had that infuriating, knowing grin as soon as he saw her. She turned away quickly before her face reddened.

Lisa looked different. Prettier, somehow. It took Beth a few moments to realise that Lisa had put on more make-up than she usually wore. It made her eyes seem much larger and the eye shadow she had applied emphasised the green and gold flecks within them. When she slipped her jacket off, Beth could see that Lisa was wearing a semi-transparent cream blouse. The outline of her bra was just visible when she lifted her arm to point at the whiteboard.

Was it for her benefit, Beth wondered? She was going out with Lisa that evening. In her preoccupation with the previous night's events, she had almost forgotten about that completely. It didn't seem quite so appealing any-more, somehow. Perhaps she should try to find some excuse to beg off?

Would the three men ask her out again? Brian had already suggested it. He was quite sweet, but Steve had been, surprisingly, the more gentle lover. As for John – she still didn't know how to take him.

'I don't think you've been paying attention this morning, Beth. Is something bothering you?'

Beth jumped at the sound of the instructor's voice right beside her. Lisa was bending over her desk, her eyes running all over her body.

'I'm sorry. I was miles away.' Beth sensed herself colouring.

'You've hardly started the exercise.' Lisa was examining her laptop screen. 'Is there something you don't understand?'

'What? Oh, no. I'm just having trouble concentrating.' Beth forced herself to pay attention to her work as she began hitting the keys of the keyboard furiously.

Lisa patted her shoulder. 'I'm looking forward to tonight, too,' she whispered, her own cheeks glowing. Beth smiled sheepishly. It was a good job Lisa couldn't read everything that had been going through her mind!

She was surprised when Lisa disappeared during the coffee break. She had expected her to stick close. Despite her comment, perhaps she was having second thoughts, too?

Beth moved over to the window and gazed out, sightlessly. She sipped her coffee pensively and tried to pull her muddled thoughts together. Suddenly, she felt a hand run down her back and over her buttocks.

'Sleep well, Beth?'

She didn't have to turn around to know it was John. 'Yes, thank you.' She was slightly disappointed when he lifted his hand away. She struggled in vain to think of something else to say to him and was relieved when the door opened and Lisa came back in.

Lisa looked round then headed straight over to them and put her hand possessively on Beth's arm. 'I've just hunted out a few additional training notes I thought you might find useful,' she told her. 'Mostly to do with stock market flotations, plus a bit about company mergers. If I can find time later, I'll get them photocopied for you.'

Beth noticed John moving away and felt a twinge of

disappointment. Teasing Lisa was fun, but there was something about John. She had never met a man before who could truly and totally dominate her like he could. She would give anything for the chance to make him squirm and beg for her the way she had done so submissively for him.

'Thank you. Perhaps I could copy them myself if you show me where the photocopier is?'

'Oh well, yes. If you don't mind then that would be a great help. I've got to attend a staff meeting at lunchtime, so I won't have much opportunity.' Beth noticed that Lisa's fingers were still resting on her arm.

'The only problem is there's always such a queue in the main office during break times.' Lisa continued. She pursed her lips thoughtfully, then brightened. 'There's an old machine in one of the storerooms down the corridor that I sometimes use.' She moved across to her desk and opened the drawer.

'Here's the key to the storeroom. It's the last door on the left. You can't miss it.' Lisa smiled coyly. 'The machine is a bit slow, but it will still be quicker than queuing.'

Beth took the key and moved her hand away quickly before Lisa could see her fingers were trembling. 'Thank you.' She remembered her promise to let Lisa have her room number. 'I'm in room 309, by the way,' she added. 'Have you decided what we're going to do tonight, yet?'

Lisa's eyes sparkled. 'I thought dinner at a small restaurant I know, then, perhaps, a club?'

'A club?' Beth wondered just what kind of club Lisa had in mind. She had heard of lesbian-only clubs. She wasn't certain that she actually wanted to go to one. Being with Lisa was one thing; she wasn't sure she fancied facing a room full of lust-filled women all ogling her body.

'Or I could take you back and show you my flat if you prefer,' Lisa added softly, almost as if sensing her thoughts. 'Nice and cosy. Just the two of us.'

That sounded more like it. Beth smiled. 'Let's just see how we feel later, shall we?'

By lunchtime, Beth had managed to pull herself together and was beginning to grow quite excited about the coming evening. She had had a taste of what it was like to be dominated by a man. What would it be like to be dominated by a woman?

Despite Lisa's warning, Beth couldn't believe how antiquated the photocopier was. She hadn't seen one like it for years. No wonder it was stuck away in a locked storeroom; it would have been more at home in a museum.

Beth switched on the light and pushed the door to behind her. It was a small room and the only other things in it, apart from the copier, were an old wooden chair and a couple of boxes of paper. The walls were painted a lurid green that looked like mould and the air smelt damp and musty.

Beth brushed the dust off the chair and put Lisa's folder down. She opened it to take out the first page of notes and sighed when she saw how many sheets there were. Thanks to the primitive design of the ancient machine, she would have to copy each sheet individually. She lifted the lid covering the glass and placed the first sheet face down. As soon as she had closed it again, she pressed the copy button.

The antiquated machine juddered alarmingly and the front panel lit up like a Christmas tree. Beth cursed and thumped the button again; nothing happened. She looked round, then spied the paper tray sticking out of one end. It was empty. She opened the top box of paper, grabbed a handful of sheets and quickly loaded the tray. The warning lights went out. She pressed the copy button again and, with a groan of protest, the old machine finally whirred into action.

As she mindlessly repeated the action of placing each sheet in turn under the lid, Beth's thoughts drifted back to John. What a body he had. He must work out every day to keep himself in such good shape. She found herself wondering what he and the others were up to and if they had looked for her to join them for lunch.

It would be fun to get John on his own. Steve and Brian were both very nice but, well, she had never met a man quite like John. Would he be very different, away from the others? Had he been showing off last night for their benefit or was he always so forceful?

Just as she finished the last sheet, she heard voices outside in the corridor and realised it was them. She heard Steve make some comment and then all three men laughed. She wondered if they were talking about her and moved closer to the door to listen.

'I've just got to get my jacket.' John's voice came quite clearly through the thin wood. 'Why don't you go on and I'll catch you up.'

'Sure. If we find Beth we'll keep her warm for you, shall we?' Brian's voice.

She heard them all chuckling and experienced a rush of anger at their presumption. Then, as their footsteps moved away, her heart suddenly began to race. This could be just the opportunity she needed. She remembered her earlier thoughts about dominating John and, as she glanced down at the now silent photocopier, a daring and delightful plan began to take shape in her mind.

Beth quickly removed the paper tray and replaced the unused sheets in the box. Then she picked up her copying and opened the door. Before she could lose her nerve, she hurried down the corridor and peered into the classroom. John was standing by his chair with his jacket in his left hand. His muscles rippled and flowed under his tight shirt and Beth shivered at the memory of his touch.

He looked up as she entered and she saw an amused grin spring to his lips as he recognised her. 'Hello, Beth. Is there something I can do for you?'

'Yes, actually.' But not what you're thinking, she added silently. 'I'm trying to do some photocopying, but I'm having trouble with the old copier. I think it's out of paper but I'm not sure how to reload it. Do you know anything about photocopiers?'

John pulled a face. 'I'm no expert,' he began, then grinned. 'Still, I'd be more than happy to have a look,' he continued cheerfully as he placed his jacket back over the chair. 'Anything for a lady. Besides, two heads are better than one, aren't they?'

Her pulse racing, Beth began to lead the way along the corridor to the storeroom.

'I heard you offering to do teacher's copying earlier,' John commented softly as they reached the door. 'It's nice to see you two girls so getting on so well together,' he added. 'Very cosy.'

Beth felt herself flushing from top to toe. Oh God. He hadn't guessed about that, had he? Was that why none of them had made a move on Lisa? Could they sense that she wasn't interested in men? After last night, they couldn't think the same about her. Did John know she was seeing Lisa that night? She pushed the thought away hastily and entered the room. John followed.

'It's not exactly the latest model.' She waved her arm towards the copier while pushing the door closed behind them with her other hand. She had already noticed the bolt on the inside and she slid it quickly across.

'You're in luck, Beth. I've used one of these old things before.' John moved round to the other side of the machine and slid the paper tray out. He glanced round then, seeing the box of paper, bent down and took a handful.

As he filled the tray, Beth leant against the door and watched him. He moved surprisingly gracefully for such a big man, she decided. Efficiently, too. No wasted effort. She noticed the way his muscles were tightening under his shirt and felt a sharp pang of longing to run her fingers over his broad chest. She reached behind her and slid the bolt open again, then closed it deliberately with a loud click.

John spun his head round in surprise as Beth pushed herself away from the door, an enigmatic smile on her face. As her actions registered on him, his lips twisted into that infuriating grin he was so good at.

'So. There is something else I can do for you.' He looked around the room eagerly, as if searching for a convenient place to take her.

Beth walked towards him slowly with her heart in her mouth. She could hardly believe her own daring. 'Yes. As a matter of fact, there is.'

As she reached him, she lifted her hand and slowly undid his belt. John grabbed her by the shoulders and pulled her towards him. Beth let go of the belt and put her hands flat on to his chest, pushing him forcefully away. She took a step back, out of arm's reach.

'Last night I played your games,' she told him. 'Now, it's my turn.' She was delighted to hear her voice so firm and sure. She wanted him to be in no doubt that she meant exactly what she said.

John smirked. 'You enjoyed last night, Beth. Don't try to deny it.'

'Yes, I did,' she agreed, returning his grin. 'But, it was still your game. Now, it's mine. You can walk away now or you can become my plaything.' She mimicked his warning of last night and gave him a few seconds to think it over. John said nothing.

'The rules are, you can't touch me unless I tell you and then only where and how I tell you.' Beth continued, watching his face carefully. If anything, his grin grew even bigger.

'Sure, Beth.'

'Sure, Beth,' she mimicked him. 'That's not what I want to hear.'

'Yes, ma'am.' He could barely contain his laughter.

Beth couldn't help wondering if he had played this game before, too. She tried to stifle the sudden pang of jealousy. The knowing grin on his face was really starting to annoy her. He was the most arrogant sod she had ever met, she decided. Probably even worse than Simon.

'Yes, what?' She raised her hand as if to slap his face.

John stopped grinning. 'Yes, ma'am. I am your property to do with as you will. I am here for your pleasure, not mine.'

'That's much better,' Beth couldn't help smiling. He had definitely done this before!

'I will only touch you where you say and I will please you as well as I can,' he added obediently, as if really beginning to enter into the spirit of her game.

Beth nodded silently and a shiver of lust rushed down her backbone at the implication of his words. She stepped forward again and resumed undoing his belt. She thought she could see a trace of doubt creeping into his eyes but, as she moved her fingers down to his zip, she soon discovered that it had not dampened his desire. Slowly, so that he would feel every tooth parting, she began to open his fly. Remembering the ID badges and her fantasy, she allowed her little finger to run down his erection.

John drew a deep breath when she first touched him and only released it with a rush when she finished undoing the zip. As she moved her hands up to undo the button, Beth let her fingers slide inside the opening. She pretended to be having trouble with the button while her little finger gently stroked the tip of his swollen cock. John's whole body stiffened at her touch and she heard him gulp as he swallowed painfully.

Beth kept her eyes glued to his face the whole time. She could see the little twitches in his facial muscles as she teased his button and fondled his tip. His whole body was rigid with concentration and she had a feeling that it would be easy to push him over the top. She was almost overcome by her feelings of power and elation at the look on his face. It was time to move on.

Beth clasped the sides of his trousers firmly in her

fingers and started to lower them slowly down over his hips and buttocks. As she moved, she gradually crouched down. She was disappointed to see that his shirt had dropped down in front, covering him from her eager gaze.

Resisting the urge to reach up and pull it away, Beth continued her downward journey, allowing her hands to run softly over the outside of his legs as she moved. She was so close to him that she could see the little hairs standing up on his skin as his body shivered at her soft caresses. She took her time.

Finally, she stood up again and stared wordlessly into his face. Little drops of sweat had formed on his brow and upper lip and his tongue was running repeatedly across his lower lip. His Adam's apple bobbed up and down nervously.

'I'm going to enjoy this, slave.' Beth leered at him suggestively, trying to imitate the look he had put on his face each time he had threatened to spank her.

John smiled weakly. His heart didn't seem to be in it. Beth's eyes narrowed.

'Well, slave. What's wrong? Aren't you glad that your mistress is enjoying herself?'

'Yes, ma'am,' he responded softly. 'I'm happy to be a part of your pleasure.'

He was doing very well so far, she decided, remembering how humiliated she had felt when he had made her openly confess her thoughts and desires. She stepped back and put her hands on her hips as she strutted up and down the small room. His eyes followed her every step. Beth frowned. His shirt was still in the way. It should be her who was getting the best view, not him.

'Pull your shirt up under your arms,' she commanded.

As he obeyed her, Beth's eyes lighted on his muscle-bound chest. She couldn't resist moving in closer to push the material aside and expose his nipples. She leant forward and nipped first one and then the other nipple with her front teeth. John flinched but made no sound.

Could he feel his own nipples hardening through all that muscle? She lowered her head again and felt him flinch in anticipation of her teeth.

Smiling, she ran her tongue over each nipple in turn and then began to use her fingers to tease them even more. Oh God. They were even bigger than hers. Was he enjoying this, she wondered? Was he imagining how it would feel if he were doing it to her? She could sense her own nipples starting to rise.

With her knees bent, she ran her tongue down his chest, kissing and licking every inch of his skin all the way down to his navel. She smiled at the way his thighs were tensing every time she touched him, revelling in the sense of power it gave her. She reached round behind him and ran her fingers gently down his spine. It was like wrapping her arms around a giant oak tree. She noticed that several of the muscles in his left buttock were jumping nervously.

Beth pushed her fingers inside his pants and cupped the curves of his buttocks in her palms. She had to press herself up tight against his body just to reach round him, so that his cock was pushed hard into her stomach. As she bit one of his nipples again, she flattened her body against his muscular stomach. She could hear his heart thumping rapidly in his chest cavity and feel the spasms of his rigid penis as it twitched and shuddered against her.

Beth arched her back and drew her stomach in, then pulled herself back as far as she could so that John had to strain forward to continue to press against her. Every time his cock made contact with her body, she squeezed his buttocks. His flesh was so firm that her hands seemed to make little impression on them.

She was just about to change her tactics when John suddenly gave a small groan and thrust his hips forward so urgently that his upper body slammed against her. The force of the blow almost winded her and the shock of it made her sink her teeth into his nipple. John gasped in pain and pleasure and, for a moment, she thought he was about to come.

'I thought I told you not to touch me without permission.' She refused to show any compassion.

'Sorry, ma'am.' He backed away.

Beth glanced round the room and spotted a long metal rule leaning against the wall in the far corner. She removed her hands from his pants and moved across the room to pick it up. Although it was worn and dusty and broken off at one end, it was still long and wide enough to suit her purposes.

'Turn around, slave, and take your punishment like a man.'

John shuffled round awkwardly to face the photocopier, his legs hampered by his trousers rucked up around his ankles. Beth leant round him and placed the ruler on the top of the copier where he could see it, then slipped his underpants off his bottom and on to his thighs. She was tempted to bite the inviting cheeks but she wasn't certain that she would even be able to sink her teeth into his solid flesh.

After she had left him to stew for a few seconds she picked up the ruler again, raised her hand and slapped his right cheek soundly with the flat edge. Although he must have been expecting the blow, he jumped violently, his muscles twitching. She gave him six more slaps, each one harder than the last. His bottom began to turn bright pink.

'Turn around.'

She was surprised to see his face was as red as his buttocks. She looked down and almost laughed when she saw how his pants had tangled up in his erection, pulling it out in front of him.

'Look at the mess you are in,' she reprimanded him as she put the ruler down on the copier again.

'I'm sorry, ma'am. It won't happen again.' John reached down and tried to untangle his pants. Beth moved closer and slapped his hand away. She crouched between his legs, finished extracting his swollen prick and pulled his pants down to his ankles. Her eyes lingered on his hardness as if it were the first erection she had ever seen.

John's body trembled as he swayed towards her. She knew he wanted her to take him in her mouth. His prick was so stiff and swollen that she could see every vein standing out clearly. The tip was already damp and shiny with his lubrication. She stood up slowly and reached for him with both hands.

'I need a permanent reminder of this,' she told him as she ran her fingers slowly up and down his shaft. 'A sort of souvenir, you might say.' As she spoke, she stared up into his finely chiselled face, searching for a reaction. His features seemed frozen, apart from the slightest twitching of his jaw muscles.

'You would like me to have a reminder, wouldn't you?' She increased the speed of her caress and felt him shudder.

'Yes, ma'am.' His words came out in a breathless rush and Beth realised that he had been holding his breath again. She smiled victoriously.

'Good. Bend over the photocopier,' she commanded as she released him.

John hesitated, obviously puzzled about her intentions.

'Right up over the glass,' she added. She saw comprehension dawn. For a moment, she though he was going to refuse and she reached for the ruler again.

With a small sigh, John climbed up on to the copier and leant forward. Beth smiled and hit the copy button. The copier whirred and she saw the beam of light passing along the glass. There was a loud thud as the paper chugged through the system and popped out the far side.

Beth walked round and picked up the sheet. John's eyes followed her. Beth pursed her lips and sighed with disappointment. 'Not good enough.'

She picked up several spare sheets of paper and

covered the exposed areas of glass around his body, then pressed the copy button again.

'Much better,' she told him a few seconds later as she studied another copy. 'Now, lift yourself up higher so that you aren't squashing all the best bits.'

John smiled at her words and raised his buttocks so that his cock and balls were only just resting on the top of the glass. Beth took her time readjusting the papers around him to cut out any unnecessary light and, at the same time, admiring the view. Finally, when she saw his muscles tensing from the effort of holding himself in such an awkward position, she pushed the button again.

'Perfect.' She examined the latest copy closely. 'Although I'm not sure it is quite as enthusiastic as it could be.' She placed the copy on top of the others and slid her hand between his legs and up on to his penis. 'Definitely room for expansion.' As she pushed the button to take more copies, she started to wank him slowly with her fingers.

'That's more like it.' She squeezed him firmly and then pulled her hand away. 'Now, you wank.'

It was quite difficult for John to get himself into position and Beth had to rearrange the surrounding papers several times before she got it right. She took three or four more copies, then stood back to enjoy watching him. From where she was standing, she could just see his balls moving with each stroke. She felt her own arousal increasing rapidly.

'Don't stop, but don't come either,' she ordered huskily. She picked up the last copy and examined it carefully. There was no doubt about what it was, or any doubt about what he was doing. She was tempted to make him go all the way. What a picture that would make!

She dismissed the idea regretfully. Even with his cooperation, the chances of pressing the copy button at the exact moment to catch his eruption were very slim.

'OK, that's enough. Get off and stand in front of me.'

She smiled to see that he was still holding himself but that, unsure what was required of him, he had stopped moving his fingers. His cock looked about ready to burst and his face was swollen with lust.

'You've pleased me, slave,' she told him. 'So I've decided to reward you with your fantasy.' She shivered at the look of hungry anticipation in his eyes as her words sank in.

Slowly, Beth lifted the skirt of her dress to waist level. She looped her fingers through the elastic of her lace panties and was just about to pull them down when she had a much better idea.

'Slave, kneel in front of me and take down my panties. Slowly.' As he began to lower himself, she added, 'When you've done that, you may satisfy me with your tongue and play with me with your fingers.'

John needed no further encouragement to obey those commands. Beth's idea of slow and his definitely did not match. He practically ripped her panties off in his eagerness, while his hands squeezed her buttocks and pulled her tightly on to his waiting tongue. As soon as her panties were around her ankles, Beth stepped out of them and opened her legs to give him full access. She sighed as his tongue began to dart back and forth over her sex lips, then gasped as he sucked her swollen clit right up into his mouth. As his fingers prised her cheeks apart, he pulled her even harder on to his mouth.

Beth placed her hands on his shoulders to steady herself, whimpering as one of his hands began to slide over her buttocks and the other reached up under her crotch to finger her sex. As his thumb began to push against the tightness of her anus, she bit her lip with shock and pleasure and tasted the coppery tang of blood on her tongue.

She was still so keyed up from the previous night that it would take very little to bring her to climax. As if sensing the extent of her arousal, John sucked harder on her clit. His tongue flicked rapidly back and forth over the sensitive flesh, and Beth dug her fingers into his firm flesh and groaned with delight as the pleasure engulfed her.

Shakily, she pushed him away. 'That was very good, slave,' she whispered as she struggled to come back down to earth. 'You can stop now.'

John reluctantly let go and fell back on to his heels. His cock was jerking from side to side as if it were waving to her. His eyes burned with passion.

Still holding her dress up, Beth crouched down in front of him. She reached out and gently slid her finger down the length of his erection. John's whole body shuddered.

'We can't leave you in that state now, can we?' she whispered, squeezing him gently.

'No, ma'am.' John's voice was tight with need.

Smiling, she straightened up and stepped back out of reach. She hooked the toe of her shoe into her panties and flipped them up into the air towards him. They landed on his chest and dropped down on to his prick. John's face darkened as her intention dawned upon him.

'Well, get on with it.' Beth stood back further, her hands still holding her skirt up. 'If it's good enough for a waiter, it's certainly good enough for you.'

John took a long, deep breath. Letting it out slowly, he took hold of the skimpy lace panties and began to rub himself with them. To her astonishment, his face had turned crimson with embarrassment again.

'Faster,' she demanded heartlessly.

John closed his eyes and began to pump himself urgently.

'Don't you dare close your eyes,' she scolded. 'I want you to look at me while you wank yourself with my knickers.' To her surprise, Beth realised that the commands were coming very easily to her. She knew she was being a bit crude but it did not worry her. She was thoroughly enjoying herself. It was no more than he deserved.

John opened his eyes and did as he was told. She

noticed that his gaze kept flickering down away from her face, not to look at her body, but to hide his shame and humiliation. The knowledge of the power she had over him at that moment gave her nearly as much satisfaction as his tongue had just done.

She looked down at his cock again and noticed how his balls were already drawing up tight against his body. His breathing was laboured and his fingers were moving more and more rapidly. She realised that he was certain to come at any second. Too fast, much too fast. She would never tire of watching a man masturbating because of her.

'I think you were right,' she breathed. 'I would have enjoyed watching the waiter wanking with my knickers.'

As she spoke, Beth reached out to slow him down and prolong her teasing. She was too late. With a loud groan, John dropped the panties and let go. The first jet of hot spunk was rapidly followed by another, then another. He groaned again and his face contorted with the violence and pleasure of his orgasm.

Beth lowered her dress and smoothed the material down. Silently, she picked up her latest batch of photocopying and turned to leave. Unbolting the door, she stepped out into the corridor and headed back towards the classroom. She smiled as she heard the door slam shut behind her and the bolt slide back across.

Beth was pleased to see how subdued John seemed that afternoon. For the first hour or so he said practically nothing and kept his head averted from her gaze. She could barely suppress her grin of triumph. Perhaps he would think twice before he tried to get the better of her again. She pulled the photocopies she had taken of him out from under the rest of the copying she had done and examined them keenly. She would certainly never forget John.

Lisa began to wander round the room to check work and Beth quickly pushed the copies out of sight under a folder. Maybe she should do some more photocopying tomorrow, too? Perhaps she could persuade Steve or Brian to give her a hand. Would John tell them what she had done to him? Somehow, she doubted it.

Later, as she stood sipping her afternoon coffee at the open window, she sensed someone standing just behind her. Thinking it was Lisa she turned to smile at her.

'Mind you don't catch cold,' John cautioned her. 'You really shouldn't stand by an open window like that when you haven't got any knickers on. What would you do if the breeze lifted your skirt?'

Beth gulped. She glanced round quickly to make sure no one else had heard his words. Obviously, he wasn't as subdued by his experience as she had thought.

'Do you want them back, by the way?' John put his hand into his jacket pocket as if he was about to produce her undies. 'Only you ran off before I had a chance to return them. Of course, they are a bit sticky . . .'

'No! Stop it.' Beth saw several of the other trainees walking back into the room, including Brian and Steve, who were already heading towards them. 'Don't you dare get them out here,' she hissed.

'Yes ma'am. Whatever you say.' His grin stretched from ear to ear.

Chapter Six

The phone rang and rang. Simon waited impatiently for a few more minutes then slammed the receiver down angrily. Where the hell was she? His wife never seemed to be around when he wanted her, which was not often. He glared into the empty adjoining office. If only Beth wasn't away on that damned training course all week. Maybe he could find a way to take her with him to Rome instead of his wife. That way, not only would he have her all to himself for a whole weekend, he wouldn't need Marie to find someone to look after the damned dog while they were gone.

It was only Wednesday. Beth would not be back until the following Monday. It had been the longest week he could remember. Why had he ever let her go in the first place? She didn't need any extra qualifications to do what he wanted her for, business or pleasure. She had been so damned insistent about it. He began thinking about what had happened the previous Saturday. His memories of what he had done to her were so powerful that he could feel his cock beginning to push hard up against his underpants.

God, if she were here now, he would tear her clothes off her and put her across his knee. He would spank that sexy arse of hers until she begged him to ram himself up inside her. If there was ever a body designed for fucking, it was hers. He wanted her, desperately.

Simon lowered his hand and opened his zip. He slipped his fingers inside and took his already throbbing cock in his hand. He fondled the tip softly and groaned aloud with his urgent need.

The way she had writhed and sobbed when he had taken her across the desk like that. Had she really minded? She hadn't stopped him taking her a second time. She could have struggled harder. He remembered the soft gasps, the way she had opened her legs for him. His hand started to move slowly up and down his erection, his excitement building as he continued to fantasise about what he wanted to do to her.

He was so carried away by his thoughts and actions that he barely heard the knock on the door. It was only when it was repeated, louder and more insistently, that Simon opened his eyes with a start.

Shit. There was someone at the door. It must be his eleven o'clock appointment, Madeleine West. Mrs West was a rich, middle-aged widow with lots of money she wanted to invest in the stock market and not a clue how to go about it. Simon planned to help make her – and himself – even richer.

But not now. He glanced down at himself. His cock was throbbing almost painfully. He could already see the dampness of his lubrication glistening on the dark, swollen tip. Christ, a few more seconds and he would have been there. He couldn't stop now.

'Mr Henderson. Coo-ee. Are you there?' Simon heard the sound of the door handle turning. Shit. Why hadn't he thought to lock it? He stuffed himself back inside his trousers and forced the zip up. Normally, he would have hurried over to the door and taken her arm to help her to the leather visitor's chair. He didn't dare stand up. He grabbed the phone quickly.

'. . . Look, I've got an important visitor now so I'll have

to call you back . . .' Simon put his hand over the mouth-piece. 'Mrs West.' He waved his hand towards the chair opposite his desk. 'Please, do come in and take a seat. I'll be with you in a minute.' He returned to his imaginary conversation.

'Yes, I realise that there's a lot of money at stake, but I can't discuss it now. I'll talk to you later.'

Madeleine West closed the door behind her and waddled across the room. She flopped down heavily into the chair and stared at him expectantly. Simon replaced the receiver and put on his most winning smile.

'Sorry about that. Please forgive me for not getting up, but I've, um, hurt my back. Golf,' he invented quickly. 'It's so painful, I can barely walk.'

Madeleine's face changed from displeasure to sympathy. 'Oh, you poor love. My dear departed Charley used to suffer with his back. Would you like me to rub it for you?'

'No!' Simon flushed with horror at the thought. The last thing he wanted was for her to come round behind his desk while he was in this state. The way he was feeling at the moment, even the tubby Mrs West seemed less undesirable than usual. If he pulled the blinds down and closed his eyes, maybe . . .

The realisation of what he was contemplating was enough to steady him. He glanced at her pasty-looking skin and shuddered. His erection began to subside.

'So long as I sit still, I shall be fine. Just seeing my favourite client and knowing how much I shall enjoy helping her capitalise on her investments is more than enough to make me feel better,' he flattered her outrageously.

Mrs West preened herself at his words and sank down on the leather chair. 'I've decided to let you invest the whole two hundred thousand,' she told him as she rummaged around in her enormous handbag for her chequebook. 'After what you said last week, I'm sure I shall be in safe hands with you.'

Simon barely stopped himself shivering at the idea of

having her in his hands. Watching her begin writing the cheque, however, made him feel almost as good as screwing Beth had done. If there was one thing in life even better than good sex, it was large quantities of other people's money.

'I must say, that's a very pretty hat you're wearing.' He could afford to be generous. The money he made out of her would easily finance his whole trip to Rome. 'You must tell me where you got it. I'm sure my wife would like one just like it.'

Mrs West beamed with delight.

It was all so very easy, he thought contemptuously, as he returned her smile. Like taking candy from a baby.

After Madeleine West had finally gone and Simon had tucked her cheque securely away in his desk, he allowed his thoughts to drift back to Beth. Pictures of her delightful tits and taut rump flashed though his mind and his cock surged back to full size. Determined not to be caught out twice, Simon crossed the office and locked the door.

Even before he reached his desk, his cock was already between his fingers again. As he began moving his fist faster and faster, groaning with pleasure, he realised he could not remember when he had last been reduced to masturbating over anyone. Normally, when he felt the urge, he just called one of his many female acquaintances to take care of him.

Maybe that's what he should do now. No one sprang to mind. Besides, he couldn't wait. His thoughts of Beth were just too strong and demanding. He kneaded himself gently and caressed his balls. Jesus, he was about to lose it, he couldn't hold on any longer. He grabbed himself again, pumping frantically.

One thing for sure. He was going to have to make Beth pay for reducing him to this. His come began spurting into his fingers. Just you wait, Beth Bradley, he threatened. He could hardly wait for next week.

* * *

106

It seemed to take Beth forever to get ready that night. First, she couldn't decide what to wear. Nothing seemed quite right and she still had no real idea what Lisa would find attractive.

After three or four attempts, she finally settled on a short, mid-blue woollen dress with front zip. Under it, she would wear her front-fastening half-cup bra with matching white lace panties and, to finish the outfit, suspenders and stockings.

When she came to do her make-up, Beth found she was so nervous that her hand wouldn't stop shaking. She had soon managed to smear mascara everywhere except on her lashes. By the time she had cleaned up and started again, the hands on her travel clock were showing two minutes to seven.

The phone rang, making her jump.

'A Ms Williams is waiting for you in the lobby, madam.'

'Thank you. Please tell her I will be right down.' Beth brushed blusher on to her already glowing cheeks and gave herself a final quick scan in the mirror. Nervously, she picked up her shoulder bag and headed for the door. Yet another new experience beckoned. This was turning out to be quite a week.

Lisa was dressed in a knee-length flared black skirt and a green silk blouse. She had curled the ends of her blonde hair under and was wearing a gold-chain necklace that disappeared inside her cleavage. Her legs were clad in stockings and she had sling-back high heels on. She looked very pretty, very young and very desirable.

As Beth stepped out the lift and started towards her, she noticed the receptionist eyeing them both up. He certainly didn't look bored now. She swallowed hard and tried to calm her nerves. Stop being so silly, she chided herself. You've spent all day with this woman in the training centre. You've had lunch together, chatted about most things and discovered you have a lot in

107

common. It's just like going out with Ann or one of the other girls.

It wasn't, of course. Beth had never even contemplated doing with any of her girlfriends what she was about to do with and to Lisa.

'Hi, Lisa.' Beth greeted her warmly. 'Right on time. You look very pretty this evening. A skirt suits you.' Beth could picture the gap of bare skin at the top of Lisa's thighs. She imagined herself undoing the suspenders and rolling the stockings slowly down Lisa's legs. Her own legs turned to rubber.

Lisa grinned. 'Thank you.' She had made an effort to dress as Beth had suggested and was pleased Beth had noticed. She ran her eyes slowly over Beth's trim figure. 'And you, of course, look as lovely as always. I've booked us a table for seven thirty. It's not far, so I thought we would walk since it's such a nice evening.'

Long before they had reached the restaurant they were talking and joking together again like old friends and Beth felt herself slowly relaxing.

The restaurant was small and cosy, with a dozen or so tables and a tiny bar. The waiter led them to a secluded table in the far corner, well away from the other diners. Beth had the feeling that Lisa had booked it deliberately. Was this, perhaps, where she brought all her women? It was a strange thought.

As they walked across the room, Beth noticed a couple of men sitting at the bar, eyeing them up. The taller one turned to his friend and whispered something. They both laughed and Beth flushed. Were they just discussing their chances of making a pick-up, or had they recognised Lisa and her as ... as what? Lesbians? The label made her shudder.

'What a lovely place,' she gushed, as they sat down. 'Do you come here often?' she added before she could stop herself.

Lisa shook her head. 'Not really. I've been here once

or twice with my mother. The food's good and it's very friendly and relaxed.'

It certainly wasn't the answer Beth had expected and she wasn't quite sure what to make of it. She took her time examining the menu, trying to calm her fluttering heartbeat.

In the end, they both chose the same. Melon to start, followed by steak and salad with a side helping of french fries. Lisa asked the waiter for a carafe of the house wine, which proved to be both full bodied and fruity.

They filled the awkward moments while they waited for the food to arrive with chit-chat about books and films they had both enjoyed. Beth took several deep gulps of the wine, feeling in need of something to help relax her again.

'So, are you getting everything you hoped for out of this week?' Lisa questioned as she poured oil and vinegar dressing on to her salad.

'Oh yes. It's even better than I had expected,' Beth responded enthusiastically, thinking more about her extracurricular activities than the course. 'I never expected to learn so much,' she added with a smile. The wine seemed to be working.

Lisa reached out and placed her hand over Beth's. It was the first deliberate touch of the evening and Beth felt a small tingle of anticipation prickling her skin.

'And, have you decided what you want to do after we've eaten? I'll leave it up to you.'

Beth paused. She was very tempted to agree to going on to the club Lisa had suggested. She was more than a little curious to see what such a place would be like. She thought about being alone with Lisa at her flat, undressing her, running her hands over Lisa's slim body.

'I'd very much like to see where you live,' she replied slowly. 'If that's all right with you, of course.'

Lisa licked her lips and fondled the back of Beth's hand with her fingertips. Her touch was feather-light. 'I'd like that, too,' she whispered.

Her voice sounded slightly husky. Beth looked up into her face and saw a tell-tale flush of colour on Lisa's cheeks. Her pupils were dilated and her lips slightly parted so that Beth could see the tip of her tongue. What would it be like to kiss another woman?

Lisa's home was on the edge of the city centre, less than ten minutes' walk from the restaurant. It was more like a mews town house or a maisonette than a flat, and Beth fell in love with it immediately.

'It's gorgeous,' she enthused as she wandered round the main living-room and examined Lisa's collection of expensive-looking porcelain figurines. 'How long have you lived here?'

'Oh, about three years. I had to wait for it to come on the market. These sorts of places are in great demand.'

'I can see why. I'd love something like this,' Beth replied as she continued to wander round, exploring. A slinky Siamese cat jumped down off the window-sill, purring loudly as it wrapped itself around Beth's legs. Beth automatically reached down to stroke its silky fur.

'That's Suki,' Lisa smiled. 'Don't let her take advantage of you. She can be very persistent when she likes someone.'

Beth continued to stroke the cat. She couldn't help smiling at the fact it was female. Didn't Lisa have any males in her life at all?

'Would you like a coffee, or something stronger?' Lisa questioned.

'I'd love a gin and tonic if you've got it,' Beth replied quickly. The effects of the wine were already wearing off. If she had ever needed a little extra courage, it was now.

'No problem. Just make yourself comfortable on the settee. I'll get the ice and lemon.' Lisa disappeared with Suki following her, meowing demandingly. Beth perched nervously on the end of the long, soft couch and gulped hard to try and steady her hammering pulse. She wondered which door led to the bedroom. She swallowed again and folded her hands on her lap to try to stop them trembling.

When Lisa returned, carrying their drinks, she placed them on the coffee-table and sat down beside Beth so that their thighs were touching. Beth tried not to flinch at the touch. She failed.

Lisa stared up into her face thoughtfully. 'You've never done anything like this before, have you, Beth?' she asked softly.

The question took Beth by surprise. She flushed and shook her head. Lisa smiled encouragingly and leant towards her. Beth had a feeling that her admission had boosted Lisa's own confidence. She felt a rush of relief. Somebody had to find the courage to make the first move. She was too tense to think straight.

'Just relax. It's not so very hard,' Lisa whispered as she placed her lips gently against Beth's.

Beth closed her eyes and returned the kiss. It didn't seem all that different from kissing a man. When she felt Lisa probing her lips with her tongue, she willingly opened them to allow her to slip the tip inside. A tingle of desire shot through her. Kissing always made her weak at the knees.

Lisa pulled Beth into her embrace. Beth jumped with shock as she felt Lisa's hands running over the outer curve of her breasts. Her body instinctively stiffened and she opened her eyes again.

Lisa immediately stopped kissing her and moved her hands away. Beth felt a tinge of regret. Was Lisa turned off by her lack of responsiveness? She hadn't meant to react like that. It wasn't unpleasant, just unusual. Gingerly, she lifted her own hand and placed it on Lisa's tiny breast. She moved closer and leant forward to kiss Lisa's lips tentatively.

'I'm sorry,' she whispered. 'It's just that I've never felt this way before. I'm not sure about anything except being here with you.' She brushed her lips softly across the other girl's mouth again.

Lisa smiled and seemed to relax at her words. Beth squeezed Lisa's breast gently and immediately sensed Lisa's whole body quiver. Encouraged, she moved her hand inwards, seeking the nipple. It felt hard and swollen, even through Lisa's clothing. She felt Lisa shivering again and was suddenly consumed with an overwhelming urge to fondle Lisa's naked breast. She raised her other hand and started to undo the buttons of Lisa's blouse.

Lisa moaned softly and moved her own hand up to help. The blouse fell open, exposing her bra. Beth pushed it up with her fingers so that Lisa's firm breasts popped into view. She ran her fingers tentatively over the nipples again and felt them grow even harder. She realised that Lisa was beginning to undo the zip on the front of her dress.

'Put your hand up my skirt,' Lisa whispered as Beth's zip came open, exposing her to Lisa's eager fingers. 'Yes, that's it,' she sighed as Beth started to slide her hand slowly up the silky stocking. As she spoke, Lisa undid the catch of Beth's bra and pulled it open. She lowered her head and ran her tongue lightly over Beth's left nipple.

Beth stopped moving her hand and gasped with pleasure. Lisa's touch was so soft, so gentle. Like the touch of a feather. Men could be so rough sometimes in their enthusiasm. As a woman, Beth guessed, Lisa would know exactly what felt good and what didn't. Suddenly she no longer had any fears about what she should, or shouldn't, be doing. All she needed to do was to caress Lisa the way she, herself, liked to be caressed.

She moved her fingers further up under Lisa's skirt, remembering how she had already fantasised about doing this. Her yearning deepened. The skin on Lisa's inner thigh was so soft and smooth. She could feel her excitement building as she moved slowly upwards. This must be what a man feels, she realised. The thought sent little tremors of desire rushing up and down her legs.

She ran her fingertips lightly over Lisa's mound. Lisa moaned again and lifted her buttocks off the couch, pushing herself up against Beth's touch. 'Oh, yes,' she whispered.

Beth felt a surge of desire pulsing through her, so strong that she almost climaxed. She could imagine exactly how what she was doing to Lisa felt. It was almost as if she was masturbating herself, only much, much better. She slipped her fingers under the lace edge of Lisa's panties and caressed her clit.

Lisa writhed from side to side and sucked one of Beth's nipples into her mouth, teasing it with her tongue. It was Beth's turn to groan with pleasure. Lisa lifted her head and sat back, so that Beth's fingers slid down on to her thigh. She smiled softly.

'Slowly, Beth,' Lisa whispered, seeing how excited she was becoming. 'There is no rush. We have all night. Let me get those things off you.'

Beth leant back on the couch and allowed Lisa to pull her dress over her head and slip her bra straps off her arms. Then, clad only in her panties and stockings, she sat back up and helped Lisa out of her own blouse and bra. Lisa stood up and undid her skirt. She dropped it to the floor, stepped out of it and held out her hands. Beth ran her eyes appreciatively over Lisa's suspenders and stockings. It was easy to see why the sight of them drove men wild.

'Come on. We will be more comfortable in the bedroom,' murmured Lisa.

Beth allowed herself to be led across the living-room and through the doorway. Lisa flicked a switch on the wall and they were immediately bathed in a soft, pinkish glow from the two wall lights.

The room was decorated in beiges and greens and dominated by a huge double bed covered with a lacy

113

spread. Lisa led her, unresisting, to the bed and pulled her down on to it. She ran her fingers over Beth's nipples again and smiled at the way Beth shuddered at her touch. She leant over her and kissed them gently.

Beth lay back and closed her eyes again. Lisa's tongue was as soft as cotton wool. She sighed with joy as she felt the tip of Lisa's tongue leave her breasts and begin to slip slowly down her stomach. Instinctively, she reached for Lisa's breasts. As she cupped them in her hands, she gently teased the rigid nipples with her fingertips.

Lisa pushed her tongue into Beth's navel, caressing it with slow, circular movements that made Beth arch her back eagerly. The tongue moved on down, and she felt Lisa's fingers peeling her panties down over her hips. She squeezed Lisa's breasts harder and heard the other woman's breathing quicken in response.

'Oh, you have shaved,' Lisa murmured. 'I like that.' Beth felt Lisa's tongue begin its slow journey across her naked mound. She clenched her teeth in expectation of what was to come.

Even so, nothing had prepared her for the shock of Lisa's tongue caressing the swollen bud of her clit. The sensation was so exquisite that she bit her tongue and twisted her body to one side in an effort to escape.

'Please,' she begged. 'That's too much.'

Lisa lifted her hand and caressed her cheek. 'Just relax, Beth,' she whispered. 'We have all night.'

Beth nodded, too excited to speak as her orgasm built up and threatened to engulf her completely. She knew that as soon as Lisa touched her clit again, she would not be able to stop herself. She gritted her teeth as Lisa lowered her head back down between her thighs.

Lisa ran her tongue down Beth's left thigh then back up the right thigh. Beth let out a sob as the tip of Lisa's tongue started to probe her outer lips and slide up over the bud of her clit again. Lisa began flicking her tongue back and forth, her touch as soft and light as the breeze. It was more than Beth could stand.

With another sob, Beth climaxed. Her whole body convulsed with the intensity of it. 'Oh yes,' she sighed breathlessly as her body writhed helplessly under Lisa's unrelenting tongue and pleasure engulfed her. She slumped down on to the bed and sighed contentedly.

She sensed Lisa lying back down beside her and felt the other woman's fingers begin to caress her nipples again. Beth raised herself up on her elbows and gazed down at Lisa's perfect body. She was lying back peacefully with a slight smile on her face. Beth recognised it as the satisfied smile she often wore after she had successfully brought a man to climax. She leant down and kissed her gently on the lips.

Lisa raised her own head and responded with some urgency. Beth could almost feel the need burning deep within Lisa's womb. She was overcome by a desperate desire to return the pleasure to this woman who had so quickly and easily brought her to fulfilment.

As if reading her thoughts, Lisa moved closer to her. She reached up to pull Beth back down on the bed and straightened her legs out as she snuggled against her. For the first time ever, Beth found herself lying breast to naked breast with another woman. Her nipples were pushed up hard against Lisa's swollen tips and she could feel the other woman's soft pubes caressing her own shaven mound. It was incredible.

Lisa increased the intensity of her kisses, moaning softly as she pushed her tongue enthusiastically into Beth's willing mouth. Beth lifted her leg and placed it over Lisa's thigh, pulling her body even tighter against her. Her clit was pushed hard against Lisa's sex and she felt Lisa shiver with passion and thrust herself urgently against her, rolling her hips to increase the pressure on her own swollen bud.

Beth felt the juices of her excitement flowing from her. She put her finger to her mouth and licked it then slipped it down between Lisa's thighs, forcing them apart. She smiled as she saw Lisa's face register delight and heard the urgent gasp of pleasure escape from her lips.

Beth ran her finger over Lisa's clit and on down to the opening of her vagina. The two women were so close together that the back of her hand was brushing against her own sex as she moved and she was masturbating both women at the same time. It was one of the most exciting and erotic moments of her life.

She became aware of the dampness of the other woman's passion on the tips of her fingers. Lisa was so wet; she might have just got out the bath. Barely hesitating, Beth pushed her thumb up inside her and caressed her G-spot.

Lisa whimpered urgently and pushed herself hard against Beth's hand, moving her hips up and down so that Beth's thumb was pumping in and out of her like a tiny penis. Beth could see Lisa fondling her own breasts with her hands and hear her desperate moaning.

She was very aware of the urgency gathering between her own legs again. Without withdrawing her thumb, Beth lowered her middle finger on to Lisa's clit and began to tease it softly. Her whole hand was now pushed against Lisa's mound, kneading her, caressing her. Beth slipped her other hand between her own thighs, using her own lubrication to rub herself.

She felt Lisa's vagina tighten as the spasm of her climax rushed through her body. The knowledge that Lisa was coming was so exciting, so stimulating, that Beth almost lost control again herself, just imagining how it had felt. She withdrew her hands almost reluctantly and sat up on her heels, her breathing ragged.

Eventually, Lisa sat up beside her and placed an arm around Beth's shoulders. She planted a gentle kiss on her cheeks. 'Thank you, Beth. That was very good. And now we can take the time to really enjoy ourselves.'

For a moment, Beth looked startled. She had expected it to be over now that they had both come. Nevertheless, she was still tingling from the thrill of seeing and feeling Lisa climax. She remembered that this was not the first time Lisa had suggested that one orgasm was only the beginning. She shivered with anticipation.

Lisa crawled across the bed and reached to open the drawer of the bedside table. Beth allowed her eyes to examine Lisa's tiny buttocks. She reached out and ran her hands over one cheek, smiling at the way Lisa's muscles tightened. She raised her hand and smacked Lisa gently. Lisa squirmed with delight.

'Lie back and open your legs,' Lisa instructed. As she turned round, Beth could see that she was holding a vibrator in her left hand. Her eyes widened. She did as she was told, then closed her eyes. She heard the urgent buzzing as Lisa flicked the switch, then jumped as the cold plastic made contact with her inner thigh. She moaned as the tip of the vibrator slipped up inside her vagina. Unable to help herself, she began to push against it, forcing it deeper and deeper inside her, entering at an angle she was not able to achieve when using a vibrator on her own.

She moaned and bit her lip as she felt the fingers of Lisa's other hand seek out her clitoris. The double sensation of stimulation in both places at once was unbelievable. She knew she could not take much more of it without coming.

As if sensing her thoughts, Lisa began to slide the vibrator slowly back out, at the same time reducing the pressure of her fingers to the softest of caresses. Beth rolled her hips and sobbed with frustration. She was desperate to come.

'Please,' she begged helplessly. 'Oh God, Lisa. Please don't tease.' She pushed herself up, trying to force the vibrator deeper inside her. 'I want . . .'

'Yes? What is it?' Lisa questioned. 'Don't be afraid to say what you want.'

'I want to feel your tongue there again,' Beth whispered, still rolling her hips.

Lisa smiled knowingly. She pushed the vibrator back up inside Beth's vagina and then leant over her and flicked her tongue across Beth's throbbing clit. Beth shuddered and clenched her muscles tightly around the vibrator. She turned her head and saw Lisa slip her hand down between her own thighs and begin squeezing her mound. Her face was flushed and her breathing was shallow. Beth sensed that Lisa was getting ready to climax as well and another tremor of ardour raced through her body.

Lisa pushed her head even lower and encased Beth's sex bud with her lips. As Lisa sucked softly on it, Beth shuddered all over and a small whimper escaped her lips. She was so close now. A shiver of excitement raced through every limb. Lisa sucked harder, while one hand pushed the vibrator back and forth in Beth's vagina and the other hand caressed her own swollen clitoris.

Beth stiffened, sobbing incoherently as another powerful orgasm rushed to overwhelm her.

'Oh Jesus,' she gasped. She heard Lisa moan softly in response and felt her slump forward over her stomach.

Beth was not sure how long it was before she recovered enough to move again. She opened her eyes and gazed down at Lisa's head still resting on her lower body. She smiled contentedly and ran her fingers through the other woman's blonde hair.

Lisa sat up and smiled at her. 'Well? It wasn't so bad, was it?' she questioned teasingly.

Beth grinned sheepishly and shook her head. She could hardly believe how much she had just enjoyed herself, or remember why she had been so apprehensive about it. It hadn't been anything like she had imagined it would be. The whole experience had been so different from sex with a man. Very slow, very sensual. Not better, just very different and very, very good.

Lisa patted her on the leg. 'I'll make us both some coffee.' She got up and slipped on the robe that was hanging over a chair. 'Come on through when you are ready.'

Beth stood up and glanced down at herself. She was covered in sweat. 'Would you mind if I took a shower?' she questioned.

'Of course not. I should have offered. It's through here.' Lisa began walking across the room towards another door on the far side. Beth followed her. As Lisa opened the door into the bathroom, Beth put her hand on her shoulder.

'I don't suppose you would like to join me?' Beth suggested softly.

Lisa's face lit up. 'I was hoping you might suggest that,' she whispered as she pulled her robe from her shoulders and dropped it to the floor.

As they stepped into the shower and Lisa turned the water on, Beth picked up the sponge and soaped it thoroughly. She ran her eyes over Lisa's trim figure then reached out excitedly to caress her puckered nipples.

Chapter Seven

*B*eth ran her eyes carefully over the example financial plan she had just completed, double-checking to ensure she had missed nothing important. She wanted it to be as good as possible. Lisa had just told them that Geoff Stevens was taking the final lecture session the following morning, and that he would probably want to review some of their best work. Beth was determined hers would be one of those selected.

Geoff Stevens! His name was spoken almost in the same breath as that of God in the financial world. Simon worshipped him in an envious, greedy sort of way. Beth knew that he would die for an opportunity to spend a few minutes fawning at Geoff's feet in the hope of learning something useful. She doubted he would have sent her on this course at all if he had realised that she would get to meet the great Geoffrey Stevens.

Beth rubbed her eyes and suppressed a yawn. The week's hectic social activities were really beginning to catch up with her. Thank goodness she had made no plans for the coming evening. All she wanted to do was curl up in bed with a good book and then sleep for at least eight hours. One could definitely have too much of a good thing.

Sensing a presence hovering nearby, she looked up. Lisa was standing behind her. Beth had been both amused and flattered to find Lisa wearing a dress that morning. Considering how she obviously felt about it during work hours, it was the highest compliment the young woman could have paid her.

'OK, Beth?'

'Yes, fine, thanks. I'm just about finished.' Beth was surprised and pleased to find she felt no embarrassment about the previous evening. They had done nothing to be embarrassed about. They had just been two good friends enjoying each other's company.

'Good.' Lisa patted her shoulder gently. 'I'm sure I can see to it that your work is one of those Geoff Stevens gets a look at. He's a wonderful man, Beth, with a brilliant financial mind. What he doesn't know isn't worth knowing. Make sure you take full advantage of him.'

Beth nodded. Even if she didn't learn anything from him, she would still enjoy Simon's professional jealousy over the meeting. She wondered what Geoff would be like. Lisa was obviously more than impressed. She smiled, realising that he was the first man Lisa had ever expressed an interest in, albeit purely professional.

Suddenly, she spotted John watching her with an amused twinkle in his eye. Lisa was still resting a hand on her shoulder and Beth drew a sharp breath and forced herself to return his stare. Her eyes dared him to make anything more of it. John flashed her a knowing grin and lowered his head. In spite of herself, she experienced a brief rush of longing as she remembered his submission to her in the storeroom.

Brian and Steve had both asked her out again, yesterday and today. If it hadn't been for her evening with Lisa, she might have been tempted the previous day. She loved the longing look in their eyes and it was flattering to be so in demand. Today, however, she was less tempted. She needed a rest. She had to be at her very best the following day, both mentally and physically, in order to impress Geoff Stevens.

Lisa patted her shoulder again and moved on. Beth finished a final check of her work and decided that it was time to call it a day. Lisa had already told them they could leave as soon as they were finished and several of her fellow students had already handed their work in and left. She glanced at her watch. Twenty past four. She had plenty of time for a long soak before dinner. Then she planned to curl up in bed with the crime thriller she had bought herself during the lunch break.

'Sure you won't at least come out for a quick drink later, Beth?' Steve caught her as she headed for the door. 'It's our last night. This time tomorrow, we'll all be on our way home. We may never see each other again,' he added mournfully.

Beth grinned. In their closed little world that wasn't very likely. There was a good chance that they would all bump into each other again sooner or later at some conference or other.

'Honestly, Steve. I've already got plans for this evening. Sorry.'

There was no way she was going to admit that she was staying in, too exhausted to take any more excitement. She wondered if he would assume that her plans were with Lisa, then shrugged. Who cared what he thought?

Steve put an exaggerated expression of despair on his face and shrugged his shoulders at Brian. 'Well, I tried,' he muttered. Beth laughed.

Brian looked round for John and shook his head. 'We'll just have to drown our sorrows without her,' he called. 'Unless you can talk her round? See you down in the bar around eight.' John stared at Beth thoughtfully, then nodded silently.

Brian squeezed her hand. 'Don't forget. If you change your mind, we'll be in the bar of the St Anne's.'

'Not tonight, Brian.'

'We could always come and tuck you in later, if you want,' he added with a wink.

'In your dreams,' Beth laughed. 'See you all tomorrow.'

When she asked for her key at the desk, the receptionist shook his head. 'Are you sure it's not in your bag, madam? You didn't hand it in this morning.'

Beth frowned. 'I'm sure I did.' She rummaged hastily through her handbag. She was certain that she remembered dropping it on the desk that morning as usual. Or was that yesterday? She must have had it last night, or rather early that morning, when she got back from Lisa's. Damn!

'Perhaps you left it in the room? I'll get the spare key for you, madam.' Beth noticed that his eyes were focused on her chest again. She felt too foolish about the missing key to pay it much attention. She took the spare key with a nod of thanks and hurried to the lift.

After a long, hot bath, Beth decided to take advantage of room service again, too weary to be bothered with dressing to eat in the dining-room. She couldn't resist another feast of prawns at Simon's expense and she also indulged herself in a slice of raspberry shortcake with whipped cream. It would do her good to get to the gym the following week.

After she had finished eating, Beth hunted for the missing key in vain, then gave up and spent an hour or so making a list of things she would like to discuss with Geoff Stevens, should she be lucky enough to get the opportunity. She couldn't help feeling excited about meeting him face to face. He was such a legend.

By eight thirty, she was dressed in a short lacy nightie and tucked up under the duvet with her murder mystery. It was ages since she had read a good book and she was soon engrossed in the twists and turns of the complicated plot. Exciting as it was, however, by ten o' clock, her eyes refused to stay open any longer and she switched the bedside lamp out and snuggled down sleepily.

She was running across a wide, grassy field in the middle of nowhere. It was dark. The ground ahead of her was illuminated by a huge harvest moon, hanging low on the horizon in a star-splattered night sky. It was clear and balmy and a soft breeze gently caressed her naked flesh. The grass was damp under her bare feet. Someone was following her and she needed to reach the woods just visible on the distant horizon.

She had no idea why. She couldn't even remember where she was or what she was doing there. She only knew it had something to do with solving the recent spate of unexplained deaths in the sleepy little village that lay a mile or so behind her.

Without warning, the scenery changed. Now, she was lying on her back in a bed of rose petals, listening to someone giving a lecture about property investment. She could hear music playing in the distance, and the clatter of dishes. She tried to lift her head to look round but a hand pushed her back down and she heard Lisa's voice telling her to relax and enjoy herself. She jumped as she felt something soft and furry brush up against her legs, purring loudly.

A car horn blared somewhere nearby and Beth heard a clock striking. She counted the chimes. Thirteen. That couldn't be right. Where had Lisa gone? She felt gentle fingers starting to undo the ribbons on the front of her nightie and a shiver of desire tore through her body. Lisa's touch was so sure, so knowing. The nightie came open and Beth felt the material pulled away, exposing her breasts and crotch.

She opened her eyes to look up at her lover. The room was pitch dark. She couldn't see anything except a vague shadow hovering at the foot of the bed. She tried to reach out to turn the bedside lamp on. A hand caught hers and held it fast.

'Lisa?' Beth twisted her head round and strained her eyes. 'What are you doing? Put the light on. I want to see you.' Beth was having trouble collecting her thoughts. She couldn't remember where she was or how she had got there. She wasn't entirely sure she was even awake. There was something about what was going on that seemed more like a dream.

Her unseen lover took hold of her other arm and lifted both arms above her head. She felt a cord being wrapped round her wrists and secured to the bedhead.

'What are you doing?' she repeated, tugging against the restraints.

Somewhere nearby, a door slammed and Beth heard footsteps in the corridor. Of course. She was in her hotel room. She must have closed the heavy shutters over the windows. That was why it was so dark. What was Lisa doing in her hotel room?

'Just close your eyes and relax.' Beth became aware of something caressing her stomach. It was as soft as velvet. A shiver ran down her spine and she felt the goose-bumps springing up all over her body. Unable to help herself, Beth writhed with delight.

'That's it. Just close your eyes and enjoy.'

Where had he learnt to touch her so softly? It took a second or two for that thought to sink in. It was a man's voice speaking to her from out of the darkness. Muffled and indistinct, as if deliberately disguised, but definitely a man's voice. Who was he? Where was Lisa? What on earth was going on? Why couldn't she think straight?

'Who's there? What's happening?' A wave of panic went through her and Beth began to pull harder against the constraints holding her wrists. A velvety touch moved up her body and brushed lightly across her nipples. Beth gasped with shock and pleasure. Jesus! How was he doing that?

'There's nothing to be frightened of. You're just dreaming. That's all. Relax.'

The words were almost hypnotic. The soft velvet continued to tease her breasts. It was the most incredible sensation she had ever experienced. Tingles of pleasure were running down her writhing body. Every caress sent ripples of longing deep inside her. Her clitoris was throbbing as if she had been using her vibrator, yet, incredibly, nothing had touched her there yet. The voice was right. She had to be dreaming.

'That's it. Close your eyes.' The voice was closer. His tongue ran over her neck and up on to her ear. Teeth nibbled her earlobe and warm breath whispered in her ear. 'Enjoy.'

Beth whimpered urgently. Her body felt as if it was on fire and she couldn't keep still. The soft breathing in her ear was causing the muscles in her legs to twitch. Unseen fingers seemed to be running up and down her thighs. The velvety touch continued to stimulate her breasts. He had to be wearing some kind of fur glove. Her nipples had grown so large and rigid that they were almost painful and her lubrication was already seeping from her engorged sex lips. She had never been so ready.

'Take me. Please.' The words fell from her lips before she could stop them. She rolled her hips again, trying desperately to rub her thighs together. If her hands hadn't been tied, she would have been unable to stop herself from pushing her fingers hard up inside her. Her clitoris and vagina were throbbing urgently. The velvety touch began sliding slowly, so slowly, over her stomach. The lips caressing her neck began to move down towards her hardened nipples.

'Oh Jesus. Please.' Beth was sobbing uncontrollably now. She felt his lips licking her breasts and his teeth nibbling her engorged nipples. Her lower body spasmed and a violent climax rippled through her. It was the first time she had ever come without any stimulation of her clitoris or vagina and the sudden intensity of it took her by surprise. She cried out in pleasure.

'That's it. Let yourself go.' The voice was as soft and

silky as the gloved hand. Who the hell was he? What was happening to her?

'John?' She whispered. 'It's you, isn't it?' Her lower body was still trembling and her legs were as wobbly as jelly.

'If you want it to be,' the voice responded softly. 'What does it matter?'

It could be Brian, she thought. She had always suspected that Brian might be a bit of a dark horse. She remembered his offer to come and tuck her in. On his own, without John taking charge, he might be capable of something like this.

'How did you get in?' She felt his gloved hand beginning to caress her thighs again and found it difficult to believe that she would be able to respond so soon. She remembered the missing key. Had someone deliberately stolen it? Who? One of the three men? When had they had the opportunity? Beth remembered the way the hotel receptionist had been looking at her. Surely, he wouldn't dare?

'Anything's possible in a dream.' The voice seemed to reply to her thoughts. His tongue began to tease her nipples again. They were still puckered and swollen. She sighed gently and closed her eyes, allowing the pleasurable sensations to wash over her. It had to be John. As he continued to caress her with tongue and glove, her clit began to tingle and pulsate with renewed desire. Her whole body had become so sensitive that when the corner of the duvet flopped across her stomach, she cried out as if she had been slapped. She sighed with relief as he pushed it gently away and soothed her burning flesh with his cool lips.

She started to fantasise about him plunging his rigid cock deep up inside her. She longed to wrap her legs around his back and bury his shaft inside her to the hilt. She wanted to squeeze and tease him with her muscles, torture him until he could take no more and had to pump his seed helplessly into her. The idea was so exciting that she hardly knew what to do with herself. As she continued to writhe from side to side, her breath coming in short, sharp pants, she heard herself begging him to take her.

'Please. I want you inside me,' she sobbed.

'Like this?'

Beth gasped as his fingers penetrated her. She immediately clasped her legs around his wrist and tried to pull him in deeper. She felt him begin slowly caressing the ridges of her vagina. Sweat was trickling between her breasts and pooling in her navel, as she burned with need for him.

'Yes, oh yes!' She thrust against him.

'Or, perhaps, like this?' She groaned as she felt his fingers withdraw, then cried out in shock as something icy cold was pushed right up inside her. 'Oh Christ!' She bit her lip to try and stem her desperate sobbing. Whatever it was that he had pushed into her was so cold against her burning flesh that the shock was breathtaking. Helplessly, she felt herself climaxing again.

As she gradually relaxed, Beth could feel liquid running out of her. For an awful moment, she thought she had wet herself. Then the truth dawned. Ice. He had pushed a chunk of ice up inside her. She could feel it melting, feel the water running down her thighs. Then she felt him begin drying her gently with a soft towel.

Beth took a deep breath and shook her head. This couldn't be happening. If her hands had not been tied, she would have pinched herself hard to make herself wake up.

'Who are you? What do you want?' she whispered weakly.

'I am whoever you want me to be and all I want is to make you happy. You are happy, aren't you?' She still couldn't recognise the voice.

He finished drying her. She felt his fingers starting to rub her nipples again and his gloved hand gently caress her mound and clit. It was still so sensitive from her last orgasm that even the soft velvet was more than she could stand.

'Yes, but no more,' she whispered. 'I can't take any more.'

'Oh, but you are wrong,' he responded quietly. 'So wrong. Believe me. We have only just begun.'

Beth licked her dry lips and whimpered softly, partly with fear, partly with anticipation. He was the one who was wrong. He had to be. She couldn't possibly climax again. She was completely sated. Utterly fulfilled. She just wanted to sleep. She sighed with relief as his hands moved off her.

The room was so quiet and so dark that, after a moment or two, Beth began to think she was alone after all. She strained her ears but could hear nothing. Had she imagined the whole thing? No. She couldn't have. Her hands were still tied and her body was still trembling with the after-effects of her passion. Had he sneaked away and left her like this? Panic engulfed her as she imagined the hotel maid finding her, trussed up and naked.

'Where are you? Untie me.' She pulled against the cord round her wrists, straining to sit up.

'Not yet.' Beth jumped as his now naked body pressed down hard against her. She sensed that he was going to take her. Amazingly, despite her weariness, she was already trembling with renewed desire.

She jumped again, then gasped aloud as his prick pushed up hard against her thigh. Automatically, she spread her legs and raised her buttocks up off the bed to meet him. She felt his fingers grasping himself, guiding the tip into her.

'Oh!' After the cold of the ice, his cock felt burning hot. Instinctively, she wrapped her legs around him, pulling him deeper into her and sighing with pleasure. She tensed, waiting to feel the exquisite sensation as he began pumping in and out.

He didn't move, just lay there on top of her with his

129

stiff cock impaling her body. She could feel it twitching and throbbing inside her. The sensation drove her mad. What was he waiting for?

Beth pushed her buttocks firmly into the mattress and forced herself down as far as she could. Thrusting hard, she pushed her pelvis forward and pulled him deeper into her. At the same time, she squeezed her vaginal muscles tightly, then pulled back and thrust her hips again. She heard him sigh softly and felt his body stiffen against her, fighting her. His cock throbbed in response to her movements.

'That's it. Enjoy yourself.' She could hear the intense concentration in his voice as he struggled to keep himself from responding. The feel of him pulsating inside her, yet refusing to react to her desperate efforts, was pure torture. How could he stand it? A few short minutes ago, she had been certain that she could not climax again. Now, she was just as certain she was not going to be able to help herself.

She pulled away and thrust again, then stiffened as his fingers reached down between her legs to seek out her tormented sex bud. With a touch as soft as butterfly wings, he began slowly caressing it. Deep inside her, she felt his swollen penis throb again.

'Oh God!' She was past caring if anyone might hear her cry out. She was past caring about anything but her desperate need to make him respond to her. How could he just lie there like that without moving? He wasn't human. She was being fucked by the very devil himself. She sobbed again and pushed against him with all her strength. The bonds at her wrists were cutting into her skin but the pain only served to intensify her passion. She tried to wrap her legs even tighter around him to pull him deeper into her. His lips ran over her breasts again and his tongue began to circle her aching nipples. His fingers continued to rub her clit and his massive cock pulsed and twitched tantalisingly inside her.

Her orgasm seemed to start at the roots of her hair.

130

The tingling ran down her neck and spine, spreading out to encompass her chest and stomach. Ripples of pleasure rushed through her womb and down her vagina. Her muscles tightened around his cock as if physically trying to squeeze his seed out of him. Hot shivers travelled down her legs and into her feet, curling her toes.

With a final shudder that shook her body from head to foot, Beth collapsed back on to the bed, her head spinning. She was so weak that she was afraid she would never be able to move again. She was gasping and sobbing, trying to catch her breath.

'Are you all right?' he whispered.

All right? He had to be joking. She wondered whether anyone had ever actually died of ecstasy. If so, she had probably just come as close as it was possible to come and still survive.

'Yes,' she whispered feebly. 'Oh yes.'

She heard him grunt with satisfaction. Suddenly, he began to plunge himself furiously into her, his cock ramming in and out like a giant piston and his breathing harsh and ragged. She realised that his whole body was rigid with tension and sensed the enormous self-control it had taken for him to resist her for so long. She experienced a surge of gratitude at his selflessness. Now, it was his turn.

Fighting her weariness and ignoring the protests of her sated body and super-sensitive clitoris, Beth lifted her body and thrust against him, gyrating her hips. He groaned loudly and increased his pace, pumping in and out of her in a mad frenzy of pent-up passion.

The sweat was dripping off him and running in rivulets down his body on to her own. She could smell his body odour, harsh and musky. His cock was so big and stiff it felt as if she were being split in half. She heard herself whimpering with a mixture of pain and raw passion at the extent of his arousal.

When he came, his release was so powerful, so thrilling, that she felt herself climaxing again as spurt after

131

urgent spurt burst from him. It was as if now that he had finally let himself go he was never going to be able to stop. They were both sobbing helplessly, their bodies trembling and shaking with the intensity of it. When it was finally over he just lay motionless on top of her, too spent and weary even to withdraw.

Beth closed her eyes and gradually drifted off to sleep.

When she awoke the following morning, the sun was streaming in through the open shutters. She was not surprised to discover that she was alone. She must have been dreaming. Sex like that couldn't happen for real. No man could do to her what her dream lover had done. She refused to look at the damp patch in the bed or acknowledge the tender ache between her thighs.

After a long, hot shower, Beth began to dress ready for the morning session at the training centre. She put on her favourite skirt and then selected a long-sleeved blouse with buttoned cuffs that hid the red welts on her wrists.

As she left the room, she checked the door carefully. It was shut and locked. If anyone had been in her room, they must have had the missing key.

On the way down, she shared the lift with a man who had just left room 308. He smiled warmly at her.

'Lovely day.'

'Yes.' Beth flushed. Why was he grinning at her like that?

When he saw her, the receptionist gave her a huge smile. 'We've found the missing key under the desk,' he told her. As he spoke, his eyes began undressing her again. Beth's flush deepened. Had he had the key all along?

As she hurried along the road towards the training centre, it seemed to Beth as if every man she passed was staring at her with a knowing grin on his face.

* * *

Beth sat, spellbound, as Geoff Stevens lectured. She had never heard anyone speak with such passion or enthusiasm. To her, despite her enjoyment of some aspects of the work, the financial service industry was really nothing more than a way to earn a living, a means to an end. Clearly, to Geoff, it was his whole *raison d'etre*. In a way, she realised that she envied him. It must be nice to revel in one's work as much as he so obviously did.

The lecture was a long one, taking up most of the morning and covering a broad spectrum of topics, some of which were rather over her head. As he delved into the more complicated aspects of corporate finance and risk management through the use of derivatives, Beth found her attention wandering.

She was still in a state of shock about her previous night's adventure, which did little to help her concentration. It was almost as if she had lived through some kind of supernatural fantasy; entering a an erotic dream world in some parallel universe, where anything could and did happen. It must have been John, mustn't it? But then, it might have been Brian or Steve. It could even have been the receptionist. It could have been a complete stranger. Beth shivered as she remembered the odd looks she had received that morning.

As the morning progressed, she did her best not to look at any of the three men. She needed time to collect her thoughts. During the coffee break, Beth stood alone by the window, hoping to avoid conversation with anyone. Her efforts were in vain. Within moments, she saw John heading in her direction. She fixed a smile on her face.

'He's good, isn't he?' John nodded towards the crowd gathered around Geoff. Beth nodded silently. Noticing Steve and Brian coming in their direction, she cleared her throat.

'So, what did you three get up to last night?' The question was out before she could stop herself.

John grinned. 'Actually, we went to a strip club,' he

told her. 'It was very good. You should have joined us.'
She noticed Steve and Brian nodding in agreement.

'What did you do?'

Beth flushed crimson and swallowed hard. John smiled knowingly.

'Been dreaming about me, have you, Beth?'

'Excuse me.' Beth pushed past them and hurried off towards the toilet. They couldn't have been at a strip club together. It must have been him.

After coffee, Geoff moved on to a brief discussion about playing the stock market. Beth struggled to concentrate. He was an extremely attractive man; tall, slim and well proportioned. His dark, wavy hair was flecked with silver and his deep brown eyes were framed by lashes most women would kill for. His mouth was wide and sensual and when he smiled, two deep dimples formed either side of his lips. Only his nose spoilt the perfection of his features. Long and narrow, it was slightly crooked, as if it had once been broken and not set properly. Beth decided that it gave him added character. Losing the thread of the lecture again, Beth ran her eyes over his well-tailored grey suit, enjoying the way it hugged his figure and emphasised his broad shoulders and slim hips. She had always liked the combination of grey suit, crisp white shirt and dark red tie on a man. She wondered what his taste in women was like. Was there a Mrs Stevens?

True to her word, Lisa not only made sure that Geoff had an opportunity to review Beth's work, she also made a point of personally introducing them during the buffet lunch afterwards. There were many advantages in being the teacher's pet.

'I must say, I was very impressed with your class work. Your financial plan showed great flair,' Geoff told her as he shook her hand warmly. 'Where are you currently working?'

'Thank you.' His handshake was firm and his skin cool to her touch. 'You are very generous. I'm with a small private company down south. Personal assistant to Simon Henderson.'

Geoff nodded his head without commenting and Beth could not tell whether he knew Simon or not.

'I believe this is the last day of your course,' Geoff continued as he helped himself to another slice of quiche. 'This is very good, isn't it? I adore buffet lunches. Just as well, considering how many I get invited to.' He took a swig of his wine.

'Tell me. Have you got all you hoped for out of the week?'

The colour rushed to her cheeks as Beth reflected on her recreational activities. 'Oh yes. It's been wonderful,' she murmured. 'I haven't been back in finance very long and I've got great hopes and plans for the future.'

'I would enjoy discussing some of your ideas with you in more detail, Beth. You seem to have a keen insight into our business. We must get together sometime. My own corporate headquarters are down south, too. Not all that far from you as it happens.' Obviously, he did at least know of Simon.

'I'd like that.' Beth was sure he was just making polite conversation. She was suddenly conscious of several other people hovering anxiously, waiting for a chance to impress the great Geoff Stevens. She was rather hogging his attention.

'Have you done much consultancy work?' Geoff continued.

'Um, well, no. As I said, I haven't been back in the business for long . . .' Beth tried not to laugh at the idea of Simon letting her loose on her own. Despite her title, she knew she was little more than a clerk or secretary in his eyes.

Geoff smiled at her confusion. 'You should. I'm certain you would be good at it. Besides, it's very lucrative.' His face broke into a broad grin. 'How are you getting home, by the way?'

'Train,' Beth responded. 'It's such a long journey and I'm not very keen on driving.'

'Nor I,' Geoff responded. 'That's why I have a chauffeur. Why don't I give you a lift and make use of the time to pick your brains? For a fee, naturally.'

Beth was startled. It was very tempting. A chauffeur-driven car would be much more comfortable than the train. She hated the underground journey across London. Simon would be green with envy at her spending so much time with Geoff.

'Well, if you're sure it's no trouble?'

'No trouble at all. It would be my pleasure.' Geoff patted her arm. 'We should be ready to leave about two thirty if that's OK?' He looked around and then pulled a face. 'Now, if you will excuse me, I need to go and make myself agreeable to my hosts. If I'm not nice to them, they may not invite me again.' He took another bite of his quiche. 'They do the best buffet I ever get.' He gave her a conspiratorial wink and grinned again.

Beth found herself grinning in response. He was nothing at all like she had imagined. She had expected he would be pompous, stuffy and self-opinionated. In fact, he was one of the nicest men she had ever met. A real gentleman. She was really looking forward to the journey home. There was so much she would like to discuss with him.

'You two seemed to be hitting it off OK.' Lisa came up beside her just as Geoff moved away. 'I told you he was worth getting to know, didn't I?'

'He is fascinating,' Beth agreed. 'He's offered me a ride home so we can continue our discussions.' Beth glanced at her watch. 'I suppose I'd better get back to the hotel and finish packing. I was too lazy to do it earlier.'

'I shall miss you, Beth,' Lisa responded softly. 'It's been such fun having you here this week.'

Beth smiled at her choice of words, then gave Lisa a sudden hug. 'I shall miss you too, Lisa. Thanks again for everything. If you're ever down my way you must look me up.'

Lisa returned her hug. 'I hope you mean that, Beth. I'd love to see you again.'

'Why don't you come and stay with me for a few days in the summer?' Beth found that she really liked the idea. 'We could have a great time. I'll write to you, OK?'

'OK. Take care of yourself, Beth.'

Feeling suddenly sad, Beth escaped quickly before she found herself having to say goodbye to the men, too. She wasn't much worried about Steve and Brian but she would certainly miss John. Miss him a lot. It must have been him last night. Mustn't it?

Chapter Eight

*B*eth made a last quick check round the room to ensure she had not forgotten anything. She couldn't help smiling to herself as she remembered some of things she had got up to here during the past few days. Was this room often host to such antics? If so, it was a wonder the bedsprings stood up to the strain!

Downstairs, she paid her bill quickly, using the business credit card Simon had given her, then picked up her small case and headed towards the main entrance. Before she reached it, the door swung open and a tall man strode in, his eyes scanning the lobby. Seeing Beth, his lips widened into an amused grin and he headed confidently towards her.

'Ms Bradley?' he questioned.

Beth nodded, puzzled.

'I'm Daniel. Mr Stevens asked me to collect you and your luggage. I understand we are giving you a ride home.' He raised his left eyebrow as if implying that there was something strange or unusual about the idea. His voice was both deep and sensual and Beth felt an immediate physical attraction for him.

Realising that he must be Geoff's chauffeur, she examined him with interest. He was extremely handsome in his black three-piece suit, crisp white ruffled shirt and dark green tie. His short hair was beautifully cut and as black as midnight. His eyes were an unusual shade of deep blue, almost violet, and his features had a roguish, almost Romany look that made Beth think of a gypsy or a pirate.

She could almost see him with a patch over one eye, swinging a cutlass and swigging a bottle of rum. Her heart fluttered and a warm glow spread through her body as she fleetingly pictured herself captured and helpless at his mercy.

As Daniel reached for her bag, he raised his eyebrow again and gave her a slightly quizzical look. 'Mr Stevens is still at the training centre making his final farewells,' he explained. 'We'll pick him up as we leave.' He took her arm. He had a strong but gentle grip. She noticed that his hands were large and beautifully manicured.

'This way, ma'am.' He began to guide her towards the door. As they moved, he gave her several sideways glances, his face clearly bemused. Beth had a feeling he wanted to say something but was not sure how to begin.

'Is something bothering you?' she questioned. 'You seem surprised at the idea of me travelling with you.' Surely, he couldn't be such a snob as to think her not good enough to travel with the great Geoff Stevens, could he?

Daniel immediately looked awkward. Beth noticed his hand had tightened on her arm. She shivered slightly at the strength in his fingers.

'Um, well.' Daniel looked around as if to make sure no one else was within hearing distance. 'It's nothing. Just that, well, Mr Stevens hasn't taken any interest in women since,' he paused, seeming to search for the right words. 'Well, not for a long time, anyway.'

Before Beth could react to this startling piece of information, Daniel let go of her arm and stepped away. He turned to face her and gave her a long glance, starting with her legs and working his way up. Beth automatically drew her breath in and held herself tall and straight. She was almost tempted to give him a quick twirl.

'Finished?' she questioned in an amused yet slightly sarcastic tone. She placed her hands on her hips and hoped he wouldn't notice the slight flush on her cheeks. 'Do I pass muster?'

Daniel licked his lips. 'Yes, ma'am. Very nice. I can see why Mr Stevens is interested. I wouldn't mind a round or two myself.' He winked at her suggestively.

Beth found it difficult not to laugh at his sheer nerve. 'Well, you can both just keep your hands to yourselves,' she replied stiffly. 'I'm acting as a consultant, nothing more.'

Daniel smiled and started to move towards the door again. Beth's curiosity began to get the better of her. 'What do you mean, he's not interested in women?' she demanded. It wasn't the impression she had formed of Geoff from what she had seen so far. She realised, however, that he had done nothing to make her believe he was interested in anything but her mind.

Daniel frowned. 'I've already said too much,' he replied softly.

It was Beth's turn to frown. She couldn't stand secrets or mysteries. 'If you tell me what you mean, Geoff won't find out.' She paused. 'Otherwise, I might have to ask him.'

Daniel swallowed and looked around again. 'He can't, well, you know,' he whispered.

'No, I don't know.' Beth was fascinated. She was also enjoying her position of authority over the clearly reluctant Daniel.

Daniel opened the hotel door and held it for Beth to walk through. He followed and hurried past her towards Geoff's car. Beth stood on the hotel steps and examined it appreciatively. It was a Bentley. It was silver grey; shiny, spotless and quite beautiful. Beth noticed one or two passers-by eyeing both the car and her speculatively, and she experienced a rush of self-importance at their interest. She assumed what she hoped was a suitably haughty expression and started to walk towards it.

Daniel, meanwhile, had already put Beth's small case into the boot. As she approached, he moved round to open the rear door. Beth began to climb in then stopped, poised with one leg slightly forward to pull her skirt tight across her buttocks. She pushed her chest out so that her blouse was clearly outlining her breasts. She noticed with satisfaction that the pose was not lost on Daniel. His eyes were devouring her greedily.

'Well,' she repeated her threat. 'Are you going to tell me, or do I ask him myself?'

'It's all the stress, you see.' Beth was amazed to see that Daniel's face appeared to be red with embarrassment. 'As I understand it, he can't, well, let's just say that he doesn't seem to get in the mood any more these days.' Daniel took her arm and helped her into the back seat of the car.

'Thank you.' Beth realised that he could not be sure if she was thanking him for his help or his information. She wasn't entirely sure herself. One thing she did know, however, was that she loved a challenge. Seducing someone like Geoff, such an expert businessman, could be extremely interesting.

She sat down and glanced around her. The carpet on the floor was even more luxurious than the one in Simon's office. She leant back on the wide beige leather seat and marvelled at how deep and soft the seat was. It was like sitting on a feather bed. The car was fitted out like a small mobile office: television, telephone, fax. There was even a small fridge. She thought about the cramped, stuffy train carriage on the way up and grinned broadly. This was definitely the only way to travel.

As Daniel closed the door behind her, Beth remembered that the windows were heavily tinted. From the outside, she had not been able to see in at all. Inside, looking out, she could see quite clearly. It was a bit like peering through a one-way mirror.

She watched Daniel walk round and climb into the driving seat. He had removed his jacket and she enjoyed watching the way his trousers clung to his hard body so that she could clearly see his muscles tightening and relaxing as he moved. For such a big man, his movements seemed remarkably smooth and graceful. He also looked extremely fit and alert. Beth wondered if he was a bodyguard as well as a chauffeur.

It took them less than a couple of minutes to reach the training centre. Geoff was already standing on the steps waiting for them as Daniel pulled up. Beth was busy examining the contents of the fridge, so she failed to notice the slight smile playing across Daniel's face or the thumbs up sign he gave his employer as he leapt out of the car and hurried round to open the door again.

'Everything taken care of, sir,' Daniel muttered as Geoff hurried down the steps and slid inside beside Beth.

'Good. A nice, smooth ride, please, Daniel.'

'I don't think that will be any trouble, sir. No trouble at all.' Daniel was still grinning as he closed the door behind his boss and returned to the driving seat.

Geoff pushed a small button on the control console and the opaque dividing window between the driver and the rear seat slid up quietly. He turned his head and smiled at Beth.

'Comfortable?' he enquired as he sat back in the deep leather seat. 'How about a drink?' As he spoke, he pushed another button and a door slid open in front of them, revealing a well-stocked drinks cabinet.

Beth nodded. 'Please. A sherry, if you have one.'

'Dry or sweet?'

'Oh, dry, please.'

Geoff leant forward and lifted a bottle of sherry and a glass.

Although Beth hadn't noticed them pull away, she realised that they were already moving again. The car was so quiet and smooth that it was almost impossible to feel any motion at all. As Geoff poured her drink, Beth examined him surreptitiously, her excitement already mounting at the thought of the challenge confronting her. Using the old trick, she slid forward in her seat so that her skirt began to ride up her thighs.

'Thank you.' She took the drink from his hand and sat back, careful not to pull her skirt down again. As she turned towards him, the lacy top of her stocking peeped out from under the hem. She watched him carefully as he poured himself a hefty malt whisky and then sat back beside her, placing the drink on a convenient shelf in the door.

'Now, for your fee.' Geoff took his wallet out of his jacket and began to count out a number of fifty-pound notes from a thick wad.

'That's really not necessary, Geoff.' Beth was still uncomfortable about the consultancy idea. 'Why don't we just consider the lift as fair payment? I'm sure I shall learn more from you than you will from me.'

From what they had discussed so far, Beth had a feeling that if anyone could help her find a way to improve her finances and escape Simon's clutches it would be Geoff. Not that she minded Simon's clutches much. In fact, she was quite looking forward to teasing him again. Although she hated admitting it, her experiences during the past few days had only heightened her enjoyment of being a man's plaything.

'That may be so,' Geoff told her, 'but you have got great imagination, Beth, and your instincts are good. I am expecting to get a lot from this trip. More than you realise.' Geoff held a handful of notes out towards her.

Beth shook her head. 'Honestly, Geoff. I can't take it.' She pushed his hand back.

'Listen, Beth. The first rule of success is never give something for nothing,' Geoff told her. 'I always charge for my services. So should you, OK?'

Beth smiled. There had to be at least a thousand pounds in his hand. 'Well, I suppose, when you put it like that.' She took the money and tucked it into her bag. 'It just seems a bit much.'

'Nonsense. You're worth it. Now, I want everything you've got.'

For a moment, Beth wasn't sure what he meant. She turned sideways to face him and tucked one leg behind the other.

'Well, then, I guess I'm all yours,' she responded as she sipped her sherry.

Geoff immediately began to talk about mergers and take-overs, continuing a conversation they had begun earlier. The more he talked, the more fascinated Beth became. She realised that he was very close to the edge with some of his wheeling and dealing. Not exactly illegal, perhaps, but walking a very thin line all the same. The whole concept thrilled her.

As they continued their conversation, Beth grew more animated. She started to ask questions and put forward ideas, responding enthusiastically to his probing. She was soon thoroughly enjoying herself and warming to his sharp mind and dry sense of humour. He laughed easily and was quick to see where her questions were leading.

As she considered her answers to some of his more difficult questions, Beth began to fiddle with the buttons on her blouse, twiddling them round nervously with her thumb and finger. At first, she was unaware of her actions but, as she noticed his eyes watching her, she allowed herself to slip one of the buttons undone in her apparent enthusiasm at their discussion.

Gradually, she moved closer to him and began to touch him lightly to emphasise her remarks or respond to his jokes. She was delighted by both his wit and his astute mind. Simon Henderson might think he was clever and slick but, next to Geoff, he was a rank amateur.

'Would you like another sherry?' Geoff offered. 'You've certainly earnt it. I've never met anyone with such a quick, keen mind.'

'Please.' Beth was terribly flattered by his compliment.

144

She smiled excitedly as she realised just how much she had learnt from him in such a short time. Far more than she had got from the whole week at the training centre. Much of what he had spoken of was less than strictly ethical but, as Geoff himself had just said, if the law doesn't say you can't do it, it means it's technically legal. It's the letter of the law, not the spirit. Her smile broadened. The financial world was much like life itself really, she decided. Do it to them, before they do it to you.

Beth took her drink and snuggled up closer to him. She had undone a couple of her blouse buttons now, the most she felt she could get away with without making herself too obvious. She placed her glass on the parcel shelf and gently pushed her knee against his upper thigh.

'Actually, after all that wine at lunch, I really shouldn't be drinking at all. I don't have much tolerance for alcohol. I get a bit reckless.' When he said nothing, she continued, 'Do you ever get like that, Geoff?' She placed a hand on his chest.

Geoff smiled tenderly and patted her leg. 'Yes, of course. Everybody does.'

Beth smiled and pulled gently on his arm so that his hand slipped up her thigh and over her stocking top. As his fingers made contact with the silky smooth skin of her upper thigh, she leant forward and kissed him on the lips. His hand slid the last inch to the top of her thigh and Beth shivered as his fingers started to caress the thin material of her panties.

Beth kissed him passionately and pushed herself hard against his arm and chest. She felt a surge of triumph as he responded by kissing her neck and ear. She could hear his breathing quicken and sense the urgency in his response.

If what Daniel had said was true, Geoff hadn't done this for quite a while. The thought excited her further. She moved her leg over his lap and wriggled up on to him until she was sitting astride his legs with her skirt almost up to her waist.

145

Geoff sighed loudly and increased the intensity of his kisses. Beth lifted her hand, undid the rest of her buttons as quickly as she could and flicked the catch of her bra open. As her breasts fell free she took his hand and placed it on her left breast.

Geoff sighed again and squeezed her nipple with his fingers. His mouth and tongue were still sending little tremors of desire racing up and down her body as he nibbled her earlobes and nuzzled her neck.

Beth slid up his lap as far as she could. Geoff released her breast and placed both his hands underneath her, pulling her even closer. Beth put one hand behind his head and pulled it down towards her. She gasped softly as his tongue ran softly across her right nipple. She rose up to meet him, rubbing her nipples over the rough stubble on his chin.

With another soft moan, Geoff pulled one of her nipples into his mouth and nipped it quite hard with his front teeth. Beth whimpered and pulled away, then whimpered again as he moved across and bit her other nipple. She dropped back down on to his lap and began to roll her hips. She could feel the material around his zip getting taut and was sure that he was beginning to harden.

Thrilled at her success, Beth pulled his shirt free from his waistband and ran her hands all over his slim, muscular torso. As he sucked her nipple back into his mouth, she dug her nails into his skin and allowed another whimper to escape her lips.

She pushed her lower body down harder against his lap. She was now quite certain that his cock was expanding beneath her and she shivered with anticipation as he began to lift himself up off the seat and thrust against her. Quickly, she dropped her hands, undid the button of his trousers and began to unzip him. Her own crotch was so close that she found she was able to caress herself with her fingers as the zip came open. A rush of longing shot through her.

He was wearing boxer shorts and Beth wasted no time in slipping her eager fingers through the opening to grab him. He was as stiff as a board. She rubbed her hand slowly up and down his erection, so excited that she barely noticed he was peeling her blouse and bra off down her arms.

Suddenly, he pushed her away and buried his head in her breasts. She gasped and arched her back, feeling his fingers pinching and tweaking her swollen nipples as he ran his tongue down her neck again. His penis was pushed up against her hand, hard and urgent.

'You are so beautiful,' he whispered. 'So very desirable.'

Beth lifted her head. Her bag was on the parcel shelf and she needed to raise herself up to reach it to get the condoms Steve had left in her room. As she moved, she rubbed her knuckles across her mound, shivering with excitement. She pushed her hips forward, so aroused by the touch that she almost forgot her bag completely. She pushed her knuckles harder against her throbbing clit. As the powerful surges of her lust intensified, Beth forced herself to concentrate. She reached out, pushed her fingers into her bag, and rummaged around frantically for the condoms. She quickly pulled one out and ripped the packet open with her teeth. She let go of Geoff's cock and slid off his lap to kneel on the seat beside him.

To her disappointment, although Geoff continued to fondle her buttocks and breasts, he made no attempt to undress her further. Obviously, he was content to leave things to her. Beth reached into his flies and carefully manoeuvred his rigid cock out of the front opening in his boxer shorts. She leant forward, placed her mouth over him, and started to move her lips slowly up and down while her tongue caressed him softly and her hand stroked his balls through the cotton of the shorts.

Geoff shuffled restlessly in his seat and she heard him groan with pleasure.

'Oh God. Please. Hurry,' he whispered desperately.

With a sudden panic, Beth realised that he might not be able to stay stiff for too long if he had problems. Quickly she lifted her head and slid the condom over him. As she pumped him with her hand to keep him excited, she began trying to pull her panties down with her other hand, cursing her clumsiness and scared his enthusiasm would vanish at any moment.

Finally, in desperation, she put her lips back down around him and sucked as hard as she could while using both hands to struggle free of her underwear. As soon as one ankle was free, she lifted her head, grabbed him in her hand and mounted him again, prising her sex lips open to insert him into her before lowering her hips to envelop him.

As his hardness slid right up into her, a rush of elation shot through her. She had done it! So much for what Daniel had said. All he had needed was the proper motivation. Still gloating, Beth began to move her body up and down, savouring the sensation of his huge cock pumping inside her.

Geoff closed his eyes and groaned loudly as he pushed himself frantically against her. Beth started moving faster, squeezing him with her muscles, her own passion increasing rapidly as she thrust herself on to him. With a final desperate groan, she felt him stiffen and come. Another thrill rushed through her body at the extent of her success; the realisation of her ability to restore his manhood.

'That was wonderful,' she whispered in his ear as she slowly lifted herself off him.

'For me, too, Beth. For me too.' She noticed he had that dumb, self-satisfied look on his face that men always seemed to wear after sex. Beth grabbed a tissue from her bag, peeled the condom off him and threw it into the tiny waste bin. She had the feeling he hadn't even realised that he had been wearing it.

'Don't forget to zip me up.' Geoff smiled.

Beth gently slipped his now flaccid penis back into his

shorts and zipped up his trousers, then leant over to pick up her blouse and bra. Geoff put his hand on her arm.

'No. Don't put them back on,' he commanded. 'You look great just as you are. I like you topless.'

Beth smiled and dropped her clothes on to the seat beside her. She began straightening her skirt.

'Take that off too,' he told her softly.

Beth wriggled out of her skirt and stockings so that she was left wearing a small silk half-slip that only just covered her naked mound. For the first time in ages, she remembered that they were in the back of a car, hurtling along a busy motorway. She glanced out of the window at the other traffic and wondered if the tinted glass was really that good, or if the other drivers could see her. She suddenly felt very naked and exposed.

She snuggled down next to Geoff with her head resting on his shoulder and did her best to suppress the self-satisfied grin stretching her lips. She felt like the cat that had got the cream and the canary.

Geoff pushed another button. 'Daniel. Could you pull in at the next service area, please.'

'Yes, sir. About five minutes.'

Daniel's disembodied voice made Beth jump. She glanced up at the thick, dark glass between front and rear. Thank God he couldn't see or hear what was going on!

'Perhaps I had better get dressed?' she suggested.

'No. Please don't. I want you to stay here just like you are,' Geoff told her. 'I won't be long.'

Beth smiled and snuggled up against him again. 'Anything you say,' she whispered, closing her eyes. Was he planning to have another session with her later? Maybe, now that they had done it once, he had completely regained his confidence. Had she, perhaps, awoken some kind of ravenous sex monster? Well, there was no harm in hoping!

As they pulled into the parking area of the service station, Beth sat up and stared out. It took all her self-control not to cover her breasts and sink down into the seat. She knew nobody could see in, but she could see out quite clearly.

They pulled up close to the building. Geoff was humming contentedly to himself and Beth stifled another grin of triumph. So he should be happy, she told herself smugly, remembering what she had done for him.

'Just stay as you are, Beth. I won't be long,' he told her again as Daniel opened the door for him and he jumped out of the car. Beth noticed several people walking past and her heart leapt into her mouth. Surely, they must have seen her through the door? She watched them carefully as they continued walking towards their car, without so much as a backward glance. With a sigh of relief, she moved her hands away from her exposed breasts.

She watched Geoff walk off, then gathered up her scattered clothing and folded it into a neat pile. Glancing down, she noticed that her slip had ripped slightly up one seam, exposing even more of her upper thigh. The tear gave her an idea. Beth reached for her bag and found her emergency sewing kit. She retrieved the small scissors and, carefully, slit both seams up to the waistband so that all she was covered by were two pieces of silk at back and front. It felt very sexy; like an Egyptian slave girl.

A group of businessmen walked by the car, glancing casually at the darkened windows as they passed. Beth forced herself to sit upright with her shoulders back, breasts fully revealed and her legs apart. She giggled at their lack of response. If they only knew what they were missing!

She wriggled around restlessly, wondering what pose to take when Geoff returned. She tried sitting upright with her hands on her knees but that felt rather silly. She lay down and sprawled right across the seat, first on her back, then on her side. The torn slip dropped away completely, exposing her mound. Too obvious.

Finally, she snuggled up on her side, with her legs folded under her on the seat. She carefully arranged the silk slip so that nothing was showing and then closed her eyes. She could hear more people walking past and, somehow, with her eyes closed, it seemed even more exciting with strange voices coming at her out of nowhere.

Beth began fantasising about having sex with Daniel. He was so damned good-looking. She couldn't imagine that he had any stress-related problems. She pictured Geoff receiving a phone call – some kind of business emergency that meant he had to get back to his office straight away. 'Sorry about this, Beth, but Daniel will see that you get home safely after you drop me off.' She imagined the chauffeur opening the door of the car for her and finding her in nothing but a torn slip. She would glance down ruefully at herself and explain to him how Geoff wouldn't let her get dressed. She would claim that he had thrown her clothes out of the window on the motorway and ask him to lend her his jacket.

How excited Daniel would be at the unexpected sight of her nakedness. She imagined him licking his lips in anticipation as she struggled to open her front door. As soon as they got inside, he would rip his jacket off her shoulders and force her down on her knees. She could almost hear the sound of his zip opening.

She pushed her hand down under the silk slip and started to tease her clitoris softly as she imagined Daniel's hot cock ramming into her from behind. She was still tingling from her earlier arousal and her outer lips were damp with her juices. She could clearly picture Daniel moaning with pleasure as she squeezed him inside her until he could take no more and began spurting urgently.

Her excitement getting the better of her, Beth pushed her finger up inside her. What if her friend Ann, who was looking after her house while she was away, arrived while Daniel was still thrusting into her? She imagined

Ann watching, wide-eyed, as Daniel slipped his cock out of her and stood up to introduce himself. What would Ann do? What would she say?

She couldn't imagine Daniel missing such an opportunity. Maybe he would tell Beth to undress Ann while he recovered his strength. She had never imagined making love to Ann before, but after her experience with Lisa . . . Or maybe she would hold Ann down while Daniel took her over the back of the sofa? Beth moaned softly and increased the pressure of her fingers. She could practically hear Ann begging him not to stop while Daniel's buttocks tightened and relaxed as he pumped himself into her. Maybe she would join in, too.

She was just about to start fondling Ann's breasts in her imagination when she heard the driver's door open and realised that Daniel must be getting out to open the door for Geoff. She had almost forgotten that Daniel was sitting just the other side of the dividing glass. Hastily, she removed her hand and smoothed the silk slip back into place. She kept her eyes closed as the rear door opened and she heard Geoff climbing in beside her.

The door slammed shut with a resounding click and she was aware of the vibration of car engine as they pulled away. She imagined Geoff examining her as she sprawled back, motionless. Although he wasn't humming anymore, she was aware of his eyes examining her closely. She wondered if he was trying to peek under the tiny silk covering protecting her mound, or if he was enjoying the sight of her naked breasts and swollen nipples.

Beth felt the car pull out on to the motorway and increase speed. Her senses seemed exceptionally acute. Earlier, she had been totally unaware of the motion of the car. It had been the smoothest ride she had ever had. She smiled to herself at the unintended pun.

What was Geoff waiting for? Perhaps he needed a bit more encouragement? Keeping her eyes closed, Beth stretched lazily so that her breasts wobbled from side to side. She felt the silk cloth slide off, baring all. She smiled seductively and opened her eyes.

Her smile froze as realisation dawned. No wonder the car wasn't as smooth as before. Geoff must be driving. Quickly, she tried to cover herself while Daniel just stared at her, his wide grin providing serious competition for the Cheshire cat.

With one hand over her sex and the other clutching her breasts, Beth gazed round frantically, searching for her clothes. Daniel must have moved them; they were nowhere to be seen. She huddled in the corner and tried to collect her thoughts. Her faced burned with the memories of her recent fantasy.

Daniel continued to grin and she was acutely aware of the lust smouldering in his eyes. There was no mistaking what he had in mind and a thrill of excitement and desire raced through her. Beth forced herself to adopt a regal expression. If he wanted her, he would have to take her by force. She would do nothing to make it easy for him. In fact, she would fight him all the way. The thought was so stimulating that it was all she could do to contain herself.

'Where's Geoff?' she demanded. Talk about stupid question. She tried again. 'What have you done with my clothes?'

Daniel laughed. 'You don't need them for what I've got in mind.'

'If you think I'm just going to sit here while you ogle me, you're sadly mistaken,' she informed him. 'Now, give me my clothes at once.' As she spoke, she finally spotted them on the floor by his legs.

'Why don't you come and get them?' he challenged her.

Doing her best to forget her nakedness, Beth moved across the seat and reached down. Daniel licked his lips.

'Like I said before, very nice. I wouldn't mind a round or two with you.'

Beth made a supreme effort to look angry as he picked

up her clothes and pushed them out of reach behind him.

'In your dreams. How dare you?' she raged. 'If you think I would so much as let you touch me, let alone anything else . . . Now, just give me my clothes, you big ape.'

'Let me? I don't want you to let me,' Daniel retorted. He paused to let that sink in. 'I take what I want,' he continued. 'So you see, your opinion is not relevant.'

'I'll fight you every inch of the way,' she declared, surprised that her anger was quite genuine.

'I'm counting on it,' Daniel told her. He smiled. 'Although, to be fair, you are bought and paid for, don't forget.'

'What do you mean?' Beth realised that he was referring to her consultancy fee. The bastard had made her a prostitute. Geoff's money hadn't been for her opinions at all. It had been for her body. Her expression changed to a look of horror.

'No. He can have his damn money back. I didn't want it in the first place. I'm no whore.'

Daniel snorted contemptuously and pulled his tie loose. He had already removed his jacket and now he started taking his shoes and socks off.

'What the hell do you think you're doing?' Beth cried. 'You can bloody well put those back on again.' She shrank away into the corner with her legs drawn up underneath her. She used one hand to push the silk down between her thighs while her other hand crossed over her front, protecting her breasts.

Daniel ignored her and quickly pulled the shirt off over his head. Beth smiled as he struggled with the sleeves. In his enthusiasm, he had forgotten to release his cufflinks. She examined his chest, admiring his well-built physique. He was covered in dark, wiry chest hair running across his nipples and down his firm stomach past his navel. He was even more gorgeous than she had suspected.

154

Still smiling, Daniel released his trouser button and pulled both trousers and pants off in one fluid motion. Beth felt her breath catch as he revealed his bulging cock to her gaze. He was almost as big as John had been. She realised that he was watching her reaction and she knew she was blushing. Her body felt suddenly weak.

'Now, how do you like it?' he questioned. 'On top, doggy-style, missionary, from the back or maybe you'd just like to suck it? How about all of them?'

'How about none of them? Put your clothes back on or I'll start screaming and Geoff will fire you.' It sounded unlikely even to her. Geoff already knew what was going on. She had been well and truly set up. Jesus. Geoff probably didn't have any sexual hang-ups either. How stupid could you get?

'Maybe you'd like to come over here and stroke it?' Daniel proceeded to rub himself softly with his fingers. Beth held her breath. She had always loved watching a man play with himself like that. It drove her wild.

'No. I wouldn't,' she whispered.

Daniel grinned again. 'Think about it, Beth. If you managed to get me off then I wouldn't be able to fuck you, would I? Worth a try, I'd have thought. Or perhaps you want me to fuck you?' He was pumping himself quite hard now and his penis looked dark and swollen. Beth shivered.

Maybe he was one of those guys who preferred doing it in front of women rather than actually taking them? Sort of reverse dominance. Beth changed her approach.

'Why don't you show me,' she suggested coyly. 'I've never seen a man wank before.' Well, not for a couple of days anyway, she added silently.

Daniel shook his head. 'No, Beth. You come over here and finish me.' He stopped pumping and sat back with his legs open invitingly.

Beth realised how much she was burning to take his cock. Her whole body was tingling with desire. She wanted to jump on him and impale herself on his throbbing shaft. How should she respond? Should she play along and give him a hand job, or should she refuse to do anything at all? She noticed that his eyes were still watching her and saw the amused expression on his face.

She liked the challenge of masturbating him, the power it gave her. She remembered his words. Their journey was far from over. He was fit and healthy. And there would be plenty of time for him to recover. He looked as if he could probably get it up at least twice more before they arrived. Was that his plan? Let her think she was saving herself and then take her anyway?

Beth sighed. The decision would be a lot easier if her treacherous body wasn't dripping with passion just at the thought of him. The thrill of driving him to distraction with her touch would probably be enough to bring her to orgasm, too. She couldn't afford to give him the satisfaction.

'I wouldn't touch you with somebody else's hands, let alone mine,' she informed him bitchily.

'No? Well, in that case, I'll just have to get on and fuck you, then, won't I?'

Beth shuddered with longing at the threat. She huddled back further in the corner and tried to look suitably unimpressed. She failed miserably.

Daniel reached out and grabbed her arm. Although Beth pushed back even further against the door and did her best to resist him, he pulled her easily along the soft leather towards him.

'Don't you dare,' she cried as she struggled to pull her arm free and push him away. 'Let go of me.'

Daniel pulled her across his lap so that his erection was pushing into her stomach. She wiggled from side to side, trying to escape yet at the same time rubbing him with her skin. Daniel grabbed her leg and pulled her even harder against him. She could hear his rapid heartbeat and his shuddering breath. Another pang of longing coursed through her and she increased her struggles.

Beth stretched her arms out until her fingers found the

bracket for the safety belt. She grabbed it and tugged hard to try and pull herself free. She felt Daniel shift along the seat towards the side of the car, trapping her hands with his thigh. All she could do now was kick with her legs. She made the most of this until he reached out and took hold of her thighs.

'Damn you. Let me go,' Beth shouted.

'But I've only just got you where I want you.' Daniel began to stroke her bottom and Beth renewed her efforts to bruise his shins.

'Behave yourself,' Daniel commanded. He slapped her hard.

Beth shrieked with shock and rage and Daniel immediately slapped her again.

'Keep quiet and keep still or you won't be able to sit down for a week.'

Beth stopped wriggling. Her buttocks smarted and a warm glow spread through her bottom as the sting wore off. She could almost picture the handprints on the soft white flesh.

'Much better.' Daniel started to stroke her again. Beth closed her legs as tightly as she could and gave herself up to the sheer bliss of his silky touch.

'Now, how about that hand job you promised me?' he suggested as he pushed one of his fingers between her clamped thighs. Beth tightened the muscles as hard as she could to trap his finger. Undeterred, Daniel began to caress her aching clitoris.

'I didn't promise you anything.' Beth gritted her teeth as his finger delved deeper and deeper into her slit. He could hardly fail to notice how wet she was.

'Well, what if I do you first?' he offered. 'How does that sound?' He relaxed his grip and Beth immediately rolled off his lap on to the floor. She looked up and saw her clothes on the seat behind him. Immediately, she made a grab for them.

Daniel was too quick for her. He caught her hand and forced her fingers over his groin. As she made contact with his erection, Beth automatically opened her fist and then closed it again around him before she realised what she was doing. She could feel him throbbing and couldn't resist giving him a soft squeeze, even as she used her other hand against the seat to try and push herself away.

Suddenly, Daniel let go of her and Beth fell back against the drinks cabinet. Before she could recover he grabbed her arms and pulled her up. Effortlessly, he swung her up on to the seat as if she were a rag doll.

Beth thumped his chest frantically with her fists. She heard him grunt with pain as one blow found its mark. She felt his hand tighten round her wrist and she swung at him with her other hand. He deflected her easily, laughing as he secured her other wrist.

'That's it, Beth. I love it. Especially when you surrender to me. I can already imagine your hands rubbing me.' He pulled her hands together and pushed his cock into them, forcing her fingers up and down over his length.

'Good girl. You catch on quickly, don't you?' He held her still again. 'Not yet, though. I promised to do you first, didn't I?'

Beth rolled her hips urgently and strained against his clasp. Daniel ignored her. Easily holding both her wrists in one hand, he began to slide his other hand slowly down her stomach towards her crotch. With a supreme effort, Beth finally managed to break free and back away out of reach.

Daniel pulled her along the seat, twisted her left arm behind her back and rolled her on to her stomach. He grabbed his tie and looped it round her wrist, then reached for her other hand. Beth buried it underneath herself.

'Stubborn woman.' Daniel knelt on the small of her back and used both his hands to tug her right arm free. This was a mistake. Beth quickly slipped her left hand under her as he pulled her right one back. Her fingers brushed against his erection and, immediately, he pushed himself into her fingers.

'Not yet, Beth. Not yet.'

'Let me go.' Beth emphasised each word. She gasped as he slid his body down her back so that his pubic hair and balls tickled her skin, making goosebumps spring up all over her body. His cock thrust urgently between her buttocks.

'Now, let's have the other arm, shall we?'

Beth laughed. She was quite sure that she could keep this up for hours. She had forgotten the end of the tie trailing from her wrist until she felt him start to tug on it. Helplessly, she felt her arm slip out from under her. Daniel grabbed her wrist and tied her hands together at the small of her back. He sat up and nodded appreciatively.

'Anyone ever tell you what a nice bum you've got? My prick feels great nestled between those soft buttocks. Does it feel good for you?' She felt him prodding her with his cock as he spoke. The feel of it was driving her insane. Frantically, she tugged her arms, trying to free her hands. It was hopeless. She felt him slide off her and start to roll her over.

'Definitely a body made for pleasure.' Daniel stroked her right breast and then ran one finger down her body, smiling as her skin twitched. 'I love shaved beaver. It shows a woman who enjoys being naked.' He trailed a fingertip over her naked mound.

'Open up. It's difficult fingering you with your legs together.' He pulled her thighs apart and pushed his hand between them.

Beth clamped her lips together to stop herself from moaning. She made a feeble attempt to roll away from him then, realising it was hopeless, she lay still. She was determined not to let him get her too excited. So long as he didn't succeed, she wouldn't have to do anything. The very thought of him trying to satisfy her all the way

159

home was extremely pleasant. He had a wonderful touch. She set the challenge.

'You won't make me come, no matter what you do,' she informed him calmly.

'We'll see. If I succeed, then you'll do whatever I want?'

'No, I won't,' she contradicted, 'because you won't succeed.'

Daniel nodded approvingly. 'I thought you'd given up on me for a minute.' He moved his finger over her nipple and caressed it softly. Beth shivered. Daniel grinned and lowered his head over her breasts. His tongue darted in and out, first on one nipple then the other. He wrapped his tongue round one and then slowly ran his finger down her stomach, over her mound and on to her inner thigh.

As he began the return journey, Beth sighed contentedly, savouring her pleasure. She could endure that indefinitely. Although delightful, it was not enough to push her too far. If he wanted to win then he would have to do a lot better than this. She smiled happily as his hand traced an ever-expanding circle over her breasts and stomach. He was wasted as a chauffeur; he should have been a masseur.

Gradually, she felt him moving both hands and tongue down her body. A small shiver of excitement ran up her legs as he tickled the back of her knee and, as he moved his fingers up towards her thigh, she raised her hips slightly to allow him access to her buttocks. His fingers were as soft and delicate as silk.

A small sigh escaped her lips as his tongue circled her navel and glided on down over her mound and outer sex lips. She felt a rush of wetness between her thighs and realised that she needed to concentrate a bit harder. Seemingly oblivious to her reaction, Daniel carried on down her leg and sucked her big toe into his mouth. She jumped with surprise and allowed him to raise her leg as he started to kiss his way gently back upwards.

Beth clenched herself ready for his attack, certain he would take full advantage of her exposure. In fact his lips barely caressed her sex before moving on up her body. She lowered her leg back on to the seat as his tongue licked her breasts and then slipped on up to her neck.

Daniel nibbled her earlobe, then blew gently into her ear and started to kiss her eyelids. As he lowered his head, she turned her mouth away. Kissing always turned her on and she was determined to make him work. Firmly, he pulled her head round towards him again and planted his lips on hers.

Beth screwed her eyes tightly closed and did her best not to respond. She sighed as his other hand began to slide slowly down her body towards her mound. She moaned softly as he pushed his fingers into her slit and gently teased her sex bud. His tongue relentlessly probed her, forcing her lips open and darting in and out.

His fingers slipped deeper between her legs, exploring every inch of her. Beth started to panic. He couldn't fail to notice how excited she was. It might not be as obvious as a man's erection but her dampness was still a dead give-away. His tongue pushed harder and deeper into her mouth and Beth felt her desire building. She pulled back against the seat and resumed her struggles.

Daniel let go and began to chuckle. He tweaked her erect nipples with his fingers then rolled her on to her side and ran his hand down her spine. Beth sighed with relief. Thank God he had stopped when he had. Did he realise how close she had come – or had he thought she was making another attempt to get away? She felt his hand fondling her bottom and she took a few deep breaths to steady herself.

Still chuckling, Daniel rolled her on her back and crouched over her head. Looking up, she could see his rigid cock thrust out in front of him as he leant over her and took himself in his hand. She gasped as he pushed his cock against her breasts and started to rub the damp tip round her nipple. He lowered his head, and covered her mound with his mouth. His penis pressed forcefully between her breasts as he leant over her. As his tongue began to circle her outer lips, she felt the urgent thrill of approaching climax. Desperately, she squeezed her thighs together, forcing his head away. Losing his precarious balance, Daniel slipped off on to the floor.

'Now, that wasn't fair.' Daniel grabbed her legs and pulled them off the seat. He pushed her upright and put his hands on her knees to force her thighs open wide. Pushing his hands under her, he lifted her up and pulled her exposed vagina on to his mouth. His tongue flowed effortlessly into her, seeking her G-spot.

'Oh God.' Beth writhed with passion as he sucked and licked her. She knew she was lost. She felt him pushing deeper and deeper inside her, thrusting in and out, varying the speed and the depth. His hands squeezed her buttocks, pulling her backwards and forwards against him. The more she struggled, the harder he held her.

She came suddenly and violently, shuddering uncontrollably at the intensity of her release. Incredibly, he continued licking and sucking her, long after the final spasm of her climax had faded away. On and on until she felt herself beginning to respond again. Finally, he slid his hands from under her and sat back on his heels. He wiped his mouth with the back of his hand and smiled mischievously.

'Well. That wasn't so difficult, was it?'

Beth stared at him wordlessly, her breath still coming in short little pants. Daniel got up and knelt across her lap with his cock pressed against her breasts. He reached round behind her and untied her hands.

'Now it's your turn.' He placed her hands on his cock and stared at her expectantly.

Beth pulled her hands away and placed them at her sides. 'No. I never agreed to do anything.'

Daniel grabbed her hands again. Beth struggled

against him, trying to ignore the feel of his erection pushing on to her mound. She twisted away and slid down off the seat so that her knees were on the floor and her breasts were pushed up against the leather seat. She sensed the smack coming too late to dodge. Her eyes began to smart as his hand slapped her bottom again and again.

'Are you ready to keep our bargain yet?'

'I made no bargain. Ow!' She received another sharp smack. Her buttocks were on fire and hot tears began to trickle over her lids and run slowly down her cheeks. He whacked her again.

'OK!' She gave in. 'I'll do it.'

As soon as he let her go, Beth raised herself to a crouch and rubbed her stinging buttocks tenderly. Daniel sat himself on the seat, directly in front of her with his legs open wide. His erection seemed to have grown even larger. Beth raised her hand and ran her fingers slowly down it, teasing him. His whole body tensed.

She lowered her mouth over his cock and ran her tongue around the tip. As she slipped her hand down the shaft, she cupped his balls in her other hand and caressed the delicate skin underneath them. Daniel writhed with pleasure and tried to force himself even deeper into her mouth. Beth instinctively closed her lips round him and sucked hard. She heard his groan of delight and a tremor of power rushed down her spine.

If this was what he wanted, so be it. She had become quite good at telling just when a man was right on the edge. She would bring him right to the brink, then stop. She would tease and torture him until he was begging her to let him come, then tease him some more. By the time she was done with him, he would be in such a state he wouldn't even be able to remember his own name.

She began to move her head more quickly, pumping him rapidly in and out. Daniel clutched the back of her head and moaned urgently. Beth felt her own juices beginning to flow again.

Chapter Nine

*I*t was quite late by the time Beth arrived home. Another short stop at a service area shortly after dark had given Geoff the opportunity to return inside the car with her, while Daniel resumed his duties behind the wheel.

Beth used the changeover time to slip back into her clothes. Unsure of what to say to him, she had taken the easy option and not mentioned what had happened at all. Geoff had followed her lead and, after an uncomfortable silence that had lasted for a few miles, they had resumed their financial discussions almost as if nothing else had happened.

Despite her comments to Daniel earlier, Beth had found it impossible to openly give Geoff his money back. What would she have said? She opted for leaving the wad of notes in the drinks cabinet. When he found them, she was certain that Geoff would get the message. Damn her pride. A thousand pounds would have come in very handy.

Although she had wanted to be angry with them both she knew, in all honesty, that they hadn't done anything she had not willingly gone along with. It had been fun, even if Geoff hadn't been in such dire need of her services as she been led to imagine! Just the thought of how neatly they had set her up made her smile. Compared to that, what she had done to Simon didn't seem nearly as clever as it once had.

Geoff had been the perfect gentleman for the rest of the journey although, once or twice, she had noticed the hungry way he was looking at her and had wondered if he had been excited by imagining what she and Daniel had been up to. She was only thankful that the dividing window was tinted. It suddenly occurred to her that it might be tinted the opposite way round from the other windows, allowing Geoff and Daniel a clear view inside. She was slightly shocked to discover how excited that possibility made her feel.

When they dropped her off outside her house Geoff thanked her then wished her well with her future career and expressed the hope that their paths would cross again before too long. Daniel just smiled appreciatively as he helped her through the door with her case. He had even tipped his chauffeur's cap and given her one last, lingering gaze before he turned to leave. She was sure that she could detect a hint of amusement in his eyes and she felt herself glowing with a mixture of embarrassment and desire.

As soon as she had dumped her case in the bedroom, Beth ran herself a hot bath and had a long soak. She was too exhausted even to think straight and decided on a light supper of soup and sandwiches, then an early night. While she was waiting for the soup to heat, the phone rang.

'Beth? It's Ann. I thought you must be home by now. Good week?'

'Mmm.' A sequence of sexual encounters raced through her mind, each one more exciting and erotic than the last. How could she even begin to describe it? If anyone else had told her about such a week, she would have thought that they were suffering from a somewhat overactive imagination.

'Yes. Very, er, interesting.'

Her voice must have given her away. 'I sense a man,' Ann responded immediately. 'Don't tell me you found time for some romance, too? Honestly Beth, since Jonathan, there's just no stopping you, is there?'

'Not exactly,' Beth replied slowly. Romance wasn't the word that immediately sprang to mind to describe her recent experiences. She remembered a conversation she had had with Ann a year or so ago when she had confessed some of what she and young Jonathan had been up to. At the time, it had seemed quite shocking.

'Thanks for the bread and things.' Ann had been in earlier that day, as arranged, to switch the heating on and leave a few essentials.

'Don't change the subject,' Ann complained.

'I'm not. Look, Ann, it's been a really long day. All I want to do right now is curl up in bed and sleep around the clock. I'm too tired even to think.'

'OK, you win. Keep your secrets for now. I've got to go and see my parents over the weekend but I'll pop round one evening next week, shall I?'

'Fine. Thanks again for the shopping.' As she hung up the receiver, she found herself wondering exactly what she was going to tell Ann when she saw her.

Simon glared impatiently at his watch when Beth walked through the door the following Monday.

'You're late,' he complained. 'We don't keep training course hours here, you know.'

Beth checked her own watch. It was two minutes after nine o'clock. What had put Simon in such a foul mood already? She had expected that he would be glad she was back.

'Sorry,' she responded meekly. 'The bus was late.' She noticed that he was staring at her body and was surprised to feel a slight shiver of disdain. He wasn't going to make a habit of leaping on her, was he? Teasing him until he couldn't help himself had been great fun, but she hadn't really thought about what working with him afterwards would be like. It was fine if she initiated it, but she didn't like the idea of him assuming he had any rights to her body.

'Well, how was the training course, then? I hope I got my money's worth.'

Beth smiled at that. 'Very illuminating,' she replied. 'I even got to meet Geoff Stevens. He gave me a lift home on Friday.'

Simon's eyes narrowed. She had known that name would get to him. *'The* Geoff Stevens?' he said, clearly surprised. 'What was he doing there?'

'He gave the final lecture. What a brilliant mind that man's got!' Beth enthused. His body wasn't to be sneezed at either, she reflected silently.

Simon shrugged. 'He's just been lucky, that's all. Had a few good breaks. I don't suppose you managed to persuade him to put any business our way?' Geoff was renowned for using smaller financial companies to spread the risk of investment or even hide some of his larger deals.

It was Beth's turn to shrug. 'The subject didn't actually come up,' she replied. 'He did admit to having heard of you, though,' she added generously.

Simon brightened. 'Really? How? What did he say?'

'Nothing. Only that he seemed to know your name.' She tried not to smile at his inflated ego.

Simon snorted rudely, then ran his eyes over her body again. 'We don't have any appointments for an hour or so,' he remarked pointedly.

'I'll use the time to catch up on the backlog of filing, then, shall I?' Beth was already on her way to her own office. What had she ever found attractive about Simon, she wondered? He might be a great lover, but that didn't make up for him being a chauvinistic pig. Could she use what she had learnt from Geoff to find a way to escape Simon for good? She would have to give it some very serious thought. She remembered the way Geoff had flattered her knowledge and praised her skills. Could she, perhaps, go in business for herself as a consultant? She almost blushed again at the memory of what else Geoff had used the word to mean.

'By the way,' Simon called her back. 'I have to go to Rome at the weekend. There's a chance for a big deal there if I play my cards right.'

Beth's heart sank. He wasn't going to ask her to go with him, was he? She could just imagine what a trip like that would entail.

'The thing is, the people I'm going to see, they want me to take my wife along too . . .'

'How nice,' Beth interrupted quickly. 'Mrs Henderson must be thrilled.'

Simon frowned. 'I'm not sure that she will be able to go,' he replied slyly. 'We've got a large dog, you see. Marie adores him. She refuses to put him in kennels in case he pines.'

'Well, can't you get someone to stay at your home and take care of him? What about your son?' Beth vaguely remembered that Simon and his wife had a teenage boy.

'Chris is away at college,' Simon replied. 'I don't think Marie will be able to find anyone she trusts in time.' He paused. 'I have to be seen taking my wife with me,' he added.

So, she was right. He was asking her. She was almost tempted. She had never been to Rome and Simon was a wonderful lover. He was also a complete bastard. Besides, if she was going to make a name for herself in the financial world, she needed people to know her for herself, not mistake her for Simon's wife or, worse, his mistress.

'Well, I suppose I could stay at your house, if you like,' she offered. 'I love dogs, so I would be quite happy.'

'I couldn't ask you to do that,' Simon replied quickly.

'Really. It's no trouble. I'd love to do it. I'll get your wife on the phone for you now, shall I? I'm sure she will have lots of shopping she needs to do for the trip.'

* * *

As Beth closed her own office door behind her, Simon frowned. That hadn't gone at all the way he had planned it. How had she so easily outmanoeuvred him like that? He wanted her in his bed in Rome, not curled up at his house, petting the dog. Marie wouldn't be any use to him in Rome. She knew nothing about finance. She wasn't even all that good at flirting with potential clients.

There was something strange about Beth today, he decided. What had happened to her while she was away? A week or so ago, she had been practically begging him to take her. Now, she seemed to be deliberately avoiding him.

He felt a slight twinge of doubt as he wondered if she thought he had taken advantage of her. He quickly dismissed it. The way she had been begging for it, she could hardly blame him. Perhaps she thought she was too good for him, just because she had spent a few hours with Geoff Stevens. It was a pity that she hadn't managed to get anything useful out of that meeting. He would kill for a chance to do some business with Geoff Stevens. He found himself wondering what else Beth and Geoff might have got up to.

Simon glanced at his watch again. He could hear Beth in her office and he felt himself stirring as he remembered the way she had whimpered and cried while he had taken her over the desk. She had certainly enjoyed it. She'd been wet and ready for him. Was she playing games again?

He got up and walked across the thick carpet towards her door. When he pushed it open, Beth was leaning over the filing cabinet so that he could just see the tops of her stockings under her short skirt. He shivered with anticipation as he felt his cock begin to stiffen.

'Beth?' His voice cracked slightly and he cleared his throat quickly. 'About the other day . . .'

Beth straightened and turned round on her heels.

'I'm sorry about your clothes. Maybe you'd like to buy some new ones to replace them?' Simon reached for his

169

wallet. Women could never resist the idea of buying new clothes.

'It's not important,' she responded softly, her cheeks colouring. Simon's eyes darted down her cleavage. He could clearly see the outline of her half-cup bra. His fingers itched to rip it off her and run his tongue across those luscious breasts.

'I insist.' Simon opened the wallet and peeled a couple of notes off. 'Buy yourself something really sexy,' he told her.

Beth smiled. 'If you're really serious, why don't you bring something back from Rome for me?' she suggested cheekily. 'Italian fashion is world-renowned.'

Simon hesitated. He liked the idea of picking out something especially for her. It would be difficult to go shopping without his wife, but he might be able to slip away. He would get her something so blatantly sexy that it would make her blush to look at it, then he would make her wear it around the office. His cock stiffened further. He nodded silently and returned the money to his wallet.

Maybe he would invest in one of those new digital cameras. With no film to develop, there were no restrictions on what you could use them for. He could take pictures of her posing for him and look at them on those nights when Marie wasn't being cooperative enough. He could even put them on the computer. Maybe he would design a screen saver of Beth stripping!

He took a step closer and reached out to run his hands down the sides of her body and over her hips. He felt her stiffen slightly and try to pull away. Was this more of her games? First begging for it, now playing hard to get. Did she want him to force her again? The idea inflamed him.

Simon grabbed Beth round the waist, pulled her roughly towards him and ran his lips down her neck. His cock pushed up urgently against her body and he began to throb with desire.

The phone rang and Beth slid easily from his arms. She walked over to the desk and picked up the receiver.

'Henderson's. Good morning. Yes, he is. Just one moment, please.' Beth put her hand over the mouthpiece. 'It's Bob Jarvis, calling from Rome. He says it's urgent.'

Simon tried to calm his breathing. His heart was thumping and he could almost feel the blood boiling in his veins. He had wanted her all week. He would go mad if he didn't have her again soon. Perhaps he could get rid of Bob quickly. There would still be plenty of time before his first client arrived.

'I'll take it at my desk,' he told her, his eyes still locked on her cleavage.

Beth lifted her fingers from the mouthpiece. 'I'm just putting you through now, Mr Jarvis,' she said.

Simon sighed heavily and turned to walk back to his own office. As he moved, he pushed his hands down inside his waistband and tried to adjust his throbbing cock. He would just get rid of Bob and then . . . Simon caressed his swollen tip softly with his fingers, his imagination running riot.

As soon as Beth had put the call through to his phone, she walked over and closed the door between the two offices. She leant back on it and closed her eyes for a moment. Her body was trembling and her legs felt shaky. Despite her growing dislike for him, she was already damp at the possibility of Simon taking her again. If the phone hadn't rung when it had, she knew she wouldn't have done anything to stop him.

She took a quick, shuddering breath and walked slowly over to her desk. Damn it to hell. This wasn't what she wanted at all. If he thought he could take her whenever he felt like it, he would become even more insufferable. His fingers could do wonderful things to her body, her treacherous imagination reminded her.

Beth sat down and propped her head on her hands. Sooner or later, of course, he would tire of her, just as he tired of all his conquests. The stories about Simon were littered with broken hearts. She had no intention of becoming another of his discarded playthings. Somehow, she had to find a way to string him along, keep him interested in her until she got her own plans sorted out.

Maybe it wouldn't hurt to provoke him again. After she had pushed him over the edge, she would submit to him, do whatever he asked without a murmur. Even better, she could plead and beg with him to let her go. She knew how much he liked that. It would be so easy. The way he had been acting, the problem was more one of stopping him than of letting him. She was in no doubt about how aroused he had been. The idea of it sent a small shiver down her back.

Pushing her thoughts to one side, Beth began to examine the new computer on her desk. She had forgotten until today that Simon was arranging for this new system to be installed. Why he thought that the two of them needed to be networked was somewhat beyond her. If the door was open, as it was most of the time, he only had to raise his voice to speak to her.

She wasn't totally convinced that she needed a computer of her own at all. Up until now, they had managed perfectly well with her using the one in his office when he was out with clients. Still, it was rather fun to have a computer all to herself. It made her feel more important. If only he would let have a few clients to take care of on her own as well. She knew that she had been perfectly capable of handing that much even before the training course in York.

Beth turned the computer on and waited impatiently while it powered up. After her week in York, at least she felt more confident about using it. When she had first started with Simon, she had known next to nothing about computers despite the lessons that had been part of her refresher course. Even so, she felt very wary at the sight of the myriad of complicated and intertwined software

172

packages the new machine boasted. She knew that Simon would be livid if she crashed the system.

'I just don't understand why people find computers so difficult to master,' he had told her a couple of weeks ago when she had expressed concern about what he was proposing. 'They are perfectly simple, so long as one approaches them logically.'

It was all right for him. He had a degree in computer programming to go with his various certificates and diplomas in financial subjects. You could say a lot about Simon, but no one could accuse him of being stupid. Except maybe, Geoff. Simon was a financial amateur next to Geoff.

Finding Windows Explorer, Beth scanned the contents of the system curiously, fascinated to see what Simon had already been up to. She was not surprised to see that hardly any of the client files had found their way on to the system yet. No doubt that boring task had been awaiting her return.

When she spotted that he had already set up his own folder, Beth moved the mouse over it and clicked to open it, curious to see what else he had been doing. Perhaps it was his electronic little black book with the names and phone numbers of all his willing females. She pictured the fun she could have setting up conflicting rendezvous with some of them. That might teach him a lesson.

To her surprise and frustration, she found he had restricted access with a password. She experienced a flash of anger and disappointment. Was he just hiding the names of his girlfriends, or had he got some other secret he didn't want her prying into? Well, secrets were like a red rag to a bull so far as Beth was concerned. One way or another, she would get in.

Beth cocked her head to one side to make sure that he was still talking on the phone, then made a few wild stabs at guessing his password. She was sure it would be something stupidly obvious. He was too contemptuous of her limited computer skills to imagine she would get the better of him. What could it be?

She tried a few obvious things: his name, his wife, his son, even her own name. Nothing worked. She tried to remember if he had told her what their dog was called, although, considering how scathing he had been about the animal, she wasn't too hopeful. Damn! Beth tapped her finger impatiently on the mouse button. What silly word had he used? She wasn't even sure why she was so anxious to get in to his precious secrets. She just had a feeling they might contain something useful.

Outside, she heard Simon making his farewells to Bob. Was the trip to Rome still on or had Bob called to cancel it? She quite liked the idea of spending the weekend at his home. It would be fun poking around, seeing how he lived his private life. She was curious to see what he would bring her back to wear, too. She was certain it would be skimpy, transparent and totally impractical. She strained her ears to hear what he was doing now.

When the door handle to her office began to open, Beth quickly moved the mouse and clicked for the screen saver to appear. She remembered what he had been doing when the phone rang and felt a sudden thrill at the idea of him storming in to ravish her again.

Just as her door began to swing open, the door to the main entrance buzzed. His first client of the day was slightly early. As Beth jumped up to answer the door, she heard Simon curse under his breath and return reluctantly to his desk. The grin on her face as she greeted his client was wider than she normally used to greet even their most valued customers. His diary for the rest of the day was virtually solid. Tomorrow, he was out all day at a conference in London. It would be Wednesday before he had a chance to get her alone again.

Beth wasn't all that surprised when Ann turned up soon after she got home that evening. She knew her friend's curiosity had been aroused by their brief conversation on Friday night. She wasn't entirely sure how much she was prepared to reveal about what had gone on. Some of it was just too private.

'Ann.' She gave her friend a quick hug. 'It's good to see you.' Beth was shocked to realise that she was comparing Ann's body to Lisa. She had never looked at Ann that way before. In many ways, Ann and Lisa were quite similar: slim build, boyish hips, small breasts, fair hair. Ann was older, of course – the same age as Beth herself. She began wondering again about her friend's preferences, and was surprised and slightly shocked to feel a brief tremor of desire at the idea of pleasuring Ann the way she had pleasured Lisa.

Ann returned the hug and then wandered into the living-room and threw herself down on the settee. 'It's good to have you back. It seems like you've been away for more than a week, somehow.'

'It seemed a long time for me, too,' Beth called over her shoulder as she headed into the kitchen to make coffee. 'I've been wining and dining like a glutton. I really need to get to the gym.'

'Gerri sends her love, by the way,' Ann continued. Loud, boisterous, redheaded Geraldine was another of their closest friends. 'She claims to be in lust again. A new instructor at the gym, if you please.'

Pretty and vivacious Gerri, who had just turned forty yet thought she was still twenty, liked to give the impression that she was a real man-eater. Privately, Beth harboured more than a passing suspicion that their friend was actually scared stiff of men.

Coffee mugs in hand, Beth made her way back into the living-room to join Ann. She settled herself comfortably down on the settee beside her friend, curled her legs up under her, and took a sip of her drink.

'I met Geoff Stevens up in York,' she said. 'He's one of the best-known financial wizards in the country. He thinks I've got great potential.'

Although Ann stared at her quizzically, she said nothing. Beth knew her friend was burning to ask if there was anything going on, romantically speaking. She was determined to keep the conversation away from that subject for now.

'Anyway, it got me thinking about my future. I don't want to stay with Simon any longer than I have to.'

Ann looked surprised. 'I thought you loved your job?' When Beth did not reply, she added, 'Do you think this Geoff might give you a job, then?'

'Good God, no. I shouldn't think so.' Beth briefly imagined what working with Geoff every day might be like and felt a tingle of excitement. 'He suggested that I would be good at consultancy work. I'm thinking about going it alone.' It sounded exciting but, at the same time, frightening now that she had put it into words.

Ann looked doubtful. 'Do you think you could? I mean, you're only just back in the field. It takes an awful lot of guts to work for yourself. And money. How would you cope with the overheads?'

Beth sighed. Trust Ann to put her finger right on the problem. She had gone to work for Simon in the first place so that she could become financially independent from her ex-husband. Now, she needed to earn enough to escape Simon. Why did everything always seem to come down to money?

'It's not all that difficult to make money in the financial world. All it takes is confidence and know-how.' Beth frowned. 'Geoff manages to make it all sound childishly simple,' she added ruefully.

Ann laughed. 'Money makes money, Beth. I bet this Geoff character is rolling in it, isn't he? When you can afford to take a few gambles and it's not the end of the world if you lose a few thousand here and there, it's a different matter.'

Beth opened her mouth to protest, then closed it again. Ann was quite right. How could she possibly hope to play in the same league as Geoff Stevens? For one brief encounter, he had willingly offered her more money than she had in her savings account. She should have kept it. She would never have spent it, of course, but it would have been a nice souvenir. It excited her to think of how she had sold herself to two men – even if she hadn't realised what she was doing until it was too late!

'Cheer up,' Ann told her, seeing her face. 'Things aren't so bad. At least you're earning better wages now than when you were at the newsagents. You don't need to rely on Tony any more and you seem to be having fun.'

Beth smiled, remembering her week in York. She was certainly having fun.

'Tony called me while you were gone, by the way.'

'What? Why?' Beth had found several messages on the answer phone from her ex-husband but hadn't got around to contacting him yet. Now, she considered the possibility that it might be urgent. 'Did he say what he wanted?'

Ann shook her head. 'Only that he couldn't get in touch with you and was worried. I think he may have had a tiff with his wife and was looking for a shoulder to cry on. I told him you were away on a training course and I wasn't sure when you were due home.'

'Thanks.' Beth felt a rush of irritation at Tony. Ever since she had asked him round for coffee one day about six months ago, he had been pestering her more and more often. She had never regretted anything as much as she regretted leading him on that day. He was more interested in her now than he had ever been when they were married.

'So, what about your week?' Ann changed the subject to one she was obviously more interested in. 'Was this Geoff your big adventure?'

'No, well, not really. Although he did give me a ride home in his chauffeur-driven Bentley.'

Ann's eyes widened. 'Wow! He really is loaded. I don't suppose he's single, too, by any chance?'

'Actually, I think he is.'

'There you are, then. Why not forget about going into business for yourself and just concentrate on marrying into money?'

'Ann! How could you? After Tony, the last thing I'm looking for is another husband.'

'Not even a stinking rich one?' Ann continued to tease. She took another sip of coffee. 'Well, if it wasn't Mr Rich, who was it that put that sparkle in your eye?'

Who, indeed, Beth wondered. Lisa? Her evening with John, Brian and Steve? John himself? Daniel? How could she even begin to come out with a story like that? She had had a more active week than a professional hooker!

'No one thing or person,' she replied. 'It was just a good week all round, I suppose. The course was interesting and useful and I met several fascinating people, male and female. I've asked Lisa, the course lecturer, to come and visit me in the summer. You'll like her, Ann. You two are quite similar in many ways.'

Beth could feel Ann staring at her in surprise. Her friend had clearly been expecting a revelation about a man, not news of an invitation for a new woman friend to come and stay. Would Ann guess what had taken place between her and Lisa? Her cheeks began to glow at the possibility. She had no idea how Ann felt about that sort of thing.

Ann was a great talker. Beth could remember several times when Ann had surprised and even shocked her a little with her revelations about her sexual fantasies. In a way, it had been Ann who had first introduced her to using a vibrator by giving her the idea of looking at sex magazines. Still, she was never quite sure just how much practical experience Ann had.

As she watched her friend watching her, she realised how much she wanted to experiment with Ann, to enjoy her body as she had enjoyed Lisa. How could she possibly broach the subject? It was much more difficult than with a virtual stranger. She had known Ann since school. Maybe Lisa could break the ice?

Suddenly, her mind was flooded with images of the three of them naked on her bed together, and a pang of desire shot through her body so powerful that it was all she could do not to pull Ann into her arms and ravish her there and then. Her limbs were beginning to tremble with excitement.

'I suppose I had better go and phone Tony and see what he wants,' she muttered softly as she leapt to her feet and fled from the room.

Chapter Ten

'This is my wife, Marie. Marie, this is Beth.' Simon led Beth through into the living-room and made the introductions. Before anyone could say anything else, there was a loud bark and a large golden retriever charged into the room, its tail wagging furiously.

'Oh, and that's the dog,' he added unnecessarily as he aimed a spiteful kick at its rear end. The animal dodged the blow easily and, coming to a stop, stretched out its nose to sniff Beth's hand.

'He's very friendly, aren't you, Sandy?' Marie assured Beth, giving her husband a reproving glance. 'He'll soon get to know you.'

'Hello, Sandy,' Beth leant down and patted the dog on the head. She was rewarded with a slobbery wet kiss on the back of her hand. Simon pulled a face. Clearly, he was no animal lover.

Marie held out her hand. 'It's very kind of you to offer to look after him like this.' She appraised Beth cautiously, as though unsure about committing herself.

Beth wondered if Marie knew about her husband's reputation. If so, she was probably wondering if Beth was one of his many conquests. The realisation made her feel terribly guilty and she pushed her thoughts away.

Marie couldn't possibly know what Simon was like. If she did, she wouldn't stay with him, would she?

'I'm only too happy to help. I'd love to own a dog but, being out at work all day, it wouldn't be fair. Sandy and I will have a great time, won't we, boy?' Sandy gave her hand another wet lick and both women laughed. Simon frowned and looked at his watch.

'Why don't you get on and show Beth where everything is?' he interrupted them irritably. 'If we don't get a move on, we'll end up missing the bloody plane.'

As Marie led her round the house, Beth examined her surreptitiously. She was quite pretty, in a washed-out, mousy sort of way. Her light brown hair was cut short and probably permed. Her eyes were grey-blue, wide set over a snub nose and narrow lips. She had a reasonable figure, perhaps a little on the plump side, and was heavily but skilfully made up. Her clothes were beautifully tailored and her jewellery looked expensive. She wasn't the sort of woman Beth would have expected Simon to be married to. What sort that was, however, she had no idea.

The house and its contents looked as expensive as Marie's clothes and jewellery. Simon might moan and groan about business all the time but, unless Marie had money of her own, he obviously wasn't doing too badly. The house alone must be worth over a quarter of a million, perhaps more.

She barely had time to take everything in, far less to learn her way around the huge house, before Simon started yelling for his wife to get a move on. Marie gave Beth an apologetic smile.

'I'd better go. Simon gets in such a state. Now, are you sure you'll be all right?'

'We'll be fine. Don't worry.' Beth patted the dog again. 'Just go and have a wonderful time.'

Marie gave her another sideways glance. Her face made it perfectly clear that she was not expecting to have anything close to a wonderful time. Beth felt suddenly sorry for her and wondered again why Marie stayed with her husband.

'Marie. Come on.' Simon's voice was tight with anger and Marie scuttled off towards the door, still calling final instructions over her shoulder as she went.

Beth heard heated words being exchanged and then Simon's voice called a curt goodbye. The front door slammed and she and Sandy were alone.

She checked her watch. It was a little after six o'clock. Simon had closed the office early so that he and his wife could catch an evening flight to Rome ready for a break-fast business meeting on Saturday morning. Beth sighed, wondering what she was doing here. The long, lonely weekend stretched out endlessly before her. She decided that she might as well get herself something to eat.

After a couple of wrong turns, she found her way to the kitchen and retrieved the exotic cold meat and salad platter that Marie had prepared for her. Sandy followed at her heels, his tail still wagging enthusiastically. According to Marie, he had already been fed that evening. Unable to resist his big brown eyes, Beth fed him from her plate. There was far too much for her, anyway.

After she had rinsed the dishes and tidied away, Beth set out to explore. A door leading from the hallway near the front of the house opened in to what was obviously Simon's private study. She gazed around curiously at the heavy wood-panelled walls and expensive leather furniture. It was a real old-fashioned male retreat. She was surprised that there were no animal head trophies on the walls or a gun rack in the corner.

She wandered around behind the huge desk and tried the top drawer. It was locked. What was he hiding here? Excited, she wondered if she could find anything in his study that would reveal his password to the protected folder on the office computer system. Feeling more than a twinge of guilt, she rummaged around the desk looking for a key.

A sudden bark caused her to jump and look round

anxiously, half-expecting Simon to pop out of the wood-
work and catch her prying. Sandy barked louder.

'What is it, boy?' Beth hurried out into the hallway,
her heart thumping. It occurred to her just how isolated
this huge house was, set back from a quiet road in an
acre of so of its own grounds and surrounded by thick,
tall hedges. No wonder Marie liked to keep Sandy
around with Simon away so often.

The dog had its nose pressed to the crack under the
front door. He had stopped barking and his tail was
wagging furiously, Nervously, Beth pushed the curtain
aside on the window beside the door and peered out. It
was already growing dark. She saw a shape moving in a
nearby bush and her heart leapt to her throat. She tried
to remember where the phone was.

The bush moved again and a large cat dashed out and
shot up a tall poplar tree. Sandy began barking again
and Beth leant back against the wall, laughing with relief.

'I promised you a walk before bed time, didn't I?' She
petted the dog under the chin. 'Right then. But, no
chasing cats, OK?' Sandy wagged his tail at a word he
recognised and dashed off to the kitchen where his lead
was kept. Still laughing, Beth followed.

Saturday dawned fine and sunny. By mid-morning it
was clear it was destined be the hottest day of the year,
so far. After a long walk in the nearby woods with
Sandy, Beth stripped off her jeans and jumper and took
a cool shower. Refreshed, she donned a matching set of
underwear that would have to serve as a bikini and
helped herself to a tall glass of gin and tonic. The
Hendersons had a large patio beside a small swimming
pool. Although it was probably still too cold to swim, a
comfortable-looking sun lounger was perfect for making
a start on her suntan.

Beth sat down and carefully applied a liberal coating
of suntan oil. She looked around to ensure that she was
not overlooked and then slipped her bra off so that she

would get an even tan across her top. Sprawled out comfortably, she pulled the old sun-hat, which she had found in the hallway cupboard, down over her eyes. The dog flopped down contentedly under the shade of a big old oak tree, his tongue lolling.

Beth closed her eyes. It was very quiet and peaceful. In the background, she could hear the birds twittering and bees humming busily. It was a perfect early summer day. She let her mind wander. Could she really start her own business? It would be wonderful to be her own boss. No more Simon telling her what to do. What was he hiding in the secure folders on the computer?

Sandy started barking excitedly again and Beth smiled lazily. You'd think it would be too hot to chase after cats. The barking changed to an enthusiastic whining.

'Hello. Oh . . . Sorry. I thought you were my mother.'

Beth jumped at the unexpected voice and pushed the sun-hat back off her face. A young man was standing a couple of feet away from her, one hand stroking the ecstatic Sandy. Beth stared.

He was tall and slim, with longish dark hair and a clean-shaven, boyish complexion. Dressed casually in jeans and scruffy T-shirt, yet wearing an expensive wrist-watch and designer trainers, he looked a lot like a younger version of Simon.

'Are you a friend of my mother?' he asked. 'Where is she?' He appeared to be having trouble not staring at her and Beth suddenly remembered that she was dressed only in a pair of skimpy panties. She made a half-hearted attempt to cover herself with one arm as she swung her legs round and sat up.

'No. I mean, yes.' This must be Simon's son, she realised. She noticed his eyes had dropped to her groin. Considering how skimpy her panties were, it was little wonder he was staring.

'You must be Chris. I'm Beth. I work for your father. I'm looking after Sandy while your parents are away.'

She stood up, keeping her arm over her chest and trying to remember exactly where she had thrown her bra.

'I see.' Chris smiled. He took a step closer to her and held out his hand. 'Pleased to meet you, Beth. You say my parents are away?'

'Yes.' Beth automatically lowered her arm to shake his hand. His skin was damp and clammy. She saw his eyes widen at the sight of her exposed breasts and quickly put her arm back to cover herself. Very clever. He obviously took after his father.

'They've gone to Rome for the weekend,' she explained. 'I don't think they were expecting you home.' His face looked quite pale and shaken. She realised that the handshake had not been deliberate after all.

'No.' Chris was frowning. 'We don't communicate much and, anyway, I hadn't planned this visit until the last minute.'

Beth shifted awkwardly from one foot to the other. 'Well, I suppose now you're here, I might as well pack and leave you to it. I'm sure you can see to Sandy.'

Chris looked puzzled, then frowned again. 'What? Oh, no. Don't go. I mean, well, I'm not sure how long I shall be staying. If Mum and Dad aren't here, I might just as well head back to college.'

'Well, if you're sure. I don't want to intrude. Sorry to disappoint you.'

Chris stared at her in bewilderment.

'About your parents, I mean.'

'Oh, I see.' He grinned sheepishly. 'Believe me, you're, I mean, it's no disappointment.' His eyes ran over her exposed flesh yet again.

Beth flushed. 'I was just thinking about getting myself some lunch,' she muttered. 'Would you like something?' It felt awkward, offering to entertain him in his own house.

Chris nodded and swallowed hard without speaking.

'I suppose I should put something on first.' Beth gave

185

up trying to find her bra and reached for the blouse hanging over the arm of the chair.

'No, don't do that.' He flushed. 'What I mean is, I don't want to cause you any trouble or anything.' He was openly staring at her now and a quick glance at his groin confirmed to Beth what he was thinking about.

Beth smiled and slipped her feet into her strapless sandals before pushing her arms into the sleeves of the blouse. It was just long enough to cover her bottom. She pulled it round and did up just one button to hold it over her breasts. She noticed with amusement that Sandy and Chris were both watching her with the same puppy-dog expression on their faces.

As she made her way back towards the house, Beth was very conscious of Chris walking just behind her. Her panties were riding up between her buttocks as she moved and she resisted the temptation to pull them out. He was certainly good-looking. His young, firm body reminded her of . . .

'So, what are you studying?' she asked quickly, determined to keep at bay her powerful memories of young Jonathan. She looked over her shoulder at Chris.

'I'm sorry?' Chris flushed and his eyes dropped to the ground guiltily as if she had just caught him doing something he shouldn't be doing.

'At college. What are you studying?'

'Studying?' He paused. 'Oh, I see.' He paused again. 'I, um, just general business studies.' He was obviously having trouble concentrating on their conversation. She grinned as he hurried forward to hold the back door open for her.

'I take it you're not too keen?' Beth headed into the kitchen and hovered by the fridge. She really ought to cover up a bit more before she got the food. It was so hot. She liked the way he was watching her.

'Dad wants me to join him in the family business.' He made it sound like a life sentence.

'So, what's wrong with that?' she moved slowly, using

all her skill to make her provocative poses seem acciden-tal. She forced herself not to look at him to check the effect.

'I want to study medicine,' he replied as he perched himself on a kitchen stool. 'I've got no head for figures.'

Beth looked up and smiled at his choice of words, noticing that he quickly averted his eyes from her.

'Why don't you just tell him, then? Your father, I mean.' It was definitely far too hot for any more clothes. She opened the fridge and rummaged around for a suitable sandwich filler. 'Are beef sandwiches OK for you?'

'Yes. Great.'

Beth turned to look at him.

'I can't tell my father anything,' Chris replied to her earlier question. 'If you work for him, you must know that. Once he's decided he wants something, there's no stopping him.'

Beth hid a smirk. 'I suppose he can be a bit forceful,' she responded. 'Still, it's your life, isn't it?'

'Is it? I'm not so sure.' Chris's words were so soft that she barely caught them. She tried to swallow her impatience. Chris didn't look like a wimp. If he took after his father at all then, surely, he had enough guts to stand up to Simon over his own future?

She fetched the butter and bread and busied herself with the sandwiches. Her breasts swayed gently from side to side with every stroke of the knife and she noticed that his eyes were riveted to them. Perhaps he and Simon weren't so different after all.

'There you go.' Beth placed a plate of sandwiches on the counter and perched herself on an adjacent stool.

'Thanks. They look great.' Chris took a huge bite and munched ravenously, as if he were half-starved. Lads his age always had good appetites. Her thoughts returned to Jonathan. Chris was older, of course. If he was at college, he must be at least eighteen, maybe nineteen. He was unlikely to be an innocent where women were concerned. Not with a dad like Simon!

Beth took a bite of her own sandwich and examined Chris again surreptitiously. He had mistaken her for his mother. Did he find her attractive? He had certainly had a good look at her body. He was still staring at her legs. The temptation to tease him was too strong to resist.

Beth raised her left leg and crossed it over her right one. Her blouse was not quite long enough to cover her groin. She leant forward slightly to take another sandwich, giving him a clear view down the top of her gaping blouse. She knew that her nipples were hardening.

Chris's eyes widened and the colour on his cheeks deepened. She licked her lips as if to clean up stray crumbs and glanced at his crotch. The way he was sitting, it was not easy to tell if he was responding physically to her body or not. She noticed that he was no longer eating, just holding the sandwich between his clearly trembling fingers.

'Are you going to eat that,' she teased, 'or just play with it?' She raised one eyebrow.

Chris jumped and stared at the sandwich in bewilderment. Finally, he sighed and took a small bite. His eyes returned to her chest. Beth felt the first tingles of her own desire prickling the tops of her thighs. The idea of seducing Simon's son was deliciously tempting.

'So. Are you going to stay around this afternoon or do you have to leave straight away?' she questioned. 'It's awfully hot to be stuck in a car,' she added.

Chris shrugged. 'I don't know yet. I haven't thought. When did you say my parents would be home?'

'Not until tomorrow evening.' Beth decided to push him a bit more. 'I'd be very happy if you stayed around and kept me company. It's very lonely here, isn't it? Especially at night.'

Chris looked startled.

'I could cook us a special meal this evening,' she tempted him. 'How about lasagne? It's my speciality. I can make it as good as anything your parents may have in Rome. That's if you like Italian food, of course.'

'I love Italian food,' Chris replied. 'If you're sure it's no trouble.'

Beth smiled sweetly. 'Like I said, I'd be glad of the company.'

To her disappointment, Chris disappeared up to his room as soon as they had finished their sandwiches. Beth washed the dishes and tidied up the kitchen, then decided she might as well return to the sun lounger. As she settled back down and removed her blouse, she pretended not to notice the sound of an upstairs window opening.

Later, when she rolled over on to her stomach, she glanced up at the house and just caught a glimpse of him ducking out of sight from the window. Although she kept a watchful eye, she saw nothing further of him all afternoon. She amused herself with outrageous fantasies about what he might be up to.

Around five, she headed back to the house and wiggled into her jeans and T-shirt to take Sandy for another stroll. She debated looking for Chris to see if he wanted to join them but decided against it. He might resent her intruding on his privacy.

As soon as she returned, she fed Sandy and then began to hunt around in the kitchen for the ingredients to prepare dinner. Thankfully, Marie seemed to keep a well-stocked larder. She soon found everything she needed and busied herself cooking.

By six thirty, everything was coming along fine and Beth hurried upstairs to shower and dress. She stared ruefully at the few items of clothing she had brought with her. She had packed her case for dog walking, not seduction.

With another twinge of guilt, Beth crept down the landing to the main bedroom. Perhaps Marie had something a bit more suitable that she could borrow. She smirked at the thought of seducing Chris dressed in clothes borrowed from his own mother.

When she opened the wardrobe door and saw the long rack of dresses hanging there, she gasped in astonishment. They must have cost a fortune. Any qualms about borrowing Marie's clothes disappeared when she caught sight of a beautiful green cocktail dress at the far end of the row. She lifted it down and held it against her gleefully.

It was difficult to believe that it would fit Marie. It was only a size twelve. Simon's wife would easily take a fourteen. Perhaps it was one she hadn't worn for a long time, or maybe it was bought as an incentive to lose weight. Either way, it was perfect for Beth; short and clingy, with a narrow waist and flared hips. The neck was wide and worn off the shoulder; a style she had discovered most men appreciated. She slipped it over her head and nodded approvingly at her reflection in the long mirror.

Chris appeared just as she was adding the finishing touches to their meal. She looked up and smiled warmly as he entered the kitchen.

'Good timing. I was just about to call you.'

Chris sniffed the air appreciatively. 'It smells wonderful,' he told her. Beth noticed that his voice sounded slightly nervous. 'And, you look, er, fabulous.' She smiled at him again, pleased to notice that he had also dressed for dinner. The casual yet expensively cut black trousers fitted him perfectly. His dark blue, open-neck shirt was made of silk.

'I thought we would eat in the living-room, if that's OK,' she told him. 'Your dining-room is so huge, I'd be lost in it.'

Chris laughed. 'Dad insists we eat in there. I think it makes him feel more important. You know, lord of all he surveys. When Mum and I are alone we always eat in the living-room,' he assured her. 'Do you want me to carry anything?'

190

As they made their way into the living-room Beth watched him carefully, enjoying the sight of his firm body, the smell of his expensive aftershave and the underlying scent of his masculinity. Her skin prickled with anticipation.

They sat down side by side on the wide leather couch, and Chris poured them both a glass of wine from the bottle she had already placed on the low coffee-table. He took a bite of his lasagne and smacked his lips.

'This is incredible.' He took another large forkful.

Beth made a start on her own meal. She was acutely aware of the warmth of his thigh close up against her own leg. A small shiver ran down her back. She swallowed her food and took another mouthful. As an awkward silence gradually fell between them, she glanced around the room looking for a topic of conversation.

'This really is a beautiful house, Chris. Your father's business must be even more successful than I had realised.'

Chris snorted. 'King Midas. That's what he tells us to call him. Dad has always had a talent for turning money into more money. Especially when he's playing about with other people's money.'

'His rates are quite competitive,' Beth replied. 'Not everyone in the business does as well as he seems to have done.'

'No? Well, not everyone is as willing to take the gambles with other people's dosh that he does.'

'How do you mean?' Beth was intrigued by the implication.

Chris shrugged. 'Nothing. Only that he uses other people's money to make his own and then takes a bigger percentage than they realise. More wine?' He leant forward to pick up the bottle and used the movement to close the gap between his leg and hers. As his thigh pressed harder against hers, a surge of desire shot through her.

'Please.' She turned to hold her glass towards him and

their gaze met. She could see the longing burning within Chris's eyes. Longing and something else. Fear? What was he afraid of? Perhaps he wanted her but was afraid to trespass on what he assumed to be his father's domain? Anger engulfed her. She loathed the idea that he should think of her as belonging to Simon.

'Still, you have to admit that he has done well for you all,' she continued.

Chris frowned. 'Yeah. Well, you know one reason why he's so successful, don't you?' His words sounded very sharp and sarcastic.

'He works very hard,' Beth replied cautiously.

Chris snorted. 'He's not the only one. He also makes Mum be nice to his clients. I've heard him.'

Beth smiled. 'Well. That's not so unreasonable is it? I mean, she can hardly be rude to them, can she?'

'That's not what I mean.' His voice rose an octave. 'I've heard her being nice to some of them – in the bedroom.' His eyes were flashing with anger. 'You know what really pisses me off? He takes all the credit. Never even thanks her.'

Beth was silent. She couldn't help being a little shocked. She knew Simon was a bit of a bastard but – his own wife! No wonder Marie acted like she did. Beth wondered what she herself would have done if her ex-husband had ever asked her to do something like that.

Chris was watching her closely. 'So, does he ever make you be nice to his clients?' he questioned.

Her temper flared. 'No, he bloody well doesn't,' she snarled. Even as she said it, she realised that that was probably why he had wanted her to go to Rome with him.

Chris sneered. 'Really? He will. Sooner or later. You know, I wouldn't even be surprised if he told me to be nice to one of them, male or female, if he thought it would make him some money.'

'Would you like some more lasagne?' Beth decided that the conversation had gone far enough. She hated the idea that Chris might think she was willing to be manipulated by Simon. Under the circumstances, she was on shaky ground denying any involvement with him. Damn Simon to hell.

As she stood up and bent over to pick up Chris's plate, Beth took the opportunity to let her skirt ride up her legs. Although she was rewarded by the sound of his sharp intake of breath, Chris made no move towards her. He certainly wasn't as quick on the uptake as his father.

When she returned from the kitchen with second helpings, Beth accidentally misjudged her seating and fell back so that her leg was pressed tight against his thigh. She heard his gentle sigh. Although he still made no attempt to touch her, at least he didn't move away either.

She picked up her glass, took a sip and licked her lips slowly. 'This is a great wine, isn't it.' Beth placed her glass on the table and put her hand on his knee. 'I'm so glad you decided to stay tonight, Chris. It's nice to have some company.'

She felt him flinch at the touch and saw the colour flow up his neck and cheeks. He held his body rigid, as if afraid to move. Did he find her unattractive or was he really so shy? Beth began to run her finger slowly up his thigh.

'Actually, I was thinking I should be on my way soon.' He glanced at his watch. 'If there's not too much traffic, I should be able to get back before midnight.'

'Surely, you don't want to go at this time?' Beth's fingers continued their journey up his leg. 'Besides, you shouldn't drive after all this wine. It's surprisingly strong.' Her fingers tightened round his upper thigh, giving it a gentle squeeze.

Chris jumped as if he had been stung by a wasp. He slid away from her along the settee so that her hand slipped off his leg. Beth glanced at his crotch and was delighted to see how tight his trousers had suddenly become. Obviously, he wasn't totally immune to her charms.

'What's wrong?'

'Nothing. Cramp.' Chris leant over and gingerly rubbed his leg where she had touched him. Beth grinned.

'Cramp? In your thigh? How strange. Here, let me massage it for you.' She shifted along the settee and put her hand back on his leg. She felt him jump again. He was as nervous as a kitten. Or a virgin. Surely he couldn't be virgin at his age? The idea both delighted and excited her. She squeezed his thigh muscle firmly and sensed his whole body shudder.

'Better?'

'Yes, fine. Thank you.' His voice was tight and squeaky. Beth stopped squeezing and began to slide her fingers upwards again. Chris whimpered softly under his breath. Suddenly, he leant forward and put his lips to hers. His left arm slipped hesitantly around her shoulder to pull her closer.

Thank God, Beth thought to herself. For a moment there, she had been at a loss as to how to encourage him. Bar whipping off all her clothes and leaping on him, she was rapidly running out of ideas. She opened her lips enthusiastically to his probing tongue.

Chris pulled his head away. 'God. I'm sorry. I shouldn't have . . .' He removed his arm and sat there looking like a naughty schoolboy. A quick glance at his fly reassured her that his body did not necessarily agree with his conscience.

Beth snuggled against him and rested her head on his chest. She could hear his heart thumping madly against his rib cage. 'Relax, Chris. I don't bite.' Well, not too hard, anyway, she added silently, as she pictured herself sinking her teeth into his firm flesh.

'But what about my father?' Chris whispered hoarsely.

'Let's just leave Simon out of this, shall we? He's my boss, nothing more.' Was that it? Was he frightened, or perhaps repulsed, by the concept of making it with one of his father's women? Her dislike of Simon increased further.

Beth undid one of his shirt buttons and pushed her hand inside. Chris gulped as her fingers gently caressed his smooth chest. His arm slipped round her shoulders once more and his lips returned to hers.

He might be a bit slow on the uptake but there was nothing wrong with his kissing technique. She writhed helplessly as his fingers ran across the bare flesh of her shoulder and came to rest on the swell of her right breast. A pang of lust shot through her. She pulled her hand back out of his shirt and moved it down his body until her fingers were resting over his straining groin.

Chris groaned and pushed his tongue harder into her mouth. His fingers started to explore the shape of her breast and she sensed her nipples hardening in response. The tingling between her thighs intensified. She could only guess how damp her thong must be. What was he waiting for?

Impatiently, Beth raised her hand and guided his fingers inside her dress. She sighed loudly as she felt him gently fondle her swollen nipple; his touch was as soft and light as a feather. She was desperate to feel his lips sucking her there.

Beth put her hand back on to his trousers and fumbled with the button. She almost sighed with relief as it came undone. Slowly, she started to slide the zip down, exposing his bulging underpants.

Chris sighed again and tightened his grip on her breast, squeezing it almost painfully. Beth shuddered with desire and felt her lubrication flowing. His shy reluctance, despite his obvious need, was driving her wild. She could hear her own breath rasping in her throat. Eagerly, she pulled his pants down and wrapped her fingers round his hardness.

His whole body shook at her touch. 'Oh God,' he gasped softly as he thrust his hips upward to push his throbbing cock hard into her fist.

Sensing that he was already close to coming, Beth released her grip and pushed her hand down further so that she could caress his balls with her fingertips. They were already tight and swollen. She definitely needed to find a way to slow things down still further.

Beth pulled her hand out, put his cock back in his pants, wriggled out of his grasp and sat up. Chris lay back against the cushion of the settee, his face burning with lust. She stood up and turned her back to him.

Slowly, she peeled the dress off her shoulders and let it fall to the floor, revealing her naked back and the lacy strap of her thong. She placed her hands over her breasts and swivelled round on her heels to face him.

Chris immediately sat forward and stared at her without speaking. Beth glanced down at the way his cock was straining against his pants. She saw that his hands were at his sides and guessed that he was afraid to touch himself in case he lost all control. Smiling provocatively, she moved her hands slowly down her body towards the tiny scrap of lace covering her mound. Her breasts fell forward to reveal her swollen nipples to his longing gaze.

Beth slipped her fingers down inside the lace and ran them softly over her tingling clitoris. His gasp was loud enough to smother her own sigh of pleasure. Slowly, she slipped the thong down, revealing her shaven mound. Chris gasped again and his right hand involuntarily moved round to rub himself.

Beth dropped the thong to her ankles and stepped out of it. Naked, she leant forward and took his hand, pulling him to his feet. Chris stood up submissively with his hands at his sides and his eyes glued to her mound.

Beth put her hands on his hips and hooked her fingers into the waistband of his pants. Gently, she eased them over his erection. It leapt out towards her like an angry cobra writhing its head from side to side, ready to strike. He might be a bit shy, but he certainly had nothing to be ashamed of. She stepped away to look at him.

'Finish stripping,' she whispered huskily.

Galvanised into action by her words, Chris immediately began to rip the rest of his clothes off. In his desperation, he was trying to get his shirt off over his head at the same time as kicking his feet out of his trousers. Losing his balance, he stumbled back on to the settee and fell on the floor. Seemingly oblivious to how he must look, he continued to struggle with his clothing. As he finally lifted his legs clear of his trousers, his fingers tore the remaining buttons from his shirt. He tossed both garments to one side and struggled to get up. Beth could see his balls and cock swaying under him and her fingers itched to grab him. She raised one eyebrow and stared at his socks.

Red-faced from exertion and embarrassment, Chris ripped them off and pulled himself back up on to the settee.

Beth knelt down and ran her tongue down the full length of his penis, savouring the masculine taste of him. With one hand under his scrotum, she slid her tongue back up and wrapped her lips around his swollen tip. Slowly, she sucked him into her mouth. She heard him gasp and felt him push his hips forward, thrusting into her so forcefully that she almost choked. She immediately gripped him harder with her lips, forcing him to slow his pace. Bobbing her head up and down, she continued to slip him in and out of her mouth so slowly that he was barely moving.

'Please,' he begged desperately as he grabbed her head with his hands to try to push even deeper into her. 'Oh my God, I can't . . .'

Instinctively, Beth fought against him, maintaining the slow, torturous speed that she knew was driving him mad. Another rush of excitement shot through her. There was nothing that gave her greater pleasure than holding a man right on the edge like this. The rush of power it gave her was almost as good as an orgasm. She felt her own juices dampening her thighs.

Pulling back, she let him drop from her mouth and

feasted her eyes on the throbbing veins of his swollen erection. His balls were hard against his body and she knew that he would not be able to hold on much longer. She glanced up.

Chris had closed his eyes. His face was screwed up as if he were in pain and every muscle of his body was tight with concentration. She knew he was fighting to control himself and the knowledge of his struggle was almost enough to bring her to climax. She clamped her thighs together tightly and took a couple of deep breaths to calm herself down.

Seeing that he had also relaxed slightly now that she was no longer sucking him, Beth raised her hand and wrapped it round his cock. He was so damp with her saliva and his own lubrication that her fist slid freely down his length. She started to pump him, slowly at first, then faster and harder as he began to thrust against her once again. Unable to help herself, Beth slipped her other hand between her own legs and squeezed her mound and bud. She was very close herself now.

Chris put his hands on his buttocks and pushed himself harder into her hand. Beth immediately tightened her grip, squeezing him as firmly as she could to prolong the moment even further.

'Oh, Jesus. I can't hold it!' His desperate cry was the final trigger. With a last savage pump of her fist, Beth felt her own climax tear through her body. Chris began to spurt violently into her clenched hand, groaning with every convulsion of his eruption.

Beth waited until he had nothing left to give then opened her fist to release him. She slumped back wearily on her heels. Her skin was tingling and glowing with the aftermath of her own fulfilment.

Chris flopped down heavily on to the couch as if his leg muscles no longer had the strength to hold him. His chest was still heaving and she noticed with delight that his sticky wet cock was still partly erect. She shifted forward on her knees and kissed its tip lightly, smiling as his hands began ruffling her hair.

'That was, I mean, well, you're quite something,' he whispered softly.

Beth stood up and sank down on the couch beside him with her head resting on his sweat-covered chest. She ran her fingernail down his chest.

'You're not going to leave me all alone in this great big house tonight, are you?' she whispered in her best little-girl's voice. 'Who's going to scrub my back for me?' She took his hand and pulled him up. Still holding his hand, she led him unresisting upstairs towards the shower.

Chapter Eleven

*I*n the end, Chris didn't leave to return to college until about an hour before Simon and Marie arrived home from Rome on the Sunday afternoon. By that time, Beth and Chris had enjoyed pleasuring each other several more times in a number of imaginative positions and settings.

Chris had proved to be a sweet and considerate man, nothing like his selfish, money-grabbing father. No wonder he didn't want to go into business with Simon. If his bedside manner was anything like as good as his 'in bed' manners, he would make a wonderful doctor!

The more Chris had told her about Simon, the more Beth grew to despise him. Chris might not want to go into the business, but he obviously knew more about what his father got up to than she did. His revelations about some of Simon's underhand practices had made her really angry. Geoff might walk a thin line between what was strictly legal in some of his dealings, but she was certain that he didn't deliberately fleece his clients the way Simon apparently did. As for the way he used his wife like that! By the time Chris left, Beth was absolutely determined to find a way to really fix Simon.

When the Hendersons finally returned, Simon was in

a foul mood. Obviously, his plans in Rome had not worked out to his satisfaction. Marie looked tired and weary and had little to say for herself. She thanked Beth politely for taking such good care of Sandy, then pleaded a headache and disappeared upstairs. Simon offered her a drink but Beth made excuses and escaped quickly before he got any ideas. At Chris's request, she said nothing about their son's visit. She didn't even want to think about what Simon would do if he found out what she and Chris had been up to.

The following morning, Simon seemed to be in much better humour. As soon as he had taken care of the most urgent business, he called Beth through to his office.

'This is for you.' Simon held out a large, flat box. Beth stared at him.

'You did suggest I brought you something from Rome,' he reminded her. 'Go on, open it.'

Beth took the box curiously. She was amazed that he had remembered.

The dress was red and made of a stretchy, lacy material that would hide little. It was long and slit high up both sides; the neck was wide and the back so low it would probably reveal the crease of her buttocks. It was just the sort of thing she would have expected him to choose, but she had to admit that she loved it.

'Thank you, Simon.' She held it against herself. 'It's lovely.'

Simon smirked at her. 'You can wear it next weekend,' he told her.

'Next weekend?'

'Yes. Marie and I have been invited to a weekend party. It will be a great opportunity to make some useful contacts. I want you to come with us.'

'Won't your host object?'

'No. You're already expected.'

Beth frowned. She didn't like to be taken for granted.

201

Especially by Simon. 'I'm not sure that I'm free,' she began.

'Make sure that you are. I need you to be there and I expect you to make yourself useful by being nice to the host. Very nice.' He leered suggestively and Beth flushed angrily at the implication behind his words. It was exactly what Chris had warned her would happen. She gritted her teeth.

'Like I said, I'm not sure . . .'

'It's not open to discussion,' he told her firmly. Beth's temper flared.

'How dare you treat me like some woman you pay for by the hour,' she yelled.

Simon grinned. 'Actually, I never do pay. Why pay for something when you don't need to?' He reached round and patted her. 'If you still want a job next week, you'll do as I say.' He grinned again. 'Don't look like that. I don't think you'll find it any great hardship. You already know the host; Geoff Stevens.'

By Friday night, Beth was so keyed up that she couldn't sleep. Although she was still furious with Simon, she couldn't help being excited. As she lay tossing and turning in her bed, she tried to imagine what the weekend might hold in store.

Geoff Stevens' wheeling and dealing weekend parties were infamous in financial circles. She had never expected to find herself among the guest list and she wondered how Simon had managed to wangle the invitation. Although she really wanted to see Geoff again, she had not forgotten how easily he and his chauffeur had manipulated her. What had Geoff thought when he had found the money she left in his car? She wanted to see Daniel again too, but was even more nervous about that as she recalled what had happened between them.

Still, Simon had no right to treat her like this. She remembered his conceited words. Just you wait, she vowed silently. You will pay, one way or the other.

Simon and Marie picked her up at nine thirty the following morning. She was so nervous that she hadn't managed anything for breakfast and the thought of the coming buffet lunch was already making her stomach churn.

Marie was beautifully made up and her dress and jacket superbly tailored. Beth couldn't help noticing that her eyes seemed unusually red, as if she had been crying. Marie said little during the two-hour journey and, occasionally, when she thought no one was looking, she shot venom-filled glances at her husband. Beth wondered what he had been up to this time. Had she, too, been given her instructions? Perhaps Simon imagined that, between them, they could be especially nice to Geoff.

Simon, she noticed, seemed to be in fine spirits and totally oblivious to his wife's angry stares.

'I expect great things from this weekend, Beth. I'm sure that Geoff can be persuaded to put a little business our way and I'm relying on you to do whatever it takes to persuade him.'

Beth frowned but chose not to respond to this repeat of his earlier demands. Not that she would really mind persuading Geoff! She noticed the look on Marie's face but couldn't decide what it meant: surprise, suspicion or maybe pity?

When the car finally turned into the sweeping driveway and Beth caught sight of Geoff's rambling mansion and immaculate grounds, she gasped aloud. This place made even Simon's luxurious house seem little more than a hovel. For the first time, she started to appreciate just how rich and successful Geoff Stevens truly was.

As the three of them mounted the wide steps leading up to the imposing oak doorway, the front door swung open to reveal a smiling Daniel. Obviously, he also played the part of butler when he wasn't driving. Beth felt her breath catch at the sight of his muscular body and roguish good looks. She had forgotten just how attractive he was.

'Good morning. Please come in. Sarah will show you to your rooms, then drinks are being served in the library.' As he spoke, Daniel stared at Beth and gave her a quick wink that brought a sudden glow to more than her cheeks. She could sense his eyes burning into her as they followed a pretty maid up the wide staircase.

Her room was at the end of a long corridor, whose walls were covered with expensive-looking paintings of racehorses. Its fittings and decor would have put most five-star hotels to shame and Beth grinned with delight as she bounced up and down on the huge four-poster bed. With any luck, she would get the opportunity to test it properly later.

As soon as she had hung her clothes in the massive oak wardrobe and splashed a little cold water on to her flushed cheeks, Beth hurried nervously downstairs, excited at the idea of seeing Geoff again. On the way, she met several other guests, including Simon and Marie, all heading for drinks in the library.

In the library, Geoff was standing beside a huge, horseshoe-shaped bar, talking with a serious-looking Asian man. He looked across when they came in and Beth shivered with pleasure at the tiny smile that played across his lips when he spotted her among the latest arrivals.

She moved into the room and accepted a glass of sherry from a tall, redheaded waitress. Sipping the drink, she moved over to the french windows and gazed out over the park-like grounds, wondering just how many acres Geoff owned.

'Dreaming about me again, Beth?'

Beth jumped at the familiar voice and spun round on her heels. John was standing behind her with that infuriating grin of his. Her heart flipped and her mind immediately began to relive some of their recent antics.

'John. I didn't know you were going to be here.' She looked round quickly. 'Are Steve and Brian here, too?'

'Not that I know of,' he replied, moving closer so that his thigh was touching hers. 'Still, speaking for myself, I can't say that I shall miss them too much.' He ran his hand lightly down her spine and nodded out of the window. 'Nice view, isn't it? Would you like to take a walk?'

Beth shivered at his touch, remembering the way he had played with her body that night in her hotel – if it had been him. She felt her face start to burn.

'I, um, well, yes, I suppose we –' She broke off as Geoff came up behind them and took her hand.

'Beth. How delightful to see you again so soon.' He raised her hand to his lips and kissed it lightly. 'I'm so pleased you could join us. It should be an interesting weekend.'

Beth smiled as her eyes moved from John to Geoff and then back again. She felt quite weak at the knees being so close to two of her recent conquests at the same time – although, perhaps, conquest was not quite the right word.

'Hello, Geoff. Thank you for asking me. Your house is absolutely breathtaking.'

Geoff took hold of her arm. 'Come on. There are several people I want you to meet. If you will excuse us, John?'

John nodded politely. 'I shall see you later then, Beth.' It was a statement rather than a question and Beth experienced a thrill of desire and longing as she saw the hungry look in his eyes. She could almost picture him beside her in that huge four-poster bed. She nodded without answering and John flashed her another know-ing grin. He seemed to have an uncanny knack of read-ing her innermost thoughts.

'By the way. You left something behind in my car the other day,' Geoff told her softly as her led her across the room towards the Asian man he had been talking with earlier. 'I must make sure to return it to you before you leave.'

Beth opened her mouth to argue, but Geoff squeezed her arm. 'I meant what I told you that day, Beth. The money was a consultancy fee for your business knowledge and was well earnt. To suggest anything else insults both of us.'

Beth closed her mouth again. There was obviously no point in arguing with him. If he was really that determined for her to have the money, well, why not? She had made her point. Not that she would ever spend it. Maybe she would frame it as a memento of her first consultancy fee. When she felt naughty, she could look at it and remember just how she earnt it.

'Here we are. Beth, I want you to meet Ho Chan. This is Beth Bradley. A very promising newcomer to our ranks.'

The rest of the day passed in a whirl of new faces, good food, liberal amounts of alcohol and stimulating discussions. By five thirty, Beth's head was swimming and her feet were aching. Making polite excuses to those around her, she escaped gratefully and headed for her room to shower and rest before dinner.

Without paying attention to where she was going she took a wrong turn out of the library and found herself in a long dark corridor with several doors on either side.

She opened one at random and smiled when she found a narrow staircase leading up. Thinking that it was probably a servants' staircase to the upper floor, she hurried up the steep steps and through the door at the top. It opened out on to a landing that looked vaguely familiar and Beth turned left and hurried along it, looking for her room.

Although she had no idea how many rooms opened out on to the landing, she remembered that her own room was the last one on the left before the landing ended at a huge stained-glass window. She was too weary to notice that the paintings on the walls were of hunting dogs rather than racehorses.

When she finally reached the end of the long corridor,

Beth opened with a sigh of relief what she thought to be her own door. She couldn't wait to take a hot bath.

The room she entered seemed to be some kind of huge games room with a snooker table and table tennis. Through a wide arch at the far end, Beth could see a fully fitted gymnasium with treadmills, step machines and several kinds of weights. She sighed with frustration, realising that she was now totally lost.

She was just about to retrace her steps when she heard a sound coming from the gym. Hoping there might be someone in there who could give her directions, Beth hurried across the room and peered through the archway.

Daniel was standing in the far corner of the gym with his back against the mirrored wall. He was dressed in training shorts and a T-shirt so tight that every muscle was clearly outlined. As her eyes travelled downwards she noticed the obvious bulge at his groin and suddenly realised that he was not alone.

She glanced curiously at his companion. She was obviously one of the housemaids, dressed in the short black skirt and white frilly blouse all Geoff's maids seemed to wear. She had her back to Beth and she had untied her hair so that it was cascading loosely round her shoulders.

Before Beth could move, the maid stepped in front of Daniel and bent forward to slip her hand down the front of his shorts. Daniel sighed loudly as he leant even harder against the wall, thrusting his hips forward to give the maid full access. Beth was close enough to see that his eyes were closed and to notice the look of intense concentration on his face.

Beth involuntarily stepped back into the shadow of the archway. A tingle of excitement swept through her as she saw Daniel put his hands round the maid's waist and undo the zip holding her skirt. The skirt slid down off the maid's narrow hips and Beth could just see the straps of her suspender belt peeping out under the bottom of her blouse. Daniel's hands lifted the blouse and slipped down inside her panties to fondle her taut buttocks.

Beth held her breath as the maid began to lower Daniel's shorts. He wasn't wearing anything under them and she just stopped herself from sighing aloud as his swollen cock fell free. The maid ran her hand slowly down its length and cupped his balls. Beth could feel her own nipples rising with desire. She pushed her legs together tightly as the tingle between her thighs grew more urgent. She knew she should leave. She had no right to spy on him like this.

Daniel removed his hands from the maid's panties and spun her round on her heels until she was standing with her back to him. With his arms around her shoulders, he guided them both round so that they were facing the mirrored wall with their backs to Beth.

Beth examined the maid's firm buttocks, thinking how sexy they looked framed by her panties and the bottom of her blouse. The sight of Daniel's rigid prick waving back and forth with its shiny tip almost caressing the maid's cheeks was even more exciting. Remembering how she had struggled against him in the car, Beth felt a slight twinge of envy for the maid's position.

The maid raised her hands and put her flattened palms on to the mirror as Daniel forced his hands under the bottom of her blouse and pulled her buttocks hard against his cock. Beth looked at the mirror and could see Daniel's hands moving under the maid's blouse. She could almost imagine the way he was teasing her pubes and clit with his fingers and she squeezed herself even harder as another pang of desire raced through her.

His breathing laboured, Daniel grabbed the elastic of the maid's panties and started to peel them down. Beth took a sharp breath and almost choked in her effort not to gasp as the maid's huge penis fell forward over the top of her – his – panties and stuck out proudly in front of him with its tip touching the mirror. Her legs were suddenly much too weak to hold her and Beth swayed, then grabbed the wall with her left hand to stop herself falling.

Huddled in the archway, she looked more carefully at the maid's reflection, for the first time seeing the broad shoulders, the narrow hips, the dark shadow on his cheeks and, of course, the urgent erection. Her eyes dropped back down to the reflection of his groin in the mirror and she had to fight to stifle another gasp as she saw Daniel reach round from behind to fondle his companion's stiff cock.

Beth shuffled back further and crouched down, trying to make herself as small as possible. She had never seen two men together like this, not even in films. Her heart was hammering almost painfully and her emotions were in complete turmoil. She couldn't take her eyes off them.

Daniel's companion – Beth couldn't keep thinking of him as a maid – shifted his feet backwards and arched his back, pushing his buttocks up into the air. He slid his feet apart and lowered his buttocks into Daniel's groin.

Daniel whipped his own shorts down to his ankles and then grabbed his friend's buttocks with his hands, prising the cheeks apart. She could clearly see the other man's thighs and calves quivering as he tensed his muscles, ready.

Beth held her breath as Daniel wet his index finger and pushed it gently into the man's crack. She saw his other hand grasp his own cock firmly to begin guiding it forwards. Jesus Christ! Daniel was going to penetrate him! He was actually going to – She couldn't help the small gasp that burst from her lips.

It didn't matter. Daniel and his friend were obviously too engrossed to notice her. They were both breathing raggedly and she could see the sweat beading on their firm flesh. She whimpered softly as Daniel thrust his stiff cock deep into his friend's anus. Both men grunted and Beth whimpered again as she heard Daniel's groin slap against the other man's buttocks.

She glanced in the mirror and saw the man's face tighten with passion as Daniel began to pump firmly in and out. She lowered her eyes and watched, fascinated, as his own cock twitched and throbbed in response. She experienced an almost overwhelming urge to walk over and grab it in her hand.

Almost as if she had forgotten where she was, Beth slipped her hand under her skirt and up between her thighs. She ran her finger over her mound and on to her sex. Her clit was hard and swollen with her passion and her panties were already dripping wet. With a small sigh, she pushed the damp material aside and pushed her middle finger up into her moist vagina to rub herself. Her eyes never moved from the mirror.

Daniel pulled his friend further away from the mirror and pushed him down until he was bent over, supporting himself with both hands, spread-eagled on the mirror. She saw the man push back with his buttocks as Daniel began to pump harder and faster, grunting loudly with every thrust.

Daniel leant over his friend and pulled him down even harder on to his cock then reached round with his right hand to grasp the other man's erection in his fingers. Tightening his fist round it, Daniel began to pump it in time with his thrusting. His friend groaned and stiffened the muscles in his legs to stop himself falling. His face twisted and darkened and Beth realised that he was about to come.

She started to push more urgently with her own finger, using her thumb to caress her already desperate clitoris. A long tingle of excitement raced through her and her nipples burned. She was almost there, too.

Daniel reached round with his left hand and pushed it under his friend's balls. He squeezed gently and thrust even harder with his buttocks and thighs. The other man cried out and jerked his hips. His spunk began to pump from his cock in violent bursts, splattering the mirror and dripping down Daniel's fingers. Daniel thrust his own hips again, then stiffened and groaned as he climaxed.

Beth bit her lips as she imagined his hot semen bursting from him. With a small cry, her whole body shuddered and a massive orgasm rippled through her so powerfully that she lost her balance and collapsed in a heap on the floor. Realising she was in imminent danger of discovery, she crawled across the floor until she was hidden from view round the corner.

As she huddled there, panting, she could hear the sounds of the two men moving around and talking together in low voices. She felt a tinge of panic. If they came through the arch, they would find her and know that she had seen them. She held her breath, shivering with fear and emotion.

Finally, as her breathing slowed and the strength returned to her shaking limbs, Beth pushed herself up on to all fours and crawled forward to peer round the archway.

Daniel and his lover were lying side by side against the mirror, talking softly. She glanced down. Their damp, limp cocks were both totally exposed to her gaze, pointing towards each other as if joining in the conversation. As she watched, Daniel reached across to his friend's groin and ran his fingers slowly down his cock.

Beth's eyes widened as the man's cock twitched feebly. Daniel repeated the caress and his friend's cock twitched again. He reached out and took Daniel's penis between his fingers, squeezing him softly. Gradually, both cocks began to swell again.

As she watched, the two men continued to pump and fondle each other. Within minutes, they were both semi-erect again. Daniel turned over on to his stomach and raised his buttocks invitingly. His friend got up and crouched over his legs. Taking his rapidly hardening prick between his fingers, he leant forward and used his other hand to part Daniel's cheeks.

Beth began to tremble. They were going to do it again.

She could hardly believe it. She pinched herself to see if she was dreaming as the man slowly thrust himself deep into Daniel's bottom. She heard both men sigh urgently as he began pumping in and out.

It was too much. With a small whimper, Beth pushed herself back and forced herself to her feet. As the men's passionate moans grew more urgent, Beth lowered her head and fled, trembling, out the door and down the corridor.

'Whoa!' She almost screamed as she felt herself crash headlong into someone. As she lost her balance, strong arms wrapped around her body and helped her up on to her feet.

'Where's the fire?' John still had his arms around her shoulders, bracing her. 'What's wrong, Beth? You're trembling all over.'

'John.' Beth's legs sagged as she swayed against him. 'I'm sorry. I didn't see you. I was trying to find my room only I took a wrong turning and got lost and –' she broke off as she realised that she was rambling incoherently.

John laughed. 'You look as if you've seen the resident ghost.' He held her tight. 'You're in the wrong wing, that's all. This bit's reserved for Geoff's bachelor guests. Women and married couples are housed in the south wing.'

Beth felt his hand slip easily around her waist. 'Not that I'm complaining, or anything, You are welcome to visit us as often as you like.' He stared at her pale face. 'What's got you so spooked?'

'Nothing.' Beth shook her head and pulled herself out of his grasp. 'I just panicked a bit when my room wasn't where I thought it was. Silly, really.' She swallowed hard and tried to block out the vivid images of Daniel and his friend that were still flooding her mind.

'Perhaps you've had a bit too much to drink and not enough to eat.' John suggested, patting her arm. 'Come on. I'll escort you to your room. Unless you would like to take that stroll now? It's a lovely evening.'

Beth hesitated. The fresh air would do her good. She needed to clear her head. She wondered if Daniel and his friend were still pleasuring each other or if they had finished. Her knees began to tremble again. She needed a shower. She could smell the sweat of her arousal and excitement on her body, and her underwear was cold and wet against her still throbbing bud.

'I'd love a walk,' she told John. 'But, first, I really need to shower and change, if you don't mind waiting.'

'I don't mind at all,' John told her with a small grin. 'I'll even help scrub your back if you want.' He began to guide her gently along the corridor. 'This way.'

Beth leant against him gratefully, enjoying the heat of his body through his suit and his warm masculine odour mingling with his aftershave. It would be useful to have someone to scrub her back. Her own hands were still shaking too much to be any use.

'It might take us a bit longer,' she whispered.

'There's no hurry,' John replied. 'We've got all night.'

Before they reached her room, however, they met Geoff coming along the corridor in the opposite direction. His face lit up when her saw her and Beth had the feeling that he had been looking for her. She noticed his eyes narrow slightly when he saw who she was with.

'Beth. I was hoping to find you. I've got a couple of things I want to discuss with you in private. I don't know when I shall have another chance.' He looked pointedly at John. 'I seem to keep coming between you two, don't I?' He didn't sound as if it bothered him. John shrugged philosophically.

'Our plans will keep, won't they, Beth?'

'Fine. In that case, perhaps you would like to come down to my study.' Geoff took her arm.

Beth nodded dumbly and allowed herself to be guided along the corridor. She was feeling light-headed and dreamlike, as if she were watching herself from a distance. Everything was moving too quickly, and she seemed to be having trouble keeping up with what was going on. Her head was still full of pictures of Daniel and his friend and her body had been keyed up with the promise of being alone in her room with John. She glanced over her shoulder at him and John raised his right hand in mock salute.

'Later, Beth.' His words were so faint that she only just caught them. A shiver of anticipation ran down her spine as she turned back and tried to focus her attention on what Geoff was saying to her.

She could feel his hand burning into her skin. Her head was spinning. She had believed herself to be virtually shockproof. She could still hardly believe what had happened or that she had just stood there, watching. Worse, she had actually . . . She shuddered helplessly as the memories washed over her.

Chapter Twelve

Geoff's study was every bit as luxurious and impressive as the rest of his home. While Geoff poured her a drink, Beth perched herself awkwardly on one of the deep leather armchairs that were scattered around the room. She shifted uncomfortably at the cold dampness of her underwear and wished she had insisted on showering first. She hadn't even found her way back to her room.

'Oh. Before I forget, here's your money.' Geoff handed her the wad of notes with her glass of wine. She took both without comment and held the money awkwardly in one hand.

'I'll come straight to the point,' Geoff told her as he eased himself down in a second comfy chair. 'I've an opening at my head offices. A sort of public relations-cum-personal assistant. I was rather hoping that you would be interested.'

Beth stared at him in surprise. It was an incredible opportunity and the prestige of working for Geoff Stevens would do her own career nothing but good. Simon would be livid.

'Why, thank you,' she stammered. 'I'm very flattered . . .'

'But?' He interrupted her. Beth's cheeks coloured.

'No. It's just a bit unexpected, that's all.' What was it that was bothering her, she wondered? It was a great opportunity. One that she would be mad to turn down because of some crazy whim to become her own boss. Ann had already pointed out how difficult that would be.

'Would you give me a little time to think about it?' she asked. Perhaps a year or two with Geoff might be exactly what she needed to give her the knowledge and confidence to make the final step to go it alone.

'Of course.' Geoff reached across and patted her arm in a fatherly way. 'There's no immediate hurry. Don't take too long, though. Your talents are wasted on a man like Simon Henderson.'

Beth's flush deepened, as if Geoff were referring to talents that had little to do with finance. Was he? If he knew anything about Simon at all, then he must know about the man's philandering reputation. She felt another rush of irritation at the way everyone seemed to assume that she was one of Simon's many conquests.

She opened her mouth to defend Simon's business, then closed it again. Chris probably wasn't the only one who knew what his father was up to. Someone as knowledgeable and well-connected as Geoff would be bound to know all about him and his unscrupulous business practices. She remembered that she was supposed to be here to help convince Geoff to put some business Simon's way. Suddenly, it was important to her that he should know she was not a complete innocent where Simon was concerned.

'I suppose Simon is a bit of a rogue,' she laughed. 'His intentions are in the right place but, somehow, he lacks your finesse.'

Geoff pulled a face. 'I certainly wouldn't trust him with my money. As for his intentions, well, they are debatable. There is a clear line between what's acceptable and what's not. Simon crosses it.'

216

So much for Simon's ambitions, Beth smiled to herself. She wondered why Geoff had invited Simon here at all. It couldn't simply be an excuse to get her here. There had been nothing stopping Geoff from inviting her personally, if he had wanted to.

'Mind you,' Geoff grinned, 'he does provide a little light entertainment. It amuses me to watch him fawning all over everyone. And it did give me an opportunity to try to poach you from him without being too obvious about it.'

Geoff picked up the wine bottle and refilled her glass. 'Drink up. I've got a lot to celebrate this evening. Ho Chan and I have just completed a deal that should prove extremely lucrative for both of us.' His eyes twinkled as he leant closer and put his hand on her knee.

'It's rather clever, actually, if I do say so myself. Would you like to hear about it?'

Beth couldn't help smiling in response to his enthusiasm. She had a feeling that whatever it was he had just pulled off, it was probably only just on the right side of legal. Her smile deepened. He and Simon were not so different really. As Simon once said, Geoff had had a few more breaks.

As she sat back to listen to him talk, Beth enjoyed the feeling of his hand resting on her knee. As she moved her legs slightly, she noticed the way his eyes brightened. It would not take much to distract him from finance as she had done before in his car. It wouldn't take much to distract herself, either. She was still on edge from what she had witnessed earlier and from the idea of enjoying John again. She parted her legs slightly, so that his hand slipped on to her inner thigh.

Gradually, through her growing arousal, she began to register that he had changed the subject. As she focused on what he was now saying, all thoughts of seducing him fled from her mind. She shifted in her seat so that his hand could no longer reach her and concentrated all her attention on his words. She found her mind racing ahead of him at the mention of a company that was gaining power rapidly. Another company she had heard of was in a similar position and she realised that they could dramatically increase their hold on the financial world if they worked together as one company.

'Are they going to merge?' she blurted out excitedly.

'Merge? Did I say anything about a merger?' His eyes sparkled mischievously.

'No, but you obviously think it's on the cards. The benefits to both companies and their stockholders are obvious.'

'Um. In what way?' Geoff was staring at her intently.

'Well, Donald has recently taken over as chief executive at Torrins. He's been looking to protect his market share and increase it.' Beth was thinking aloud. 'A merger with MM would not only cut his closest competitor out of the market but, by rationalising, he could reduce overheads and increase potential. MM have several factories not working at maximum capacity, whereas Torrins factories are . . .' she stared at Geoff questioningly ' . . . are they old? I seem to remember that they had problems not too long ago?'

'Health and safety inspection,' Geoff prompted her.

'Right. So, if the buildings can't easily be salvaged then it might be cheaper just to merge with Torrins and use all their capacity.'

Geoff smiled.

'Torrins's company report is due out soon,' Beth continued thoughtfully. 'The shares are already dropping. With a year like the one they've just had, they're bound to fall even further.'

'Next Thursday,' Geoff nodded. 'The report is due next Thursday.'

Beth stared at him. That information was worth a small fortune. Why did he mention it? 'Are you involved with this?' she questioned softly.

Geoff shook his head. 'No, sadly not. If I tried to take advantage of it, my actions would be spotted immediately and any element of surprise would be lost.' He smiled ruefully. 'Besides, the truth is I can't release sufficient funds at the moment to make it worth my while.'

'Is that why you invited Simon here?'

Geoff looked startled. 'Good God, no.' He patted her hand. 'No, I just wanted to test you. Up until now, your deductions have been spot on.'

'But –' Beth prompted.

'You've got great instincts, Beth.' He paused and his face grew thoughtful, as if he was searching for the right words. 'It's difficult to explain. Once in a while, you find someone special. I could have mentioned this information to half a dozen people here today. Indeed, I have brought the subject up with one or two. Although they had a few good suggestions, none of them considered a merger or remembered the annual report and its consequences.' His fingers began to play with hers. 'You, however, came to the point straight away without any prompting. I want you to think hard about my offer. I really could use your talents.'

When Beth didn't respond, he continued, 'You would be welcome to stay here during the week if it's too far for you to travel. I've got some property in town that you could use, if you prefer. I'd pay a very competitive salary. Better than most.' He smiled again. 'Well, I won't push anymore. Take a few weeks to think it over and make use of what we have just discussed if you can.'

As Beth continued to stare at him, her mind was already running on overdrive. She was suddenly certain what Simon's secret computer file must contain and equally certain of how she was going to make use of it for herself. If only she could figure out what his password was. There must be some way to make him reveal it to her.

Geoff stood up and held out his arm to help her to her feet. 'Well, it's nearly seven thirty,' he told her. 'Much as I hate to break this up, we both need to change ready for dinner. I can't completely ignore my other guests.' He squeezed her arm. 'I can see your mind is already hard at work,' he told her as he patted her gently.

Impulsively, Beth turned and wrapped her arms around him. Hugging him tight, she gave him a big kiss. 'Thank you,' she whispered. 'For everything.'

Geoff grinned. 'Oh, being nice to a beautiful woman is one pleasure I'll never tire of. Would it also be helpful if I arranged to get Simon out of your way towards the end of next week?'

Beth thought quickly. Even if she could break his password and did find what she expected to find, she would still need some time to set everything up. She nodded. 'How about Friday?' she suggested.

'Done. And now,' he guided her towards the door, 'duty calls.'

Beth nodded, her mind barely registering his words as her plans chased each other round her head. If she could pull it off, she wouldn't have to work for Simon or Geoff. She felt a slight twinge of guilt so far as Geoff was concerned but none at all about what she hoped to do to Simon.

'I know this sounds a bit silly,' she confessed,' but I can't remember how to find my room. I was lost earlier when you found me.'

Geoff laughed. 'I can't imagine you ever being lost for anything,' he replied. 'Come on, I'll escort you.'

After a hot shower, Beth dressed carefully. Since she was only wearing her red dress that Simon had bought her in Rome and a pair of sandals, it didn't take her very long. The dress was so skimpy that she couldn't resist the temptation not to wear anything under it. She would have to be very careful how she moved or she would expose a lot more than just a bare thigh.

She practised parading around the room and soon discovered that if she took small steps, she could just about get away with it. She lengthened her stride and was rewarded with a perfect view of her newly shaven mound in the mirror. She would certainly have to save the longer strides for special moments!

By eight thirty, Beth was moving slowly down the wide staircase. She was well aware of how striking she looked and not surprised to see heads turning to watch her descend. The red of the dress was perfect for her dark colouring and the cut looked like it had been made especially for her. It clung in all the right places, then fell gracefully to the floor, emphasising her figure and poise. The material was so thin and light, it felt as if she wasn't wearing anything. It was a wonderful choice. At least Simon wasn't completely useless!

She had been so shaken by Geoff's business proposition that she had completely forgotten about Daniel and the maid until she spotted some maids serving drinks. Suddenly, it all came flooding back and, between the erotic images in her mind and the soft caress of the sexy dress on her naked body, she found that she was feeling incredibly aroused. She watched the maids closely, wondering if Daniel's friend would dare to appear among them.

Beth jumped as Simon appeared beside her out of nowhere and took her by the arm. As he steered her towards a quiet corner, Beth managed to grab a glass of champagne from a passing tray. She took a big gulp to steady her nerves and felt the bubbles stinging the inside of her nose.

'Where the hell have you been?' Simon hissed as soon as they were out of hearing. 'I've been looking for you for hours.'

'I was with Geoff Stevens.' Beth took another sip of her drink.

Simon looked surprised, then pleased. 'And?'

'I . . .' Beth paused for effect and took another sip. She realised that Simon was hanging on to her every word and growing more agitated by the second. She suppressed the urge to giggle and gulped hard. 'I, I, let him be nice to me,' she confessed breathlessly.

Simon's eyes widened. 'What did he do?' He was obviously fascinated by the idea of Beth obeying his instructions. She could almost see the feeling of power it gave him.

'I can't talk about it.' She gave him a pleading look.

Simon leered crudely. Before she could react, he stepped even closer, pushed his hand inside the slit of her dress and started to stroke her mound. Beth gasped with surprise and shock.

Her first instinct was to slap his face. She hated the thought of making a scene. Her treacherous body writhed with delight at his knowing touch; she was already so keyed up that it was enough to send her wild. She took a deep breath and prayed no one was watching. The look on her face and the way her body was squirming helplessly would have been a clear indication of what was going on.

Simon's quickened his caress and the breath whooshed from her before she could stop it. She could sense her orgasm building urgently and wasn't sure whether to try and stop him before it was too late or let him finish her. As a small whimper burst from her swollen lips, a loud gong sounded, making them both jump.

'Ladies and gentlemen, dinner is served.'

Simon slowly and reluctantly slipped his fingers out from her dress. Beth swayed slightly, her knees buckling with the intensity of her need. Simon held her arm to steady her.

'You know what I like about you most, Beth?'

She shook her head, not trusting herself to speak.

'I like the expression on your face when I take you. The way you submit to my will. I want you bent over my desk, waiting for me at the office on Monday morning.'

With supreme effort, Beth found a little spark of resistance. 'I can't. It's the wrong time,' she informed him.

Simon shrugged. 'Nevertheless. I want you without any knickers. After you have shown me what you've got, we'll find a good use for those hot lips of yours.'

Beth put on her most submissive face and nodded silently. She bit her lips and blinked as if trying to hold back the tears. Simon grinned.

'Excuse me.' As Simon moved across the room to join his wife, Beth felt another shiver of lust tear through her body.

Much as she loathed Simon, she couldn't resist the opportunity to torment him. Jesus, how she loved to tease men that way, provoking them until they didn't know whether to beg her to stop or beg her not to! She remembered how she had played with Daniel and the way his body had shuddered and writhed at her touch. Monday morning promised to be very interesting. By the time Beth was through with him, Simon would be so desperate for release that he would be forced to push her away and wank himself.

As she followed Simon and his wife, Beth took another deep breath. She realised that she was dreading dinner. If she didn't find a way to calm herself down, she was going to have trouble sitting still. She started to wonder if it were possible to bring herself off by squeezing her thighs together under the table without anyone noticing. The thought made her even more excited.

As she walked into the dining-room, she spotted John. To her astonishment, he was dressed in a kilt and sporran. She stared at him in amazement, realising that she had never thought about the significance of his slight Scottish accent before. She had to admit that he looked fantastic.

John's eyes lit up when her saw her. He walked confidently over to her. 'It seems I get the pleasure of your company again for dinner,' he told her.

Memories of their last meal together rushed into her mind. She forced a smile. 'How so?'

'I'm seated right next to you.'

Beth remembered how he had arranged the seating at the restaurant. 'How did I manage to be so lucky?' she questioned.

'Oh, just fate,' he smiled. 'Besides, I happened to nip in earlier and rearrange the seating cards.' He grinned. 'Hell, you didn't want to sit next to that prick Simon, did you?'

Beth laughed, loving the sheer audacity of the man. 'Well done, John.' She reached out and pulled him closer. 'I've still got those photocopies,' she whispered impishly.

John shrugged. 'And I've still got your knickers,' he replied quickly. 'I even wore them to work one day.'

'Only once?' Beth shammed disappointment.

John nodded. 'The trouble was that all I could think about all day was you. I had such a hard on they couldn't contain me. Most uncomfortable.' He grimaced. 'Shall we sit down?'

Beth laughed as he guided her over to the huge table. She was surprised and pleased by his confession. The thought of what he must have looked like in her panties with everything poking out was both amusing and thrilling.

John held her chair as she sat down cautiously and carefully arranged her dress over her legs. As he sat down beside her, he shifted his own chair closer to her and casually moved his place setting across.

Beth glanced around curiously at the other diners. She couldn't help noticing that, although attractive, many of the other women looked overdressed with their jewellery, frills and complicated hairstyles. She saw several men examining her appreciatively and felt even more pleased with her own simple dress and loose hair. She knew that she looked stunning.

As their wine glasses were filled and the first course served, Beth turned towards John. 'So, how have things been for you since York?' she asked him politely.

'Very quiet,' he responded. 'The excitement went out of my life after you left.' As he spoke, she felt him put his hand under the table on to her thigh. 'Still, I'm hoping that will soon change for the better.'

His fingertips began to trace small circles on her leg and Beth felt the goosebumps rising over her body at his soft touch. One of the waiters came over to serve the soup and she sighed with disappointment as John moved his hand away.

Beth looked up to thank the waiter, then froze when she realised that it was Daniel's friend, this time playing a more masculine role. She wondered what he would do if he realised that she knew his secret. Would he dress as a maid for her, if she asked him? Doing her best to ignore her urgent arousal, she forced herself to concentrate on what John was saying. The last thing she needed at the moment was to let herself become even hornier than she already was.

As soon as the waiter moved away, John put his hand back on to her leg. She felt him slip his fingers underneath the slit of her dress. He began to softly stroke her bare flesh, his fingers gradually moving higher. She gritted her teeth and hoped he could not see the effort it was costing her to keep still. Did he have any idea how much she longed for him to put his hand between her legs and caress her already throbbing bud?

She almost groaned with frustration as he moved his hand away and resumed eating his soup. She glanced at him surreptitiously, trying to assess how excited he was, but his face gave nothing away. Damn his self-control. This thought reminded her of her hotel lover and it was on the tip of her tongue to ask him outright if it was him. What if he denied it? How he would revel in her admission of an unknown man possessing her so completely! She couldn't risk it.

As she finished her soup, it occurred to her that she had the ideal opportunity to discover for herself the truth about what Scotsmen wear under their kilts. She quickly dropped her hand under the table and placed it on John's knee.

Although his face showed no obvious reaction, she noticed with delight the way his muscles were stiffening as her fingers travelled slowly up his leg. As she moved higher and higher, his hand started to tremble and his breathing quickened. Resisting the urge to go all the way, Beth changed direction and began sliding her fingers back down towards his knee.

She felt him relax slightly and watched him lift his spoon to take another mouthful of soup. Quickly, she slipped her hand back up and grinned as half the soup slurped messily into his bowl. John grabbed his napkin and wiped his mouth. His hands were trembling again.

'Wonderful soup,' she commented conversationally as he tried to take another mouthful. Her hand moved even higher and he quickly put his spoon down. 'Or don't you like it?'

'I like it very much,' he assured her tightly as he carefully took a smaller amount and raised it to his lips. 'I'm just taking my time, so that I can savour every second.'

By the time he had managed to finish the last mouthful, his face was quite flushed. As the waiters began clearing away, he placed the spoon carefully back in the bowl and turned his head towards her. 'Touché.' He smiled.

Beth saw beads of sweat on his forehead as he ran his finger round his collar. 'It is rather warm in here, isn't it,' she commented wickedly.

Before he could reply, she turned round to respond to a question that the elderly gentleman on the other side of her had just asked about where she worked. She shifted her chair around slightly so that she could talk to him, at the same time managing to move it even closer to John. The waiters began serving the next course.

When she turned back, she felt the warmth of John's knee next to hers. Although the food was excellent, she ate without noticing what she was putting in her mouth. John's thigh continued to burn her and, finally, she could no longer resist the temptation to continue her exploration. As she began to run her fingers slowly up his leg, she found herself hoping that he was wearing something so that she could take it off. Her fingers drew closer and closer to his cock and John swallowed loudly and reached for his wine.

Beth grinned at the pained expression on his face as he chewed each mouthful of food slowly and washed it down with the wine. She slid her hand between his legs and jumped as she discovered his nakedness. John shifted his buttocks, trying to move her fingers closer to his penis. She pulled away teasingly and turned back to resume her conversation with the man on the other side of her.

John finished his food and leant across her to join in. He placed his arm casually on the back of her chair and turned round so that his thigh was pushed firmly against her buttocks. Suddenly, his hand dived under her dress, homing straight in on her swollen bud. She gasped with shock and quickly covered her mouth with her hand.

'Oh, excuse me,' she apologised to the elderly man. She felt John push the flap of her dress over her leg until she was completely exposed. She could only pray no one would drop anything and bend down under the table to look for it.

'It's probably the garlic,' the man told her. 'It always gets to me, too.' As he launched himself into a long and rambling diatribe about his digestive system, Beth gritted her teeth and tried to cross her legs to stop John from overexciting her.

She felt him shift his hand so that he was stroking her thigh and buttocks. Every now and then, he pushed his fingers higher and caressed her clit from underneath. She realised that perspiration was running down between her breasts with the effort of maintaining a straight face. She didn't dare let him push her over the edge. She knew that she would cry out and then everyone would know.

As another course was being served, she managed to

sit back straight in her chair but could not stop John from sliding his hand between her thighs again. She clamped them together as hard as she could so that his fingers could barely move, but the pressure was almost as exciting and dangerous as his caresses. She was almost swooning with the effort of controlling herself by the time the final dishes were cleared away and the men began to light cigars and call for brandy.

'I need some fresh air,' she whispered huskily. 'Would you like to take that walk now?'

John raised his eyebrow and, to her relief, finally pulled his hand away. 'I was rather hoping for something a little more strenuous than a walk,' he replied.

Beth carefully rearranged her dress before she stood up, swaying slightly on legs too shaky to work properly. John grabbed her arm to steady her as he escorted her round the furniture towards the french windows on the far side of the room.

Beth looked round at the other guests and noticed several flushed faces and hungry looks. She wondered if she and John were the only ones playing games under the table. Simon looked as if he had had too much to drink. He was talking to Geoff and had pulled Marie's chair out from the table so that he could put his hand on her knee.

Marie looked slightly embarrassed as her husband pushed her skirt upwards, revealing more of her leg. Geoff had an amused expression on his face and Beth was sure that he knew what Simon was offering him and was enjoying the view. She realised that it wouldn't take much to turn the party into an out-and-out orgy.

John steered her out the door and she breathed in deeply to help calm herself down. The air was thick with the scent of honeysuckle and there was a slight dampness as if it had been raining. Beth realised that the gardeners must have been watering not long ago. She wondered if they used automatic sprinklers and thought how pleasant it would be to strip off and run naked through the icy spray.

Without saying anything, John continued to guide her purposefully along various twisting paths and Beth had the feeling that he was leading her to some quiet, secluded spot he had already scouted out. His arm slipped down her back until it was resting on her bottom, squeezing it gently in time with his steps. She placed her own hand on his buttocks and considered flipping up his kilt the way the boys at school used to flip up the girls' skirts.

They turned another corner and Beth saw that they had arrived at a secluded alcove with tall hedges all around and a wooden bench in the centre. John tried to lead her over to the bench but Beth stopped short and pulled him round in front of her, then manoeuvred him until he was standing behind the bench.

As soon as she placed his hand on the back of the bench John seemed to understand her intention. As she pushed him gently between the shoulders, he obediently bent over. Beth stood behind him and took hold of the hem of his kilt. Slowly she raised it, gradually revealing the top of his thighs and the curve of his bum. She tucked the hem into the waistband and stooped down to examine him critically.

'Very nice.' She ran her hands down the outside of his thighs then pulled his legs back, forcing him to bend even lower. She slid her hands over his buttocks, smiling as he tensed his muscles. She moved down to his inner thighs and pushed them apart until she could see his balls dangling under him. She crouched even lower and shuddered at the sight of his enormous erection thrust out hungrily in the air. She pushed her hand under him, palm upwards, and wrapped her fingers round it.

John shivered and moved his legs wider apart to give her better access. Beth let go of him and stepped away. 'I didn't tell you to move,' she scolded as she lifted her arm and slapped his left buttock. It made a beautiful sound but she wasn't sure if his bottom stung as much as her own hand. She flexed her fingers and slapped the other cheek.

'Forgive me, Mistress Beth. I won't let it happen again.' Although she could hear the amusement in his voice, she thought she also detected a note of desperation and longing. It sent a rush of desire coursing through her.

Beth grabbed him roughly by the ear. She pulled him round to face her, then tugged him slowly downward until he was kneeling on the ground in front of her. Her eyes lingered over his hardness and she licked her lips as she pushed his knees apart with her foot.

God, he looked fabulous. She ran her eyes up his strong, muscular legs, noticing the way the dark hair gradually grew thicker around his crotch. His cock stuck out like a pole; hard and swollen with its single-minded desire to pleasure her body.

Beth stood in front of him with her legs slightly apart. She lifted the flap of her dress with one hand and then pulled his head towards her. John immediately put his hands on her legs and gently kissed her inner thighs. She thrust her hips forward and mewed softly as his tongue found her engorged sex. As his hands moved round her waist and began to slide up towards her breasts, she grabbed them roughly and pulled them back on to her bottom, forcing him to pull her harder on to his tongue.

John pulled her legs further apart so that his tongue could push right up inside her. Beth whimpered louder and lifted one leg over his shoulder. She dug her heel into his back to steady herself and moaned again as he thrust his tongue even deeper inside her. As she swayed, John put one hand on the small of her back to hold her. His other hand was already fondling her bottom, his fingers gradually parting her cheeks.

Beth jumped then gasped with surprise and pleasure as his fingers eased into her crack and his fingertip began to push gently on her anus. His tongue continued to slip in and out of her, moving faster and faster as he felt her responding. It was all she could do now to keep her balance. If John had not been holding her so tightly, her legs would have collapsed completely.

She started to pant desperately as his tongue relentlessly devoured her. She could sense her orgasm swelling up inside her, like a rain cloud ready to burst. Her vaginal muscles flexed violently, pushing against his unrelenting caresses. She felt him automatically thrust even deeper inside her and she shuddered and cried out as a powerful climax overwhelmed her.

Breathing hard, Beth finally untangled her leg and stepped back. John started to get up.

'I didn't tell you to move, did I?' Beth stopped him with her hand. 'I haven't finished with you yet.' She was so weak from pleasure that she wasn't quite sure what to do with him next. She stared down at him, noticing that his kilt has fallen over his groin again.

'I didn't tell you to cover yourself, either,' she complained as she took hold of his ear again and forced him down on to all fours. With her foot, she pushed his head down until it was almost resting on the ground.

'Now, pull your kilt up slowly,' she commanded as she moved round behind him to watch. Her breathing had slowed and the strength was already flowing back into her limbs. The sight of his kilt gradually rising up over his rump, revealing all, sent a little tremor of renewed desire rushing through her. She crouched down and stroked the soft skin behind his balls.

'Oh, Jesus!' John groaned with desperation and raised his buttocks into the air so that the base of his cock was completely exposed to her. It didn't seem possible that he could be so big.

'Stand up and turn around,' she whispered.

He obeyed her instantly, his whole body trembling as he stood in front of her. Beth took his hands and placed them on the hem of his kilt. She gestured upward with her hands and then held her breath as he lifted the material up to his shoulders, revealing all. She was consumed with an almost overwhelming urge to watch him pleasure himself.

'Strip,' she commanded urgently.

She watched breathlessly as he obeyed her. Naked, he stood in front of her with a slight smile on his face, making no attempt to cover himself. Beth shivered in anticipation.

'Take yourself in one hand. That's it. No, don't move your fingers. Good.' The sight of him holding his bursting cock between his fingers was so exciting Beth could barely contain herself. She slipped the straps of her dress off her shoulders and down her arms, wriggling her hips so that the whole garment slid slowly down her body.

John stared at her eagerly as his hand glided slowly up and down his shaft. Beth frowned and shook her head. He immediately stopped and gripped himself tighter, squeezing himself urgently. She saw his knuckles flexing slightly as he tried to tighten and loosen his grip without her noticing. His whole body was trembling with his passion.

'Don't tell me you need to pee?' she teased, grinning at the way his eyes silently acknowledged her revenge. His hand stopped moving.

Beth stepped out of her dress. Naked apart from her sandals, she walked slowly round him a couple of times, trying not to smile at his unblinking eyes or the way he twisted his head to follow her. He reminded her of an owl. She noticed the way his fingers were gently squeezing his cock again as he slid his hand up and down as slowly as he could.

'Eyes front,' she snapped like a drill sergeant. She whacked his buttocks with the flat of her hand. 'And keep your hand still.'

John spun his head round and did his best to stand to attention. His penis was doing a better job of it. Beth couldn't remember ever seeing anyone so big and stiff.

'Now, lie down on your back,' she told him.

As John lowered himself to the ground, she was delighted to see that he continued gripping himself. She stood over his head with one leg on either side and then crouched down, lowering herself on to his mouth. John obligingly opened his lips and started licking her thighs and mound.

Beth sighed and leant forward to rest her hands on his stomach. She used one hand to push his fingers away and then began to examine his penis inch by inch with her fingertips. She heard him suck in a deep, shuddering breath and then felt his tongue prising her sex lips apart. As he pushed it up into her, she tightened her fist around him and felt his hips lift as he pushed himself urgently upward.

Beth let go of him and deliberately moved his own hand on to his penis. John sighed with disappointment and stopped tonguing her.

'You do it,' she commanded him.

As he began to pump himself, his tongue slipped into her again. She whimpered with longing and pushed down against him, so that her breasts were hard against his chest. She watched, fascinated, as his hand started to move harder and faster.

John moaned and pushed his hips up into the air, his whole body shuddering. She could see the tip of his penis glistening and feel the urgency of his tongue as his climax approached. He was groaning uncontrollably now and writhing helplessly from side to side. His hand was moving up and down almost too quickly to see.

'Christ, Beth. I can't hold on. Don't you realise what you're doing to me? Oh Jesus!'

Beth lifted herself up and pulled away. She was not quick enough. With another frantic grunt, John exploded. His come shot out of him like a firehose, shooting up into the air and splattering over his stomach. A few drops sprayed across her left breast.

Gradually, his hand slowed and stopped. He lay back, panting, with his eyes closed. Beth knelt down beside him and pushed her knee against his chest. John opened his eyes and smiled up at her. She pouted and pointed at the small white patch of come on her breast.

John stared at her for a moment, his face puzzled. Beth frowned and pushed her chest closer to him. Slowly and reluctantly, John raised his head and started to lick her breast clean. Beth sat perfectly still, savouring the soft caress of his tongue. Finally, she stood up and picked up her dress. As she wiggled back into it, she smiled and nodded her satisfaction.

'Very good. I shan't need you again tonight.'

She walked away quickly without looking back. By the time she reached her room, she was having trouble keeping her eyes open. She was asleep almost before her head touched the pillow.

The following morning at breakfast, Simon announced his decision to leave early. Beth smiled to herself at his sour face, knowing that the weekend had proved a big disappointment to him. He was in such a hurry to leave that she barely had time to say goodbye to Geoff. She did not see John at all.

On their way home, she did her best to draw Simon and Marie into conversation, trying desperately to get one of them to say something that would give her a clue to Simon's password. When they dropped her off outside her house, however, she was still none the wiser.

After a lazy afternoon and evening in front of the television, Beth went to bed early. Her sleep was restless and filled with confused and erotic dreams of John, Daniel and Chris. At three thirty, she woke with a start and sat up straight, her heart pounding. Had Simon's son inadvertently given her the information she needed?

Beth was so excited that it took her a long time to get to sleep again. She awoke early and was in the office an hour before Simon was due to arrive. As she sat at the keyboard, her fingers were shaking so much that she could barely find the right keys.

'M, I, D, A, S.' She mouthed the letters as she typed. She almost shouted with joy when she was rewarded with a small beep and the message 'PASSWORD ACCEPTED' flashed on to the screen. Yes!

As soon as the file opened, Beth knew her guess had been correct. It was Simon's private little slush fund. Wouldn't the tax office like to have a look at this little lot?

Beth quickly closed the file again. Well, that was it. All the pieces were in place. She simply had to make a copy of the file so that Simon wouldn't see any evidence of her tampering, punch in the transaction and wait. She started to open the morning mail. Would Geoff keep his promise to get Simon out of the way on Friday? Would she have the guts to go through with it?

As soon as he arrived, Simon hurried across the office and stood in her doorway.

'Well, well,' he said. 'Caught you.'

Beth froze in panic. Oh God! He had guessed what she was doing. She opened her mouth to try to defend herself, then stopped. He couldn't see her computer screen from where he was standing. Of course. She was supposed to be ready and waiting for him without any knickers on. In her excitement, she had completely forgotten about that. She looked back up at him.

Simon frowned and pointed over his shoulder. Beth walked through the door into his office. Simon pushed her over to his desk. Before she could say a word, he pushed her down over it, whipped her dress up and ripped her panties off.

Roughly, he reached round and pulled the front of her dress apart, then pushed her bra up. Cupping her breasts in his hands, he started to kiss the nape of her neck. As he reached down to release his trousers, she could feel his erection pushing firmly into the crack of her buttocks. She gasped with pleasure and then sighed as she remembered she had told him it was the wrong time of the month. Jesus! Was he going to take her in the bottom instead? She felt a thrill of excitement and clenched her buttocks around his erection as he pushed against her.

Suddenly, he stepped away and spun her round to face him. He put his hands on her shoulders and pushed her down on to her knees. As he grabbed the back of her head with one hand, he took his hard cock in the other.

Before she could do or say anything, Simon shoved his cock into her mouth. Using both hands to pull her head harder on to him, he thrust himself right to the back of her mouth and began to push her head back and forth, pumping himself.

Beth swallowed hard and tightened her lips around him. He thrust once more and then climaxed abruptly. She heard him groan with ecstasy and felt him spurt powerfully into her. As soon as he was completely spent, he pulled back and looked down at her.

'Now dress me,' he demanded.

Beth took a shuddering breath and swallowed. He must have been thinking about her all the way to work to have been in that much of a hurry. She reached up and took his now flaccid penis in her fingers. She pushed it gently back into his pants and pulled up his trousers, then stood up and looked down at her gaping dress and lowered panties.

As Beth bent down to pull them up, Simon grabbed her hand and shook his head. Beth tried to look submissive and kicked her panties off. He raised his eyes and stared meaningfully at her breasts. Slowly, she pulled her arms out of her dress and undid her bra.

Her clothes fell in a heap on the floor. Beth stepped over them and stood, naked and shivering, with her arms crossed over her chest and her head hanging down like a young virgin slave girl. She began to fantasise that she was being displayed for sale at a slave market and that Simon was a prospective customer. The urgency of her growing passion blazed deep within her.

Simon stared at her without comment. Beth let her hands drop to her sides and looked up at him hopefully.

'What appointments do I have today?' he questioned.

'Um?' The question took her by surprise. Disappointment rushed through her at the realisation that he wasn't planning anything more. 'Just Mrs Brown at eleven o'clock, I think.' She picked up her dress and slipped it back on.

'When she comes in, I want you hidden under the desk sucking my dick,' he informed her.

Beth stared at him and then shook her head.

Simon turned her round and lifted her dress. She jumped at the sudden sting of his hand on her naked skin. He slapped her again, then again.

'All right,' she said quickly. By the time she was finished with him, this would be one idea he was definitely going to regret.

The following Friday, Simon disappeared from the office soon after arriving. He had a conceited, confident look on his face and Beth wondered exactly what Geoff had offered him by way of incentive. Whatever it was, she had a feeling that he was about to be disappointed again.

As soon as he was gone, she copied his private file on to a separate disk and then called her stockbroker and purchased as many shares in Torrins as she could get hold of. She set the amount the shares were to be sold at just prior to close of market for the weekend, then watched anxiously. To her relief, after an early fall, the shares began to rise steadily around midday.

All she could do now was wait and pray. It was likely to be a very long weekend.

Chapter Thirteen

*B*eth arrived at the office very early. She quickly logged on to the computer and typed the password. Simon wasn't an early riser on Mondays. Beth could only pray that today would not be the exception.

As soon as the data appeared, she scanned the account anxiously. The figures took a few seconds to sink in, then her face split into a broad grin. It had worked! Swiftly, Beth transferred Simon's money back to where it belonged and diverted the gains to her own, newly opened private account.

Her heart was in her mouth as she watched the screen flickering. She was terrified that Simon would walk in at any moment and catch her. She raced over to the safe and took out the backup disk she had made, then hurried back to the computer.

Finally the message she was waiting for, 'TRANSACTION COMPLETE', came up. Beth quickly closed the account and loaded the backup disk. If anything, this seemed to take even longer. Beth glanced at her watch. Eight fifty. Simon could come through the door any second. She looked up at the screen. Eighty per cent complete. Jesus! The last ten per cent had taken longer than the previous seventy. She watched the figure move to ninety per cent, then ninety-eight. It hung there, without changing. Oh God, hurry!

As the words 'BACKUP RESTORED – DO YOU WISH TO REBOOT?' flashed on to the screen, Beth sighed with relief and slammed her finger on to the return key. The computer started to shut down. Still shaking, she pushed the eject button and made a grab for the backup disk. Her fingers slipped and the disk shot across the room.

Beth cursed aloud as she raced across the room to retrieve it. She pushed it back into its box and moved towards the safe. By the time she had slammed and locked the safe door and returned the key to Simon's desk, the computer had finished rebooting. Trembling from head to foot, she logged on.

She needed a drink. She couldn't stop shaking. Beth took a couple of deep breaths to try to steady herself, then hurried into Simon's office again. Without bothering to find a glass, she grabbed a bottle of scotch from his private supply and took a large swig. The fiery liquid made her gasp. She forced herself to swallow it and took another mouthful. Gradually, she felt her pulse steady. She put the bottle back in the cabinet and returned to her desk to make a start on opening the mail.

She had done it! There was now a very large amount of money safely stashed away in her off-shore account. She didn't need this job and didn't need to take the job with Geoff. She certainly wouldn't need anything from her ex-husband anymore, either. She was free!

Coffee. Shit! She had forgotten to make his morning coffee. Beth was just getting up when she heard Simon walk through the door. She waited, listening to him stomping around.

'Late in this morning, were you, Beth?' he called. Obviously, he had noticed the missing coffee. She heard him typing something at the computer. 'You really shouldn't take advantage of my good nature like this, you know,' he called.

Beth cringed. Had he discovered what she had done?

'I shall have to punish you.' Simon stuck his head round her door and examined her greedily. When she said nothing, he went towards her and grabbed her arm. Beth allowed herself to be led, unresisting, through to his desk.

Simon sat down and pulled her across his knee. He lifted her skirt and pulled her panties down slowly. She barely flinched as he slapped her buttocks, then rubbed her smooth skin gently.

'That will teach you to forget my coffee,' he told her. Beth sighed with relief. He didn't know. As he pushed her up on to her feet, she lifted her skirt and stared at her panties round her thighs.

'Put them back,' she commanded. 'You took them down.'

Simon smiled. As he pulled Beth's panties slowly back up over her still smarting rump, he leant forward and gently kissed her thighs and mound. Finally, he stopped and began to lower the panties again, his fingers gently caressing her legs.

'No.' Beth pulled away. It was time to set the final phase of his lesson in motion. 'Not here. Somewhere else. Somewhere with a bed. Somewhere where we won't be disturbed.' She moved closer. 'Somewhere where we can really let ourselves go.' She bent forward and deliberately stroked the bulge in his trousers.

'Your place,' Simon blurted out.

'No, somewhere else.' She smiled. 'I know a very discreet motel not far away. I could get us a room and then phone you.' She gave his bulge a gentle squeeze. 'While I wait, I could get ready for you. Dress up in something really sexy.' She could tell that Simon was going for it.

'I could pretend to be one of those women who visit lonely businessmen. No, better still, you could pretend to be one of those men who visit lonely businesswomen.' She gave his erection another squeeze.

'I'm very demanding, you know.' She pushed him

240

down into the chair, lifted her skirt and sat astride his legs with her hands still caressing him. 'I expect my men to pleasure me until I beg them to stop. I only take the best. You are the best, aren't you?' She ran her finger down his groin.

Simon shivered. 'Now. Let's go now.'

'Not yet. You've got a ten o'clock appointment. We'll go at lunch-time. I'll book us a room and then you can satisfy me all afternoon.' Beth pushed her tongue into his ear.

'You'd like that, wouldn't you?' she whispered. 'I've never been properly satisfied yet.' Beth stood up, stepped away and slowly pulled her panties back up.

'OK, we'll do it.' She almost laughed at the lust in his eyes.

'You'll be begging me to stop before I'm finished with you.' Simon grinned wolfishly.

Beth smiled. 'I do hope so,' she replied in a voice filled with anticipation.

Although the rest of the morning passed slowly for Beth, she consoled herself by imagining how much more slowly it must be passing for him. At one o'clock, she picked up her coat and went into his office.

'Don't forget to bring some cash with you to pay for the room.'

Simon nodded. 'Don't take too long to call,' he told her excitedly.

For once, Beth had used her car. She drove quickly to the motel. On the way, she stopped at a post box and, with a self-satisfied grin, posted her letter of resignation to Simon. Knowing how angry he would be, she had no desire to be there when he learnt she was deserting him. A surge of elation rushed through her as she allowed herself to think about her future prospects with her newly acquired wealth.

As soon as she had registered at the motel reception, she found her room and unpacked the small suitcase she had put in the car that morning. Then she took a quick shower. Wrapped in a bath towel, she sat on the bed and phoned Simon to tell him exactly where she was. He answered it on the first ring and she smiled at the enthusiasm in his voice.

Quickly, she finished drying herself and then dressed to kill. After she had pulled the boob tube down over her breasts, she stepped into lacy panties and wriggled into a PVC skirt. Finally, she pulled on fishnet stockings and stepped into a pair of heels much higher than she normally wore.

Beth moved over to the mirror and applied a heavy coat of lipstick, then emphasised her eyes with eyeliner, dark-grey shadow and black mascara. She stared at her reflection in delight. She spun round and examined herself critically from all angles. Heavily made up, she looked just like a prostitute. Her stockings only just reached the bottom of her skirt, the boob tube was virtually see-through and the outline of her nipples was quite clear. It was perfect for the role she intended playing.

She was brushing her hair when the knock came. She moved over to the door.

'Who is it?'

'Me. Simon.'

Beth opened the door wide. Simon walked in quickly and his eyes widened when he saw her.

'Well, hello.' Beth smiled. 'Have you come for me?' she enquired with a slight lift of one eyebrow.

'Any second now,' Simon responded as he scanned her from top to toe. His eyes lingered on her breasts and the tops of her stockings.

Beth let him look for a few seconds then pushed the door closed, allowing her body to rub against him. The door clicked shut and Simon grabbed her from behind. As he kissed her neck, she felt his hands running all over her body. She let him fondle her for a while longer, then broke the embrace.

'Did you bring the money?'

'Yeah. How much?'

'Fifty pounds should cover it,' Beth replied.

Simon took out his wallet and counted out two twenties and a ten. Beth took the money and put it on the table. She took his hand and guided him towards the bed. Simon tried to grab her again but she moved nimbly out the way.

'No. This is my treat. You don't need to do anything. Just allow me to pleasure you.'

His face broke into a huge grin.

'I'm all yours.'

Beth smiled and stepped closer. She removed his jacket and hung it over the back of the chair. Standing in front of him, she loosened his tie and undid the buttons of his shirt. She placed his hands on each of her breasts while she carefully removed his cufflinks, then she opened his shirt and started to kiss his chest. Slowly, she peeled the shirt off his shoulders and down his arms. Then she knelt in front of him on the floor and removed his shoes and socks.

Simon put his hands on her shoulders to steady himself and Beth reached up and undid the catch on his trousers. As she slowly unzipped his trousers with one hand, her other hand slipped inside behind the zip so that her fingertips were caressing his erection.

Simon shuddered and took a deep breath. He let it out slowly as his trousers dropped round his ankles and Beth removed her hand. She ran her fingers up the inside of his leg and gave his balls a gentle squeeze. Simon sighed urgently and Beth smiled again as she pushed him backward on to the bed.

Leaning over him with one leg either side of his, Beth ran her hands down his chest. As they passed over his lean stomach and on to his pants, she traced the outline of his penis with her finger. She was fascinated to see that he had grown even bigger, so that the tip of his erection was now sticking out of his pants.

Beth moved on down his legs and removed his

trousers from around his ankles. She folded them neatly before placing them with his other clothes. When she turned around, Simon had moved up on to the bed and was lying back, waiting for her.

Beth pulled her panties down under her skirt and kicked them aside. She walked across to the bed and ran her fingers up his right leg, enjoying the way his body stiffened at her touch. She climbed on to the bed and swung a leg over him so that she was sitting across his chest with her back to him. She shuffled back slightly and raised her buttocks so that her sex lips were just above his mouth. She saw his cock spasm as she placed her hands on his stomach and pushed her fingers under the elastic of his pants to lift them up over his erection.

Simon sighed heavily and raised himself up so that she could pull them down over his buttocks. Beth slipped her hands round under him, allowing her nails to scratch his cheeks as she slid his pants down. Simon collapsed back on the bed, almost trapping her fingers underneath him.

She heard him moan urgently as she played with his hardness. When she started to make small circling motions round the tip with her fingers, Simon groaned and reached up to pull her down on to his mouth.

'Come here, you witch,' he whispered. He forced her sex lips open and drove his tongue deep into her. His hand slid under her and his fingers expertly sought out her swollen bud.

Beth closed her eyes for a moment and allowed the waves of longing to build up then, before she lost control, she moved off him.

'I see you are not going to behave.' She pulled the piece of cord out from where she had hidden it under the pillow, then climbed up over him again so that she was facing him. She lowered herself on to his mouth and began to rock back and forth as he licked and sucked her.

When she could take no more, Beth reached out,

grabbed his arms and raised them over his head. Simon ignored her, his tongue still busy probing her. Beth whimpered with excitement and struggled to contain herself as she tied his wrists together and attached them to the longer cord she had already secured to the headboard.

She put one hand behind his head, grabbed a handful of his hair and tugged him harder on to her. With her other hand she gently teased her puckered nipples.

Simon forced his tongue deep inside her and started to flick it in and out. Beth gasped with delight and started to caress her throbbing clit. She was so close to climaxing that she barely stopped herself from yelling aloud. She increased the pressure of her own hand and pulled his head even harder against her so that his tongue was deep inside her. She moaned loudly as she felt her climax flooding through her. Gradually, she relaxed and her movements slowed to a gentle rock. She gulped noisily, let go of his hair and moved off him.

'Well. I certainly seem to have caught myself a wild one here, don't I?' she whispered shakily.

'You'd better believe it.' Simon's grin seemed to cover his whole face. He tried to move his hands and, for the first time, seemed to realise that he was tied up. He pulled against the restraint, testing the strength of the knot and the length of the cord. Beth smiled.

'Now I shall be able to play with you without fear of you grabbing me,' she told him.

Before he could reply, Beth leant over and licked his now only semi-erect penis. She continued to tease it gently until it began to grow again. She loved watching a man growing like that in response to her touch. When he was completely stiff again, she reached under the pillow for a condom.

As she unrolled it down his length, she continued to play with him, pushing him from side to side and stroking him under the balls. She felt him gradually become stiffer and stiffer until he was as rigid as a board and his penis would no longer bend in her fingers.

Simon groaned and twisted in his pleasure, raising himself up off the bed as he tried to thrust into her hand. Beth teased until she felt sure that he couldn't take much more, then quickly mounted him, lowering herself down over him as Simon tried to push up into her.

Firmly, Beth pressed him back down on to the mattress and continued to lower herself on to him until he was fully enveloped. She began to stroke his chest with one hand and reached behind her to caress his balls with the other.

Simon grunted and tried to thrust up into her again but Beth was using all her weight to hold him down. She leant forward and bit his nipples again. Simon jumped and, with a desperate lunge, arched his back so that she was almost thrown up into the air as he pushed himself upwards. As they fell back, his cock rammed up so far into her that Beth gasped with shock, then cried out as he did it again. Instinctively, she tightened her vaginal muscles around him, squeezing him.

Simon's whole body went rigid and Beth noticed a tiny nerve on the side of his jaw begin to twitch as he struggled to keep himself under control. As he arched his back to thrust into her again, Beth dug her nails into his chest.

'Keep still,' she commanded as she increased the rhythmic caresses of her inner muscles.

Simon moaned softly and began twisting from side to side. She watched the droplets of sweat beading on his face as he drew his knees up and used his legs to push his whole body up, lifting them both off the bed. Even though she wasn't all that heavy, Beth was impressed by this desperate show of strength. For a while she allowed him to enjoy his success, losing herself in the enjoyment of the deep penetration.

As his gasps became more urgent, Beth reached round

with both hands and cupped his balls, squeezing them harder and harder to get his attention.

'Stop that. Keep still,' she repeated.

'Christ. I can't.' Simon gasped again and started to climax violently. As his seed pumped from him, he fell back on to the bed, moaning with pleasure. Beth continued to squeeze him as if trying to force every last drop out of him.

Completely spent, Simon lay still and closed his eyes. Beth lifted herself clear, peeled the condom off and wrapped it in some tissues. While he was still recovering, she picked up another piece of cord and tied his ankles so that his legs could only open about eight inches.

Simon opened his eyes and lifted his head. 'What the hell?' he tried to sit up but could only partly raise himself because of the cords on his wrists. 'What do you think you're doing?'

Beth smiled. 'You need to be restrained,' she replied as she used a final piece of cord to secure his feet to the end of the bed. She was careful to leave him enough slack to move around but not enough to leave the bed.

'If you're not careful, I'll tie you down completely so that you can't move anything but this.' Beth flicked his limp penis from side to side. 'Now, lie there and be a good boy while I go and freshen up.' She gave him another little stroke under the balls.

'I hope you're feeling fit,' she told him. 'You've got a lot more to do yet.' Beth stood beside him and, realising that her skirt was still right up over her bottom, pulled it down to cover her nakedness. Simon looked disappointed.

'Don't cover yourself. I like looking at your shaved snatch.'

Beth knelt on the bed beside him and lifted the front hem of her skirt to expose her mound. She opened her legs as far as her skirt would allow, then licked her finger and pushed it between her thighs. Simon's eyes bulged as she played with her clitoris. Using all the freedom

Beth had allowed him, Simon wriggled closer and put his head between her legs.

'So. You like me shaved, do you?' she questioned.

'Yeah!' Simon licked his lips.

As Beth continued to caress herself, she glanced round and was pleased to see that he was already partially erect again. She smiled and stood up.

'No. Don't stop. I want to watch you come.' Simon strained against the cords. 'I want –'

'I want,' Beth interrupted, mimicking him. 'What you want doesn't matter. It's what I want that counts now.' She put her damp finger to his mouth. 'Lick it,' she commanded.

Simon pulled her finger into his mouth and started to suck greedily. She looked down and saw his cock stiffen further. She smiled and pulled her hand back.

'Don't go away,' she told him as she headed for the bathroom, adjusting her skirt as she walked.

When she returned, she was carrying a bowl of warm water, a bar of soap and a towel. She placed the towel under him and started to wash his genitals thoroughly. At first, Simon thrashed about, trying to get free but, gradually, as she caressed his penis with soapy fingers, he stopped protesting and lay back contentedly.

Beth pushed a pillow under his buttocks so that she would be able to reach right under him, then sat across him so that his tongue could satisfy her again. She quickly worked up a rich lather and was delighted by the ease with which her fingers slipped up and down his soapy cock.

She sighed with anticipation as he started to probe deeper and deeper into her. King Midas certainly did have a golden tongue. She was sorely tempted to let him bring her off again, but reminded herself how draining multiple orgasms could be. She still had a lot to do. Reluctantly moving off him, she used a flannel to remove the soap from his penis and then began to pat him dry with the towel.

His cock was already rigid again and she pictured him standing in the shower, covered with soap, masturbating while she watched. It was very tempting but she couldn't afford to untie him. Not yet.

When he was as dry as she could get him, Beth stood up and dried her hands while she admired her efforts. His pubic hair was soft and fluffy, surrounding his rigid cock like a halo. It was a pity, but . . .

Beth returned the bowl to the bathroom and picked up the scissors. By the time she returned, Simon had closed his eyes again and was lying there with a self-satisfied smile on his lips. She sat over him with her back to him and took his cock in her left hand.

Simon strained forward. 'I can't reach you,' he complained, eyes still shut. Beth ignored him. Although his tongue was very tempting, under the circumstances she felt it was probably safer if he couldn't touch her. She raised the scissors and proceeded to snip his pubic hair away.

'Hey! What the hell do you think you're doing?' Simon struggled to sit up and tugged angrily at the wrist cords. Beth continued to ignore him as she carefully cut his pubes and dropped the bits on to the towel. Simon started to thrash his hips about. Beth stopped.

'Careful,' she laughed. 'You might make me cut the wrong thing.' She ran a finger up his rapidly shrinking prick. 'That would certainly ruin the rest of my afternoon.' She took another snip.

'Stop it, you bitch. Let me go. Bloody whore.'

'Bitch?' Beth questioned. 'Whore?' She pushed herself hard on to his face. 'I didn't notice you complaining earlier. Go on, lick me.'

Simon twisted his head angrily to one side and tugged furiously on the cords again. 'Let me go, damn you.'

Beth curled her fingers into his now short pubes and tugged hard. Simon grunted in shock and pain. 'Lick me.' She gave another tug, then moaned as he pushed his tongue deep inside her. 'That's much better,' she sighed. She squeezed his cock gently between her fingers and felt it twitch.

She moved off him again and examined his remaining hairs carefully, using the scissors to snip away the remaining strands on and around his balls. Simon watched in silence, holding his breath whenever the scissors touched his skin. His penis seemed to get smaller with every snip and she had to stretch it tightly in her hand so that she did not snip the skin.

As she gave the area a final inspection, she saw he was staring down at himself in horror. She heard him whimper softly and couldn't help laughing.

'Don't worry. I haven't finished yet. It will look much better after it's been shaved.' Simon whimpered again and Beth giggled. 'What a fuss over a little haircut. You men are so pathetic. It will grow back again.'

'When?' Simon whispered miserably.

'Oh, a few months.'

Simon gulped. Still laughing, Beth threw the clippings into the bin and went back into the bathroom to fetch another bowl of water, shaving cream and a razor. When Simon saw the razor, his face went white.

'Please don't, Beth. What am I going to tell Marie?'

'It's a bit late to worry about that now. You don't want me to leave it like that, do you?' She ran her hand over the stubble. 'You can always tell her that your barber got a bit carried away.' She knew it wasn't funny, but Simon was too busy staring in terror at the razor to notice.

When she placed the blade on his chest, Simon tensed as if it were a poisonous snake. Beth soaked his tackle again and began to cover it in shaving cream. She shivered at the way the cream spurted out of the can like a shower of spunk, and she rather overdid it in her excitement. When she realised what she had done, she scooped the excess off with her fingers and rubbed it into his tummy. She couldn't resist pumping him a few times with her slippery hands as well, enjoying the feel of it, even if he was too nervous to respond.

As Beth wiped her hands on the towel and then picked up the razor, Simon finally found his voice again.

'Please, Beth. I'll do it while you watch.'

Beth hesitated, almost tempted. She really didn't want to untie him. She shook her head and took hold of his prick to pull it tight. Her fingers slipped and Simon let out a terrified yelp. She wiped the tip of his cock with the towel and took hold of it again. Gently, she pulled him out to full length and began to shave the sides.

As she moved down, she pulled the skin of his balls tighter and ran the sharp blade over them, slicing the stubble away. Giving it her full concentration, Beth moved around him carefully, climbing on and off him to get into the best position. Simon barely seemed to breathe. Every time the blade touched him, his muscles tensed and his whole body went rigid.

When she had finished the crotch, Beth moved down and shaved under his balls, then moved up to do the base of his stomach. By this time, she was feeling so confident that she carefully shaped the hair at the base of his shaft into a heart. She put the blade down and washed the foam away, smiling with delight. Well, it almost looked like a heart if she squinted her eyes.

She dried her hands and ran her fingers over his hairless balls. She could hardly believe how smooth the skin felt. It was as soft as satin.

'Jesus Christ!' Simon took a long, shuddering breath. Beth grinned and ran her hand up his cock. He obviously hadn't suffered all that much. She could already feel him hardening again in response to her caresses.

She gathered up the shaving things and took them back in the bathroom. After she had rinsed them, she put them in her case and then stood at the end of the bed and stared down at him in silence.

It was quite a shock to see his cock and balls as naked as her own mound. His cock was so exposed; it seemed even bigger than ever. She shivered. It looked so rude, so sexy. No wonder men liked women to shave.

251

Beth moved round beside him. She took hold of his cock and pumped him until he was fully erect. As she put her other hand down between his legs and caressed the soft flesh of his balls again, another shiver of desire rushed through her. Simon lifted his head and stared at himself in silence. He seemed even more fascinated by his nakedness than she was.

'Now, how shall I pleasure myself next? Perhaps a hand job?' Beth pumped him harder and heard his sharp intake of breath as his cock twitched against her. 'Maybe I should suck it dry?' She bent over him and licked the tip with her tongue. Simon sighed and lifted his buttocks up eagerly.

There was a heavy knock at the door and Beth froze.

'Who the hell is that?' Simon hissed. 'Quick. Untie me.'

Beth stood up and pulled her coat around her shoulders. Before she could walk across the room, the outer door opened and someone entered the little passageway. A woman came into view and she heard Simon gasp in horror at the police uniform. Beth put her hand to her mouth in mock horror and dropped her coat as the policewoman stood in front of her.

The policewoman scanned the room quickly and her eyes widened. 'I see.' She bent down, picked up the coat and placed it round Beth's shoulders. Then she turned towards Simon, her face expressionless.

'It's not what you think,' Simon blurted out. 'She's my personal assistant. She works for me.'

'Yes, sir. I know. By the hour, I expect.' The policewoman moved over to the table and picked up the money that Simon had brought earlier. She counted it out slowly. 'Fifty pounds. Not bad for a hour's work.'

Beth opened her mouth as if to argue, but the policewoman waved her quiet. 'Don't bother. I've heard it all before. Your husband makes you do it. You've three children to feed and clothe. Your rent is due and you are going to be thrown out into the streets.' She glared at Beth.

'I really don't care why you do it.' The policewoman

moved closer to Beth and leant forward to run her hand up Beth's leg under her skirt. Beth and Simon both gasped.

'I suppose you always wear a short skirt and no knickers when you and your boss are working?' The policewoman grinned. 'Don't worry. I'm not going to run you in. It's not worth all the paperwork. The motel just wants me to make sure you don't come here again.'

She removed her hand from under Beth's skirt and gave her left breast a quick squeeze. 'I should have thought you could have done better than this, an attractive woman like you.' She put her hand back on Beth's leg and both women heard Simon gulp.

Beth glanced at Simon's reflection in the mirror. Despite the compromising position he was in, he was clearly enjoying watching what the policewoman was doing to Beth. Her eyes moved down his body and she saw that his cock was rapidly swelling. She swallowed hard and turned her head away quickly. She was having trouble stopping herself from laughing.

Ann was doing a marvellous job. Better than Beth had dared to hope. The uniform seemed to be giving her added confidence. It was almost as if she were a completely different person. Beth remembered the thoughts she had had about exploring Ann's body after her experience with Lisa. She felt a sudden shiver of longing as Ann's fingers continued to squeeze her breast.

'Do you understand?' Ann emphasised each word.

'Yes.' Beth's voice was squeaky with her growing passion.

'OK. Get dressed and go.' Ann watched in silence as Beth slammed her case closed and pushed her arms into her coat.

'What about these?' Ann picked up Beth's panties. 'You wouldn't want to go without them or I might have to arrest you for indecent exposure.'

Beth stifled another giggle, grabbed the panties and stuffed them into her pocket. She moved her head and saw Simon staring at Ann, wide eyed. 'What about him?'

'Oh, don't worry. I'll take care of him for you.' Ann licked her lips and walked across the room to the bed. Beth felt another pang of excitement.

'So, you like being punished, do you?' Ann asked Simon as she examined the cords at his hands and feet.

'Look, this is just a misunderstanding,' Simon began. He stopped abruptly as the policewoman ran her hand across his newly shaved groin.

'I've never seen a man with a bald cock before,' Ann told him. 'I can't remember if there's a law against it or not.'

Simon flushed from head to toe. 'Look, just let me go, will you?'

'What's your rush?' Ann caressed his naked cock again. 'I think you and I need to have a little chat about law and order first. Turn over.'

Simon stared at her in shock. Ann flicked his cock with her fingers. 'You're not going to disobey an officer of the law, are you?' She flicked his cock again. Simon strained against the slack of his wrist and leg ties and managed to half-roll over to protect himself.

'Nice bum. I'm going to enjoy this.'

Beth put her hand over her mouth to smother her laughter and backed out into the passageway. She could hardly believe that Simon was putting up with all this. Mind you, given the circumstances, what choice did he have?

Ann gave his backside a resounding slap and Simon flinched. She raised her hand and slapped him again, then again. His buttocks turned red.

'Turn over again.'

As Simon rolled over on to his back, Ann put her hand up her skirt and pulled her pants down. Beth looked down at Simon and saw how excited the spanking had got him. His cock was fully erect and twitching up and down. Or perhaps it was the uniform. She knew that some men got a kick out of that. Whatever the reason,

Beth was certain that Ann had now got him right where she wanted him.

Without a word, Ann climbed on to the bed and sat over him. She pulled up her skirt, revealing her suspenders, and wriggled up so that his tongue could lick her mound. She leant over and pulled his head on to her, then reached behind her and grabbed his throbbing cock in her fist.

Beth gulped at the sight of her friend and her boss together. In some ways, it was even more exciting than watching Daniel and his friend had been. She leant against the wall and lowered her hand down on to her mound. She was already dripping.

Ann climbed off Simon and put her mouth over his cock, licking and sucking it like a lolly. Simon writhed helplessly from side to side, straining against the cords at his wrists.

Beth slipped her hand up under her top and teased her nipples as she watched Ann pick up a condom and peel it down over Simon. She felt her clit tingling with anticipation and she pushed her fingers up hard inside herself.

Ann lifted herself up and crouched over Simon's groin, using one hand to guide his tip up into her. She put her hands on his chest and started to push herself up and down as if she was working out. Beth could see her friend's white buttocks bobbing up and down faster and faster as she got into her rhythm. She was consumed with the desire to go over and fondle her. Simon's balls bounced with every stroke and Beth could hear his urgent grunts as he raced towards his climax. She pumped herself harder with her finger and slid her other hand down to rub her engorged bud.

Simon groaned loudly and Ann's police hat fell from her head and bounced across the room. Ann whimpered with enthusiasm and thrust herself even harder down on to him, so that Beth could hear her friend's thighs slapping against Simon's groin. Simon groaned again and came. Beth gritted her teeth to stop herself crying out as her own orgasm enveloped her. Her ecstatic whimper was masked by the loud cry of release that burst from Ann's lips as she reached her own peak and slumped down on to Simon's stomach.

By the time Beth had recovered, Ann had already climbed off Simon and was pulling on her panties again. Simon was sprawled back on the bed, clearly exhausted by his experiences. It was only as Ann turned to leave that he seemed to remember he was still tied up.

'Wait. You can't leave me like this.'

'Oh, don't worry. I'll call room service for you.' Ann picked up the phone and pressed one of the buttons. Beth grabbed her case and slipped quietly out of the room. She was certain that Simon hadn't seen her. He seemed to have temporarily forgotten about her altogether. As she pulled the door to behind her, she heard Ann's voice on the phone:

'Could I have coffee for two in room 33, please. Thank you. Just let yourself in, will you? We are a bit tied up at the moment.' She replaced the receiver.

'I'm sure the waiter will sort you out,' Ann told Simon as she picked up her hat and headed out of the door. Beth giggled as she heard Ann's carefully planned final words: 'Of course, you may have to be nice to him.'

The two women hurried down the corridor and into the room Ann had already booked. Beth gave her friend a big hug.

'You were great, Ann,' Beth told her. 'Absolutely fantastic.'

Ann flushed with pleasure at the compliment and began to strip off her hired uniform. 'I can't remember when I last had so much fun,' she confessed. 'And, it's not over yet,' she added as she wriggled into her own clothes and stuffed the uniform into Beth's case.

The two women went back out into the corridor. A tall man carrying a tray was just knocking on Simon's door.

'Room service,' the man called as he opened the door. They hurried after him and positioned themselves just outside the open doorway.

'Oh my God,' the waiter – actually a friend of Ann – cried in surprise as he stepped into the room. 'Oh, sir. I didn't realise that's what you meant when you said you were tied up.'

Beth and Ann covered their mouths and peered round the door. Ann's friend had put the tray down and was standing by the bed, eyeing Simon up.

'Oh,' he twittered. 'I really like that shave. Very sexy. Especially the little heart.' He ran his hand up Simon's leg. 'I shall go straight home and shave myself just like that.'

Beth glanced at Simon. His face had gone completely white. 'Just let me go,' he whispered, so faintly that she only just made out his words.

'Oh, but sir. That would be such a shame.' The man's hand moved further up Simon's leg and Simon quickly rolled over on to his stomach. The man grunted with obvious delight and ran his hand over Simon's buttocks.

Beth turned to Ann. 'Your friend's gay, isn't he?' she accused. 'You never told me about that.'

Ann sniggered. 'Don't worry. He promised that he wouldn't take any real liberties. Well, not unless Simon encourages him, of course,' she added cheekily.

Beth started to laugh helplessly. There could be no doubt that Simon had been taught a lesson he wouldn't forget in a hurry.

'Come on, let's leave them to it. We've got some serious celebrating to do.' Beth grinned as she remembered her swollen bank account and her exciting future.

Still laughing, the two women turned away and headed out to Beth's car. They were already outside before Beth remembered that her panties were still in her pocket. She glanced excitedly at her friend's trim figure, already anticipating taking a few more liberties of her own.

Visit the Black Lace website at
www.blacklace.com

LOOK OUT FOR THE ALL-NEW BLACK LACE BOOKS – AVAILABLE NOW!

All books priced £7.99 in the UK. Please note publication dates apply to the UK only. For other territories, please contact your retailer.

To be published in September 2009

NO RESERVATIONS
Megan Hart and Lauren Dane
ISBN 978 0352 34519 6

Kate and Leah are heading for Vegas with no reservations. Both on the run from their new boyfriends and the baggage these guys have brought with them from other women. And the biggest playground in the west has many sensual thrills to offer two women with an appetite for fun. Meanwhile, the boyfriends, Dix and Brandon, realise you don't know what you've got 'til it's gone, and pursue the girls to the city of sin to launch the most arduous methods of seduction to win the girls back. None-stop action with a twist of romance from two of the most exciting writers in American erotica today.

MISBEHAVIOUR
Various
ISBN ISBN 978 0352 34518 9

Fun, irreverent and deliciously decadent, this arousing anthology of erotica is a showcase of the diversity of modern women's erotic fantasies. Lively and entertaining, seductive and daring, *Misbehaviour* combines humour and attitude with wildly imaginative writing on the theme of women behaving badly.

To be published in October 2009

THE THINGS THAT MAKE ME GIVE IN
Charlotte Stein
ISBN ISBN 978 0352 34542 4

Girls who go after what they want no matter what the cost, boys who like to flash their dark sides, voyeurism for beginners and cheating lovers . . . Charlotte Stein takes you on a journey through all the facets of female desire in this contemporary collection of explicit and ever intriguing short stories. Be seduced by obsessions that go one step too far and dark desires that remove all inhibitions. Each story takes you on a journey into all the things that make a girl give in.

THE GALLERY
Fredrica Alleyn
ISBN ISBN 978 0352 34533 2

Police office Cressida Farleigh is called in to investigate a mysterious art fraud at a gallery specializing in modern erotic works. The gallery's owner is under suspicion, but is also charming and powerfully attractive man who throws the young woman's powers of detection into confusion. Her long time detective boyfriend is soon getting Jealous, but Cressida is also in the process of seducing a young artist of erotic images. As she finds herself drawn into a mesh of power games and personal discovery, the crimes continue and her chances of cracking the case become ever more complex.

ALL THE TRIMMINGS
Tesni Morgan
ISBN ISBN 978 0352 34532 5

Cheryl and Laura decide to pool their substantial divorce settlements and buy a hotel. When the women find out that each secretly harbours a desire to run an upmarket bordello, they seize the opportunity to turn St Jude's into a bawdy funhouse for both sexes, where fantasies – from the mild to the increasingly perverse – are indulged. But when attractive , sinister John Dempsey comes on the scene, Cheryl is smitten, but Laura less so, convinced he's out to con them, or report them to the authorities or both. Which of the women is right? And will their friendship – and their business – survive?

Black Lace Booklist

Information is correct at time of printing. To avoid disappointment, check availability before ordering. Go to www.blacklace.com. All books are priced £7.99 unless another price is given.

BLACK LACE BOOKS WITH A CONTEMPORARY SETTING

- ❏ AMANDA'S YOUNG MEN Madeline Moore — ISBN 978 0 352 34191 4
- ❏ THE ANGELS' SHARE Maya Hess — ISBN 978 0 352 34043 6
- ❏ THE APPRENTICE Carrie Williams — ISBN 978 0 352 34514 1
- ❏ ASKING FOR TROUBLE Kristina Lloyd — ISBN 978 0 352 33362 9
- ❏ BLACK ORCHID Roxanne Carr — ISBN 978 0 352 34188 4
- ❏ THE BLUE GUIDE Carrie Williams — ISBN 978 0 352 34132 7
- ❏ THE BOSS Monica Belle — ISBN 978 0 352 34088 7
- ❏ BOUND IN BLUE Monica Belle — ISBN 978 0 352 34012 2
- ❏ CAMPAIGN HEAT Gabrielle Marcola — ISBN 978 0 352 33941 6
- ❏ CASSANDRA'S CONFLICT Fredrica Alleyn — ISBN 978 0 352 34186 0
- ❏ CASSANDRA'S CHATEAU Fredrica Alleyn — ISBN 978 0 352 34523 3
- ❏ CAT SCRATCH FEVER Sophie Mouette — ISBN 978 0 352 34021 4
- ❏ CHILLI HEAT Carrie Williams — ISBN 978 0 352 34178 5
- ❏ THE CHOICE Monica Belle — ISBN 978 0 352 34512 7
- ❏ CIRCUS EXCITE Nikki Magennis — ISBN 978 0 352 34033 7
- ❏ CLUB CRÈME Primula Bond — ISBN 978 0 352 33907 2 £6.99
- ❏ CONTINUUM Portia Da Costa — ISBN 978 0 352 33120 5
- ❏ COOKING UP A STORM Emma Holly — ISBN 978 0 352 34114 3
- ❏ DANGEROUS CONSEQUENCES Pamela Rochford — ISBN 978 0 352 33185 4
- ❏ DARK DESIGNS Madelynne Ellis — ISBN 978 0 352 34075 7
- ❏ DARK OBSESSION Fredrica Alleyn — ISBN 978 0 352 34524 0
- ❏ THE DEVIL AND THE DEEP BLUE SEA Cheryl Mildenhall — ISBN 978 0 352 34200 3
- ❏ DOCTOR'S ORDERS Deanna Ashford — ISBN 978 0 352 34525 7
- ❏ EDEN'S FLESH Robyn Russell — ISBN 978 0 352 32923 3
- ❏ EQUAL OPPORTUNITIES Mathilde Madden — ISBN 978 0 352 34070 2
- ❏ FIRE AND ICE Laura Hamilton — ISBN 978 0 352 33486 2

BLACK LACE BOOKS WITH AN HISTORICAL SETTING

BLACK LACE BOOKS WITH A PARANORMAL THEME

- ❏ THE SILVER CAGE Mathilde Madden   ISBN 978 0 352 34164 8
- ❏ THE SILVER COLLAR Mathilde Madden   ISBN 978 0 352 34141 9
- ❏ THE SILVER CROWN Mathilde Madden   ISBN 978 0 352 34157 0
- ❏ SOUTHERN SPIRITS Edie Bingham   ISBN 978 0 352 34180 8
- ❏ THE TEN VISIONS Olivia Knight   ISBN 978 0 352 34119 8
- ❏ WILD KINGDOM Deana Ashford   ISBN 978 0 352 34152 5
- ❏ WILDWOOD Janine Ashbless   ISBN 978 0 352 34194 5

BLACK LACE ANTHOLOGIES
- ❏ BLACK LACE QUICKIES 1 Various   ISBN 978 0 352 34126 6   £2.99
- ❏ BLACK LACE QUICKIES 2 Various   ISBN 978 0 352 34127 3   £2.99
- ❏ BLACK LACE QUICKIES 3 Various   ISBN 978 0 352 34128 0   £2.99
- ❏ BLACK LACE QUICKIES 4 Various   ISBN 978 0 352 34129 7   £2.99
- ❏ BLACK LACE QUICKIES 5 Various   ISBN 978 0 352 34130 3   £2.99
- ❏ BLACK LACE QUICKIES 6 Various   ISBN 978 0 352 34133 4   £2.99
- ❏ BLACK LACE QUICKIES 7 Various   ISBN 978 0 352 34146 4   £2.99
- ❏ BLACK LACE QUICKIES 8 Various   ISBN 978 0 352 34147 1   £2.99
- ❏ BLACK LACE QUICKIES 9 Various   ISBN 978 0 352 34155 6   £2.99
- ❏ BLACK LACE QUICKIES 10 Various   ISBN 978 0 352 34156 3   £2.99
- ❏ SEDUCTION Various   ISBN 978 0 352 34510 3
- ❏ LIAISONS Various   ISBN 978 0 352 34516 5
- ❏ MORE WICKED WORDS Various   ISBN 978 0 352 33487 9   £6.99
- ❏ WICKED WORDS 3 Various   ISBN 978 0 352 33522 7   £6.99
- ❏ WICKED WORDS 4 Various   ISBN 978 0 352 33603 3   £6.99
- ❏ WICKED WORDS 5 Various   ISBN 978 0 352 33642 2   £6.99
- ❏ WICKED WORDS 6 Various   ISBN 978 0 352 33690 3   £6.99
- ❏ WICKED WORDS 7 Various   ISBN 978 0 352 33743 6   £6.99
- ❏ WICKED WORDS 8 Various   ISBN 978 0 352 33787 0   £6.99
- ❏ WICKED WORDS 9 Various   ISBN 978 0 352 33860 0
- ❏ WICKED WORDS 10 Various   ISBN 978 0 352 33893 8
- ❏ THE BEST OF BLACK LACE 2 Various   ISBN 978 0 352 33718 4
- ❏ WICKED WORDS: SEX IN THE OFFICE Various   ISBN 978 0 352 33944 7
- ❏ WICKED WORDS: SEX AT THE SPORTS CLUB Various   ISBN 978 0 352 33991 1
- ❏ WICKED WORDS: SEX ON HOLIDAY Various   ISBN 978 0 352 33961 4
- ❏ WICKED WORDS: SEX IN UNIFORM Various   ISBN 978 0 352 34002 3

❏ WICKED WORDS: SEX IN THE KITCHEN Various   ISBN 978 0 352 34018 4
❏ WICKED WORDS: SEX ON THE MOVE Various   ISBN 978 0 352 34034 4
❏ WICKED WORDS: SEX AND MUSIC Various   ISBN 978 0 352 34061 0
❏ WICKED WORDS: SEX AND SHOPPING Various   ISBN 978 0 352 34076 4
❏ SEX IN PUBLIC Various   ISBN 978 0 352 34089 4
❏ SEX WITH STRANGERS Various   ISBN 978 0 352 34105 1
❏ LOVE ON THE DARK SIDE Various   ISBN 978 0 352 34132 7
❏ LUST AT FIRST BITE Various   ISBN 978 0 352 34506 6
❏ LUST BITES Various   ISBN 978 0 352 34153 2
❏ MAGIC AND DESIRE Various   ISBN 978 0 352 34183 9
❏ POSSESSION Various   ISBN 978 0 352 34164 8
❏ ENCHANTED Various   ISBN 978 0 352 34195 2

BLACK LACE NON-FICTION
❏ THE BLACK LACE BOOK OF WOMEN'S SEXUAL
  FANTASIES   ISBN 978 0 352 33793 1 £6.99
    Edited by Kerri Sharp
❏ THE NEW BLACK LACE BOOK OF WOMEN'S
  SEXUAL
    FANTASIES   ISBN 978 0 352 34172 3
    Edited by Mitzi Szereto

To find out the latest information about Black Lace titles, check out the website: www.blacklace.com or send for a booklist with complete synopses by writing to:

Black Lace Booklist, Virgin Books Ltd
Virgin Books
Random House
20 Vauxhall Bridge Road
London SW1V 2SA

Please include an SAE of decent size. Please note only British stamps are valid.

Our privacy policy
We will not disclose information you supply us to any other parties. We will not disclose any information which identifies you personally to any person without your express consent.

From time to time we may send out information about Black Lace books and special offers. Please tick here if you do not wish to receive Black Lace information. ❏

Please send me the books I have ticked above.

Name ....

Address ....

....

....

....

Post Code ....

Send to: Virgin Books Cash Sales, Random House,
20 Vauxhall Bridge Road, London SW1V 2SA.

US customers: for prices and details of how to order
books for delivery by mail, call 888-330-8477.

Please enclose a cheque or postal order, made payable
to Virgin Books Ltd, to the value of the books you have
ordered plus postage and packing costs as follows:

UK and BFPO – £1.00 for the first book, 50p for each
subsequent book.

Overseas (including Republic of Ireland) – £2.00 for
the first book, £1.00 for each subsequent book.

If you woulnd prefer to pay by VISA, ACCESS/MASTERCARD,
DINERS CLUB, AMEX or SWITCH, please write your card
number and expiry date here:

....

Signature ....

Please allow up to 28 days for delivery.